Also available in the
TOM CLANCY'S NET FORCE EXPLORERS series

Tom Clancy's
Net Force Explorers:
Deathworld

Created by Tom Clancy and Steve Pieczenik

HEADLINE
FEATURE

First published in 2001
by HEADLINE BOOK PUBLISHING

A HEADLINE FEATURE paperback

10 9 8 7 6 5 4 3 2 1

ISBN 0 7472 6190 3

Typeset by
Letterpart Limited, Reigate, Surrey

Printed and bound in Great Britain by
Mackays of Chatham plc, Chatham, Kent

HEADLINE BOOK PUBLISHING
A division of Hodder Headline
338 Euston Road
London NW1 3BH

www.headline.co.uk
www.hodderheadline.com

Acknowledgements

We'd like to thank the following people, without whom this book would have not been possible: Diane Duane, for help in rounding out the manuscript; Martin H. Greenberg, Larry Segriff, Denise Little, and John Helfers at Tekno Books; Mitchell Rubenstein and Laurie Silvers at Hollywood.com; Tom Colgan of Penguin Putnam Inc.; Robert Youdelman, Esquire; and Tom Mallon, Esquire. As always, we would like to thank Robert Gottlieb without whom this book would not have been conceived. We much appreciated the help.

Chapter One

Nick stood in front of the gateway and looked up and up at the pillars of it, there in the dark and the silence.

The polished basalt pillars were very tall. There was no seeing the top of them. They seemed to stretch forever up into the darkness. But in the empty black air between them, words hung burning in red. They said:

ABANDON HOPE ALL YE WHO ENTER HERE™

Nick stood there in the silence for a few more moments, then walked through the gates.

The first thing to assault him was the music but then that was what he had come for, what had brought him here in the first place. He was finding it difficult to believe that there had ever been a time when he hadn't known about that particular bass beat, pounding and insistent. It was such a contrast to the voice singing above it, starting out so calm and scaling over the course of almost every song into a completely abandoned shriek of cheerful rage. That was what had gotten Nick's attention the first time he'd seen a Joey Bane virteo: the *cheerfulness*. This man was angry, and enjoyed it, and didn't care who knew. The song that met you at the gateway was that first one he'd heard, the most famous of Bane's songs, and the one Nick liked the best: 'Too Jagged Off To Care.'

Nick walked in through the darkness, and the music cycled up so that you could hardly hear the moans and wailing through or under it. The noise wasn't so bad up here, anyway. This was the Top Floor, a beginners' level which, though it looked kind of impressive at first, was actually too dull and unshocking for any but the most hopeless types – mostly people Nick thought must not get out a lot, or do anything much but answer their virtmail, too scared to venture any further into virtuality. Nick had been just a little freaked by the concerted noise of human pain that first time he had come in. But then the persistent welcoming beat of the Bane music had got him past that, and then after about fifteen or twenty minutes the landscape hadn't bothered Nick at all.

It was wasteland. Gray, lowering sky, stunted dead trees, shattered boulders, the temperature warm enough to be stifling, no wind. It was desolate, a place that looked like he felt at the moment, and with the background noise, the howling and wailing, it sounded like he felt, too.

Nick shuffled along through the sterile, gray dust, his hands stuffed down in the pockets of his coverall, and made a depressed face. He could just hear what his mother would be saying now, if she could see him: 'Do you have to slump like that? Stand up straight. Look at you, you'd think you had nothing to live for. Though then again, with that last report from school . . .'

Nick frowned. He'd tried keeping his hands out of his pockets as an experiment, for nearly a week. It didn't divert her from her usual themes in the slightest. School was her favorite subject right now. He was absolutely sick of hearing her go on and on about it. *As if there aren't lots of terrific things to do besides college,* Nick thought. *And I'm passing everything, even if I'm not acing it.* But his mom wouldn't listen to anything of the kind, and as for his dad, he didn't seem to care. That by itself should have been a positive thing. 'Let the boy alone, Miriam,' he would mutter as he headed for the back of the house and the implant suite, 'He has enough problems.' And Nick certainly did. But whatever his father was interested in hearing, Nick's problems weren't it. Nick had started to wonder what he would have to do to cause a little interest.

Then he had found Deathworld.

Not that the people who used the virtual domain called it that, among themselves. 'The Circles,' was one of their private names for it, or 'Bane's Place' or 'The Bottom Floors'. Except none of the people Nick had met here so far had ever *seen* the bottom floors, reputed to be truly terrifying regions of torment and fear, and desperately cool. Nick was eager to find out whether these rumors were true, or just hype. You had to expect a certain amount of hype in conjunction with a place like this. After all, it was run by the biggest name in 'shadow jazz', a man who had made his first million by the time he was only four years older than Nick. Nick sighed. *Now there's a depressing thought. I wonder what Dad would think of that if I reminded him.*

Then again, probably it would be smarter not to. Neither Nick, in his wildest dreams, or his dad, was going to be a millionaire any time soon. That was something of a sore point with his dad. His dad's job at the vid studio wasn't terribly secure at the moment. There had just been another round of cutbacks and everybody was nervous. Nick supposed he should feel sorry for his dad, but his dad hadn't done a whole lot of feeling sorry for Nick lately. Nick shrugged. Let his dad deal with it.

The old, dry leafless tree that marked the near shore of the river was visible across the plain, and Nick made for it, kicking up the dust. If his dad was twitching over things at the moment, well, that was fine with Nick. When his dad had found out about Nick spending time in Deathworld, after the bill for the household Net account had come in last month, there had been trouble. More trouble than it merited, Nick had thought.

'I don't like you giving my hard-earned money to that man,' his father had said while eating his dinner, as Nick passed through the kitchen. 'The guy's a whacko. The domain is full of unwholesome stuff. I saw something about it on the news a few days ago. Besides, Joey Bane has enough money already without dumping ours on the pile, too. You just cut it out.'

Nick had muttered something noncommittal and escaped without making any statements about what he was going to do one way or another. But it was getting time for the new month's bill to come in, and his father would see the breakdown of the household's Net charges, and know where Nick had been.

Gonna be noise . . .

Yet Nick was peculiarly satisfied at the prospect. Whatever ruckus his dad kicked up, in Nick's personal life there was too much advantage to be derived from being here, and he wasn't going to give it up. Nick was not an outstanding student, not great at sports, no huge success with the girls, but he was *in* here, and few enough kids at school or outside of it had been able to get in. There was a waiting list, and you could sit on it for weeks or months without result.

No one was sure what made the Bane computers pick you as one of the lucky ones. The assumption at school was that there was some kind of obscure 'coolness' rating that no one understood. But being able to get access to the Circles at all, with a chance to see the dangerous stuff that was rumored to be down in those

4

lowest levels, carried its own cachet. There were rumors about what had happened to people who had ventured down into those levels thinking they were tough enough . . . and discovering differently. There had been stories of some hospitalizations . . . And everyone had heard about the suicides.

They didn't worry Nick. And as he thought about his father's reaction to his access to Deathworld, they worried him even less. His dad's annoyance pleased him somehow. *If Mom and I are supposed to make your life all nice and smooth for you,* he thought, *well, it's not gonna be that way. You haven't exactly made it that way for us. Mom can do what she wants, but for me, I'm going to enjoy myself a little. If it bothers you, tough. When I do what you want, it doesn't make any difference. Let's just see how it goes when I don't snap to attention every time you open your mouth. Right!*

And Nick grinned. It felt good to even have a chance to think such things, away from the little house where everything was always the same, and nothing ever seemed to change except for the worse, no matter what he did to try to make things better.

The Tree was closer, and Nick thought he could hear the cold sound of water flowing. Away across the dusty plain, he could see various people moving around, some of them in modern clothing, and real, or possibly so, but many more of them in clothes from other times and places, decades old, centuries or millennia old, wandering around and lamenting their fates in a hundred languages and (as the song said) 'a hundred shades of scream.'

It was noisy, but once you got past that, you noticed something. The screams tended to repeat themselves after a while, up here. Eventually you could start to work out, just by the sound, without trying to have any conversations, which of these figures were genuine people – other virtual visitors to Deathworld, the 'Guest Dead' who stopped in, as Nick did, to make some noise of their own where it was safe to do so, and to remind themselves how pointless life was. Not that Nick was all that interested in the 'Guest Dead' up at this level, especially since he didn't need them anymore. There was much more exciting business further down, everybody said. People far more dangerous, more interesting . . . and more isolated from the real world. Nick was so tired of the real world.

After he had beaten the first level, the screams and shrieks that went up on the smoky air from the tortured souls all around him stopped making much difference to Nick. Indeed, you got used to them after a while, and needed something a little more immediate, something newer and scarier, to shake you up. Though you couldn't just go and get it, for the system in Deathworld wouldn't let you down into the deeper circles until you had spent a certain amount of time in the upper ones, talking to the people you met there. When you met enough real people, and pooled with them what information you had about the level you were working on at the moment, your reward was to be allowed to progress deeper into the site, to the lower circles, where the virtual experiences got more vivid, more out of control.

Bane's voice sang through the darkness:

> 'The world gets more real,
> and things just get worse:
> run as fast as you like,
> you can't outrun the hearse . . .'

Nick kicked the dust up, approaching the Tree, and eyed the distant forms idly. In the beginning he had been surprised by the way the other people he saw had always seemed to be at a distance, no matter how long he walked toward them. Then he had discovered that this distancing was part of the domain's 'idiom,' and that it took an act of will to overcome it, not just the act of walking in a given direction. You had to go out of your way to actually talk to someone, had to strain against the fabric of this dark universe to break through. With some people you could strain against it all day and never get anywhere – they wouldn't hear you or see you. They stayed shut up in their own private little worlds. It was one of the games Bane's Place played with you, either personally or at one remove, through the domain itself. For if the Circles had a motto other than the one hanging back there between the gates, it was 'People stink. Life stinks. Everything stinks. Even this.'

The music doesn't stink, though, Nick thought as he got closer to the Tree, noticing for the first time it not only had no leaves, but also no bark. Something seemed to have bitten it off. The music was one of the best things about this place, and Nick had no time for people who suggested it was all variations on the theme of 'You're Going To Die Anyway, So You Might As Well Get Really Mad First.'

There's a lot more to it than that . . . Nick would know, for he had all the officially released song collections, and even a few of the 'pirate' segments supposedly extracted from the depths of this very domain. Beyond getting far enough down to see if those pirate 'lifts' were genuine, Nick's other great dream was to see one of the live Bane concerts some day. It wouldn't happen any time soon, for those concerts were much too expensive, the price of the tickets having to cover the (nowadays) extortionate price of actually taking a physical concert on the road. It was something few rock stars bothered to do anymore, in a time when the audience's experience could be arranged and controlled much more completely in a Net-based venue than anywhere in the real world. But Joey Bane did it, saying, 'I'm just old-fashioned that way.'

There was a hope that Nick might be able to afford one of the virtual concerts, this year or early next. *Assuming Dad doesn't blow his top when he sees the next Net access bill, and ground me.* But Nick had been squirreling away his allowance for a long time now, even diverting what should have been lunch money at school, happy to go hungry when he considered the alternative. Soon he would have enough to see The Man Himself in concert, hear in a live performance that great legendary scream of rage and despair at the end of 'Lady Macbeth,' see for himself the onstage carnage as Bane destroyed yet another ten-thousand-dollar electric lute and the instruments of everybody else in his band at the end of 'Cut The Strings.' That would be worth any amount of grief from his dad and mom. *Just a couple of hours of freedom,* Nick thought. *In the company of someone who knows what the world's really like, who doesn't pull his punches, who tells the truth about how awful everything is.* The dream had kept him going for a long while.

It wasn't so bad to hear that everything stank, after all. As long as you knew that there were lots of people who agreed with you that, painful though it might be, the truth was best. *Someday, when I move out, when I'm on my own, I'll spend as much time in Bane's Place as I want . . . and in other places, places on the edge, the scary stuff, the stuff my folks and all the deluded others don't want me to know about. They can wrap themselves up in their nicey-nice world if they like and pretend not to notice how awful things are. I'm going out where things are* real. *I'm strong enough to take it . . .*

Nick was humming the first verse of 'Nicey-Nice' as

he came up to the Tree. The air around him was beginning to mimic him with the backbeat of the song, and he could see the cold smoke coming up from the river, when he saw something that hadn't been there the last time he came. A rock. And sitting on the rock was a figure wearing the most tightly tailored black slicktite possible, with what at first glimpse looked like a big, black egg cradled in his lap. As Nick got closer, he saw it better, and caught his breath; for even in this dreary light, the 'egg' shone and glinted as if it lay under an invisible spotlight. It was a smooth, rounded shape, not really black but a brown so dark as to be mistaken for black, with a short neck – an electric lute with an ebony body, all inlaid with a spidery platinum webwork – that most famous of instruments in dark jazz, Camiun. There were people who claimed that Camiun must be a little bit alive, or else haunted, since no mere man could make an instrument sound like that. Like a soul in torment, or one just escaped from it. Joey Bane had said that on the day he discovered that the world was completely and irreversibly wicked, he would cut Camiun's strings, five minutes before he killed himself.

He's only virtual, Nick thought, stopping by the stone. But the slender, muscular, dark-clad figure gazing down into the icy gray water flowing by now shook his longish hair back, and glanced up at Nick sidewise. Nick gulped. He had talked to people here who'd claimed to have met this particular apparition. Half the time he'd figured they'd been making it up. But here *he* was, or rather one of the virtual representations of him: Joey Bane himself – the singer in his guise as Dark Poet from his second song collection, *Discourse with Spirits,* looking out across the unrelieved darkness of the landscape behind him with an expression both morose and amused. The lute in his lap hummed softly to itself, because its master's fingers were presently motionless on the strings.

'Hey, Joey,' Nick said.

That ironic smile curved itself up a little harder. Hard was the best word to describe it; it sat oddly on what would otherwise have been a young and innocent face.

'Nick,' Joey said. 'How goes the world?'

The domain's computer knew who Nick was, of course, but for a moment all he could do was shake his head. There were few enough places like this in the Net. Mostly big celebrities didn't bother going to the trouble to personalize their domains. There was usually just an introduction when you came in. In this case, whoever designed the domain had gone to some trouble to customize the output for the users. That was probably one of the reasons it was so popular. You got the chance to really talk to the star, or at least to the Net-encoded version of his personality.

'Badly. As usual,' Nick said. That was the customary response, the answer that the audience shouted back to The Man Himself at his concerts, live or visual, when he asked the question. The virtual Joey Bane smiled a little more grimly and put his hand over Camiun's strings to still the lute. It argued the point a little, fizzing and muttering under his touch.

'Yeah, yeah, everybody wants it their way,' Joey growled at the lute, and then looked up again. 'You just on your way in?' Bane's simulacrum said. 'Can't see you hanging around this level after you've solved it. Unless it's the music.' He looked bored at this possibility.

'No,' Nick said, 'I'm ready for something new.'

'Bet you are,' Bane said. 'Been stuck on three for a couple of weeks now. Hit your level?'

It was, among Banies, a rude question, suggesting you were incapable of taking the hard stuff, the real world, the truth . . . or that you were just dim. Had someone Nick's age said something like this to him, the circumstances might have become violent. But this was

Joey Bane, and that ironic look was dwelling on Nick, watching to see how he reacted.

'Don't know yet,' Nick said, in a sudden burst of humility.

Bane looked at him darkly for a moment, and then laughed. 'Nothing wrong with not knowing,' he said. 'You look pretty down, though.'

'Aaah . . .' The implant had to be feeding the Bane-domain computer his EEG and other information that would have betrayed that fact. But the thin, hard face was also kindly in a strange way, and Nick said, after a moment, 'It's just my folks.'

'Aha,' Joey Bane said. He stroked a dark, dissonant spatter of notes out of Camiun. 'The eternal problem. Can't choose 'em, can't get rid of 'em, can't do 'em without messing up the rug.' He snickered softly. 'We've still got a fair bunch of 'em down here, though. Fifth and sixth floor down, mostly.'

' "Still"? Why aren't all of them here permanently?'

'Oh, all of them spend a *little* time here,' Bane said. 'Mostly the part of their lives called "your childhood." '

Nick shot the virtstar a look.

Bane raised his eyebrows. 'Anyway, the ones who stay,' Bane said, 'the really hard cases, are mostly down on six. With the other violent types. A few manage to get further down. You ever get that far, you'll see.' He shook his head, smiled again, touched Camiun's strings and played a little minor-key imitation of an ambulance siren. 'Gets tough down there,' Bane said. 'Don't know if you're really interested in going down that deep anyway, a nice kid like you . . .'

'Won't be any time soon for me,' Nick said, 'at the rate I'm going.' He thought he might as well tell the truth, even though it was embarrassing.

Bane looked at him. 'Huh,' he said. 'Well, guess what, you've lucked into today's special offer. Every day we pick a few people for an upgrade. So come on down!'

To Nick's absolute astonishment, the earth started to rumble. Joey Bane got up, holding Camiun by the neck, and laid it over his shoulder, turning his back on the cold, gray river. 'You want to stand back, now,' Bane said, stepping away from the rock. 'You fall down the hole and land on your head, we won't be responsible . . .'

The earth shuddered harder, and from the air all around them came an upscaling moan that turned into a screech, as if the ground itself was in torment. It split open before them, raggedly, with a terrible sound of ripping stone, and the chasm went stitching and stretching itself away for what looked like half a mile to either side before it stopped, and the rumbling settled back into silence. A fearsome red glow came boiling up out of it, as if light could be made liquid: a seething light, full of screams and howls of desperation and anguish.

'Hey, *spaz*,' Nick said softly, in complete admiration.

Bane stood there tapping his foot for a moment, then shook his head. 'And am I supposed to *climb* down there?' he said to the air in extreme annoyance. 'Hey! *Tech!*'

An escalator appeared in front of them, leading down into the Pit.

'You can't get good help anymore,' Bane muttered, heading for the escalator, 'I'm telling you. Stinking roadies, I should never have let them unionize. Come on.'

The two of them got onto the escalator and started trundling down into the sulfur-smelling depths, past the thick layer of stone that made up the 'floor' of the first level. Nick was glad to see it drop away behind him, for it really was rather boring, full of nothing but 'screamers' and clueless Guest Dead wandering around trying to figure out what made this place so cool. This way of leaving the level was easier and less trouble than finding the rope ladder that was the usual way down onto the next level, the Second Floor.

They passed the last of the first rock floor, now a ceiling, and came down past that second level now. The view was better from this clear space in the middle of everything than it would be on that level itself, for the weather in there was really foul. Right across that cratery, mud-colored landscape, a terrible hurricane of a wind was endlessly screaming, full of dirt and garbage, blowing wildly assorted junk past you all the time – drink cans and snack wrappers, torn, dirty paper and old shopping bags and small showers of gravel and stones, all borne along with a grimy, near-horizontal rain. Various people were blown along there, too, or what remained of them. Until you saw their expressions, it was hard to tell whether they were chasing each other or actually fastened to each other somehow, so that where one went the other had to. Their faces, though, when you caught a glimpse of them through the murk, were furious. They snatched and grasped at the person to whom they were bound, tearing flesh as they rolled and tumbled along around the great second-level circle, blown irresistibly by that wind.

'Ah, love,' Bane said, 'ain't it grand.' He watched one particularly entangled pair of lovers go blowing by, clutching and scratching at each other, shrieking in pain and rage. 'You've been through here, of course . . .'

'Didn't think much of it,' Nick said, somewhat bemused for the moment by the sight of someone else being blown by on that wind – a thin, middle-aged, hostile looking woman, pedaling a bicycle. A faint yapping was coming from the bike's basket but it was drowned by the howl of the wind almost instantly as the woman was swept away out of sight. Where had he seen that image before?

13

'Ah, you've never been in love, then,' Joey Bane said. 'Excuse me. Lust. Well, give it a few years. You'll be grabbing at some obscure object of desire and trying to pull all the best chunks out of it whether it wants you to or not, just like everybody else. And it'll stink. But then, doesn't everything?'

'Yeah,' Nick said with some pleasure, though he tried to sound casual about it, as they dropped past the floor of that level and toward the next one. It was not a sentiment he would have gotten very far with at home. That was one of the things that made Deathworld such a trip.

'Intelligent young guy,' said Joey Bane. 'You'll go far. Well, down a few anyway.' And Nick had to grin. He knew this was all automatic; he wasn't as stupid as some of the people who insisted that all these virtreps of Bane were actually the man himself, 'slumming' in his Net domain. There were rumors though that sometimes, down in the deepest levels, you might run across one that actually *was* Joey Bane, rewarding some unusually persistent or talented Banie with a personal audience. For his own part, while he was still up in these levels, Nick knew perfectly well that the master site computer had been recording his preferences since he started coming here, that it knew where he'd been and who he'd talked to and what he'd said, and was tailoring his experience second by second to fit his needs and keep him coming back. It was probably reading Nick's body information through the implant chair right now, brainwaves and pulse and blood pressure and whatever, to make sure the things happening around him went in ways that he would like, that would make him keep coming back. But that was no big deal. Marketing computers all over the Net did that. And at the same time, it was fun. It was neat to talk to something that Bane himself had helped program to sound and react exactly the way he would.

They slid on past the level of the winds and the storm-borne couples. 'Idiotic behavior, really,' Joey was saying as he turned away from the view, 'claiming they can't control themselves, that love made them do it. Poor excuse. So now they *really* can't control themselves.' He gave Nick a narrow-eyed look that might have had a wink associated with it, but the light changed again as they plunged down past the next level of floor/ceiling and down into Floor Three, and Nick couldn't be sure what he had seen. 'You wouldn't ever try a weak excuse like that, though . . .'

'Uh, no,' Nick said.

'Yeah, right,' Joey Bane said, and didn't quite snicker. 'Third floor, gluttony, excess, and general overindulgence.'

If the weather had seemed bad on the level above, it was worse down here. Dirty sleet and freezing rain fell endlessly from blackness, and people both too fat and too thin ran along under it as if being scourged by whips, while behind them came a monstrous black-pelted shape, howling and snarling and grabbing them up in its jaws. Grabbing them up and chewing on them like newly caught rats, times three. It had three sets of jaws, three heads – huge, ugly ones like those of pit bulls – and six burning eyes. At least Nick *thought* he counted six. This was an image he had been careful to keep his distance from, the couple times he'd been down here. If the Dog caught you, it could strip you of half your 'time' credits in the domain and make you do the last couple of levels over again, which would get real boring real fast. Besides, it had been eating people when he had been here last, and the view had not been pretty. Nick's feeling at the time was that this was an aspect of 'the truth' that it was going to take him a while to get used to.

The monster bounded to the edge of the floor of that circle and began barking and slavering furiously at the two of them as they passed. 'Bad dog,' Joey Bane yelled at it, '*bad* dog! Shut your mouths, it's *me*! The neighbors are gonna start complaining again!'

The monster kept right on barking as they passed. 'Obedience school for *that* one was a waste of time,' Joey muttered as the escalator took them by. 'I tell you, this is the last time I let my sister pass off the runt of the litter on me. The poor guy's *damaged*. And he never gets enough to eat, either. He bolts his food and then he can't hold it down, and he . . . Oh, *look* at that.' Bane turned his head and yelled over the railing of the escalator, '*Tech!* You better get somebody over here to clean that up! If he slips in that and hurts himself, the vet bills are coming out of your pay.'

Nick wasn't looking, and was trying not to look like he wasn't looking, as the hound went bounding off after another trio of running, shrieking prey. 'The stomach acid eats the flooring,' Joey Bane said. 'Not the dog's fault, it's his diet. Fad dieters and runaway gourmets, what do you expect? They're so hung up on eating, or not eating, that they don't care what it does to them, or how many millions of people they starve in the process of feeding just a few a ton more than they need, or making special foods for themselves with no calories to speak of.'

Nick gulped. He was hanging on to his control as best he could, trying to stay cool, to look cool, like none of this bothered him. *It may take me a while*, he thought, *I don't care how much time I'm going to have to spend in here, but I'm going to learn to cope with it whatever I do. I am not going to look stupid in front of—*

'Fourth floor down,' Joey Bane said, looking over the rail of the escalator. 'The Haves and the Throwaways. All gamblers, really, except some of them do it with

16

stocks and bonds and margins and others do it at the gaming tables or in factories where they burn up resources that can't ever be replaced.' He made a gentle *tsk tsk* noise as the two of them passed on by and downward. 'This is an awfully underrated area. Hardly anyone spends more than the minimum time watching this bunch. It must be the suits.'

Or the screams, Nick thought, for these were truly appalling. They came out of thick, billowing darkness, and there were terrible crashing and crushing noises coming out of it as well, like a multi-car accident being continually enacted in the gloom. Nick swallowed as another crash produced a chorus of screams. They did not sound like the kind of thing you would hear in a made-for-Net drama. They sounded *real*.

'Accountants,' Joey Bane said idly as they went past one more thick rock floor/ceiling. 'Not so quiet and colorless, are they? This is nothing, though. Wait till you see what happens to the lawyers. Oh, not *all* of them, by any means. Many of them are very nice people, but the ones we get down here . . . Ah, here we are. Five.'

The music had been scaling up around them all the while. Now, as they came out on the floor of the fifth level, it crashed into the savage main chorus of 'You Said You Weren't Gonna Wait Up,' and just as Nick was about to start signing the next verse, the music started to fade away into silence. This was not one of those dark circles, and Nick swallowed when he saw what was there.

Huge cliffs reared up in the distance on all sides, and beneath them strode and strutted gigantic parent-figures dressed absurdly in clothes dating to before the turn of the last century. Bizarre floppy sweats and backwards hats, and even stranger, the non-'smart' jeans of the previous few decades, with T-shirts that hadn't yet learned the art of molding themselves to the wearer's body. They stalked around the dark rocky circle holding huge weapons in their hands. They hadn't started out as weapons, actually, but as hammers and ax-handles, kitchen knives and rolled-up newspapers. Their eyes glowed with a terrible light, and it wasn't until one or another of them had passed you that you saw the demons' wings, sinewed and fingered like those of bats, stunted and clawed. Among these awful figures, reaching no higher than their knees and running in all possible directions to get away from them, were adult figures in modern clothes, sliktites and leotites and new chitons, all terrified, all trying to get away. But they couldn't. There was nowhere for them to run, no way out, no way to climb the slick cliffs that bounded the circle here. The giant parent-demons pursued the helpless adults and attacked them with the household implements they carried. Nick wanted to look away but an awful fascination kept him watching. The punishment was deadly and endless. Broken heads resealed themselves, packing the brains tracelessly back in: broken bones reknit themselves, and bruises spread just long enough to go black, then paled back out of lividity to normal flesh again as the demons with the clubs and ax-handles chased after the abusing parents and gave them back what they had given their own children.

Next to Nick, Joey Bane was smiling slightly and singing what the lyric of the next verse would have been if the 'outer' music had still been playing: 'She hit it right on when she said it: "They only hit you till you cry . . ." ' And the tormented ones were crying as they fled, yelling and howling as loudly as they could, but the demon-parents were all deaf, and couldn't hear them, and just kept hitting. Around and around they went, the demons beating their victims while intoning phrases like 'This hurts me more than it hurts you,' and 'You'll thank me for this some day.'

Nick had heard that one often enough lately, about college. Though no one had hit him while saying it, he had been bruised enough by the words, by his mother's absolute certainty that Nick would someday actually thank her for making him so miserable. *Does she even listen to herself say these things?* He wondered furiously, but she was suffering from the same syndrome as the demons here were. She didn't hear him.

'Nasty neighborhood,' Joey Bane said after a moment, lounging against a handy rock. 'But these people should have known better. They started smacking their kids around to keep them in line, forgetting how they'd been smacked for the same reasons when they were kids, and it hadn't worked then, and it wasn't going to work now . . .' He eyes blazed. 'Or screaming at their kids day after day, telling them how stupid they are – until the kids finally begin to believe it. There are worse things than that, but not many.'

Nick swallowed. 'Do you think,' he said slowly, 'that somewhere . . . this really happens to people like that?'

Joey Bane threw him a look. 'I don't know about somewhere,' he said. 'But it sure happens *here*. That's enough for me.' He raised his eyebrows. 'You?'

Nick swallowed. 'Yeah,' he said softly.

'Right,' Joey said. 'So listen, I've got places to be.' Over his shoulder, Camiun muttered a few notes under its breath. 'Have fun while you're here. And take a good look around before you leave, so you can work out how to get down here on your own. The usual clues are here and there. Don't forget, it's not just child abusers who're down here. We've got all kinds of violence on this level.'

He started off across the circle. Suddenly, in the direction Bane was heading, Nick could see something that hadn't been there before. Where there had only been tall cliffs, now he saw the towered and crenellated outlines of the ramparts and seven gateways of the Keep of the Dark Artificer. Nick was suddenly afire with excitement again. They said that once you got in there, you could hear music that had never been heard in concert. And with the music, said the rumors, went images of fury and violence and despair that were too wild and scary for anything of them ever to have been shown elsewhere in public. *Gotta see that!*

Nick started after Joey Bane, already just imagining what the other kids in school would say when they heard that not only was he a regular in Bane's Place, but that he'd gotten through the gates of the Keep and taken the Oath never to reveal what he had seen there. *This is gonna be spaz beyond belief . . .*

But Joey stopped and half-turned. 'And where do you think *you're* going?'

'With you!'

'Not today, pally,' Bane said.

'But you said it was an upgrade.'

'One-time,' Joey Bane's virtual self said. 'And did I say sixth floor? Didn't say a word about six. Two levels, that's what you get today.'

Nick glared at him.

'What, you're complaining?' Bane said, and chuckled. 'What a little ingrate. You ought to be careful. This kind of thing can go on your permanent record.'

The good-natured mockery was somehow disarming. Nick's anger began to seep away. 'Please,' he said. 'I just want to see inside the Keep.'

'What, for free? Half the Banies on the planet want in there,' Bane said. 'What makes you so special that you get in without working for it? Nobody gets in there until they solve all the higher levels and earn the points. You know the drill.'

Nick frowned. 'This whole thing has just been a

come-on, hasn't it?' he said.

'Hey, all of life is marketing these days,' Bane said. 'Look, I'm in a good mood. You just spend the rest of the session walking around, getting to know some of these people. If "people" is the word we're looking for.'

Nick looked behind him to where the vanished escalator had been. 'But how am I supposed to get out? I haven't solved Four yet, I don't know where the entrance to this level is.'

'Oh, well,' Joey said, 'I guess that's fair. Look, you see those two over there . . .' He pointed off to one side, by the base of one of the huge cliffs, where a man with a lion's head and a woman with a tiger's were tearing at one another with terrible claws. 'They might tell you the way out if you can get them to stop fighting for a moment.' Bane looked at them and shook his head. 'Songwriters,' he said softly. 'You can get too hung up on whose name comes first in the credits.'

Nick looked at them dubiously. 'OK,' he said. 'Thanks.'

'Polite,' Joey said. 'That's what I like to hear. Guess I don't have to cut the strings just yet.' He turned away again, and started walking once more toward the gates of the Dark Artificer's Keep.

'You're gonna love Six,' he shouted over his shoulder. 'Just wait'll you see who we've got in the Lake of Boiling Blood. Not to mention the lifts from the new *Wraiths of Wrath* collection.'

Nick could hardly bear the thought of not hearing that new music before everybody else did. 'Why did you bring me here and tell me all this stuff, and then just walk away?' he yelled. 'Just to make me crazy, or what?'

'You figure it out,' Joey Bane yelled back, still walking away through the gathering darkness as behind him a demon-giant in an old-fashioned Mets uniform chased a hapless mother and father across the circle with a baseball bat. Nick caught a glance at the back of the uniform shirt as the demon passed. The name was hard to make out, but its number was 666. Nice touch, that. 'But haven't I been telling you life stinks?' Bane said. 'Don't you even listen to the lyrics? Bye bye, stinker.'

And he vanished into the darkness, laughing.

Nick stood there, heart pounding, not knowing whether to be delighted or furious. Finally he decided on furious, but it was a cheerful kind of fury, one that left him determined. 'I'll be back,' he yelled at the darkness. 'I'll do it, however much time it takes! I'll be back, and I'll meet you down on Six . . . and deeper than that!'

Only the faint sound of mocking laughter came floating back to him from the walls of the Keep, and a glint of silver and black as from away up high there, Camiun trilled once, amused.

It took a long while to get the lion man and the tiger woman to stop fighting and talk to them, but finally they showed him the way back up to Four, through a door and up a stairway hidden in the stone of the cliffs, and the tiger woman dropped a line about a 'golden key' that Nick was sure was a hint that had to do with how you were supposed to get into the Keep.

He headed upwards in a much improved mood but there was still an edge of anger on his determination to come back here and show everybody that he hadn't hit his level, that he didn't need any more favors, that he was enough of a Banie to succeed down here no matter how the program tried to get under his skin, and no matter how long it took to do it. His dad was probably going to have a spasm when he saw the Net bill, but Nick was more certain than ever that he didn't care. This was worth it.

In the gateway the abandon-hope words were still burning red when he got back up there, but as Nick approached them, they twisted and curled in the air like burning red worms, and formed themselves into new words. These said:

THE TIGER WOMAN IS A LIAR

Nick stopped and looked at that. *It's not completely true,* he thought. *She* did *tell me how to get back up to Four.*

Then he paused just on the inside of the gateway, wondering. She and the lion man had interrupted each other constantly once he got them to stop ripping each other up, and now he wasn't at all sure just which of them had told him about the way back up to Four. But he definitely remembered her telling him about the key.

So is it a false lead? Or is this a lie itself?

Nick let out a long breath. He was going to have to come back as soon as he could and start working out how to get from Three to Four, so that he could test the situation and see what the real story was. *One thing you have to give this place,* Nick thought: *it keeps you coming back.*

There was no point in lingering any longer, though. He had stuff to do at home. Nick passed through the gateway, and as usual, that big red asterisk appeared in the floor under his feet, burning like lava. Just for amusement, he stepped on it.

Instantly a vast carpet of glowing small print appeared beneath his feet, laid out and vanishing away into the virtual middle distance like the crawl in some old-fashioned space movie. It said:

©JOEY BANE ENTERPRISES 2018–2025. ALL RIGHTS RESERVED. THIS VIRTUAL DOMAIN IS A WORK OF FICTION. ANY RESEMBLANCE OR ANY MANIFESTATION TO PERSONS ALIVE OR DEAD IS COINCIDENTAL. THIS SITE IS TO BE USED FOR ENTERTAINMENT PURPOSES ONLY. YOU MUST BE SIXTEEN YEARS OF AGE

TO ENTER. BY ENTERING THIS VIRTUAL DOMAIN YOU STATE AND ACKNOWLEDGE THAT YOU HAVE READ AND UNDERSTOOD THE TERMS AND CONDITIONS FOR USE OF THIS FACILITY. YOU EXPRESSLY ACKNOWL-EDGE THAT YOU INDEMNIFY AND HOLD BLAMELESS JOEY BANE ENTERPRISES AND ITS AGENTS AND LICENSEES FOR ANY ADVERSE EFFECT WHATSOEVER WHICH MAY BE INCURRED BY THE USE OF THIS FACILITY, AND JOEY BANE ENTERPRISES AND ITS AGENTS AND LICENSEES ACCEPT NO RESPONSIBILITY FOR SUCH EFFECTS.

Nick walked on down the carpet of words with his hands stuffed in his pockets, amused, half wishing his mom could see him, half dreading her reaction, now minutes away, when she found out where he'd been. *Well, it doesn't have to happen right this second.*

YOU ALSO WAIVE IN PERPETUITY YOUR RIGHT AND THE RIGHT OF YOUR HEIRS OR ASSIGNS OR ANY OTHER RESPONSIBLE PER-SONS IN WHATEVER LEGAL RELATIONSHIP TO YOU TO MAKE ANY CLAIM WHATSOEVER AGAINST JOEY BANE ENTERPRISES AND ITS AGENTS AND LICENSEES IN ANY JURISDIC-TION NOW KNOWN OR ANY OTHER WHICH MAY HEREAFTER BE DISCOVERED, IN PERPETUITY. THIS AGREEMENT IS BINDING IN THIS FORM IN ALL U.S. JURISDICTIONS EXCEPT THE FOLLOWING: MD, NY, ME, VT. MARYLAND LAW REQUIRES THE FOLLOWING DISCLAIMER: THIS FACILITY MAY CONTAIN CONTENT INTENDED TO SHOCK OR DIS-TURB.

Nick snickered at that as he walked past it. *He* hadn't been all that shocked. Maybe people in Maryland were just too delicate to live. But he was made of sterner stuff. 'Nicey-nice,' he sang under his breath as he walked down the long strip of text, as if down a red carpet, 'wasting your time, smiling at folks without reason or rhyme: life is too short as it is; it's a crime . . . only death's certain to call . . .'

The music came up around him as he left, Joey Bane's voice singing, with Camiun providing the growling harmony under the main line, and the pulsebeat rhythm driving it all. There was supposed to be a new version of 'Nicey-Nice' out now. Nick resolved to break a little of his saved-up ticket money loose for it right away.

He turned off his implant, and vanished.

In the virtual realm, Deathworld suddenly accrued another sixteen dollars and fifty-three cents of credit.

And in the real world, several hundred miles away, someone who had been in Deathworld only an hour before was found dead.

Chapter Two

Charlie Davis was sitting in his virtual workspace, wondering how to get the steam engine to work. He could have cheated and called up the software company's helpline which would have sent him a helpful 'ghost' of James Watt, but the prospect of doing so struck him as an admission of failure. So instead he sat on the floor of the workspace, staring at the pressure gauges all over the engine's shining brass outsides and wondered what the heck to do next.

Charlie knew people whose workspaces were marvels of the 'special effects' end of virtuality. One of his buddies in the Net Force Explorers kept her workspace on one of the moons of Saturn. Another one had built himself a perfect replica of Windsor Castle, which he had filled with expressions of his own hobby, model trains. Charlie had found that a little bizarre, especially the miniature train shed which Mikey had installed in St George's Chapel. 'You should talk,' Mikey had retorted. '*Your* workspace used to be used for medical research the hard way – vivisection.'

That hadn't been precisely true, but it wasn't the kind of discussion that Charlie much felt like having with someone as pointlessly argumentative as Mikey, and he'd let it pass. Charlie had built his workspace into a duplicate of the eighteenth-century operating theater of the Royal College of Surgeons in London. It was a splendid if not very sterile space in which concentric circles of mahogany 'bleachers' surrounded an oval area where a scrubbed, wood table was set, on which some of the most important experiments in the medicines of that time had been done. The circulation of blood had been explored there, and the structure of human bone, and Pasteur had dropped by to lecture on germ theory. If the professors working there had occasionally gone a little loopy and tried things like transplanting the head of one dog onto the body of another, well, that was then, not now, and everybody was entitled to have a bad day, experimentally speaking. Meanwhile, Charlie loved the place, the warm, wooden gleam and polished-brass shine of it. It was the birthplace of modern medicine, and Charlie was going to be a doctor one of these days – though he intended to become an operative for Net Force as well. The only question was which of these goals he was going to manage first.

Then Charlie sighed heavily. 'Actually,' he muttered, 'the only question is how I'm going to get this stupid thing in front of me to work.'

It was, of course, not a real steam engine, just a mathematical simulation of one. If it was built properly, it would look and run like a real steam engine in the virtual world. Now, any workspace software worth its purchase price, if you told it to create such a thing out of nothing, would do just that and not bother you with the sordid details. But Charlie was learning how to write simulations in the programming language Caldera II, the language which virtual environments used to create things out of nothing so that they would behave real. And Caldera was desperately complex, difficult to control, easy to screw up, and otherwise just a major pain.

Charlie was not particularly interested in steam engines. What he really wanted to use Caldera for was to model the activity of neurons in the living human brain. But to create such models in any programming language, even Caldera, was an immensely subtle and difficult business – if you were interested in building models that actually worked like their counterparts in the real world, anyway, and suggested reasons for the way they behaved as they did. The steam engine was one of the 'sample' simulations which came with the most current Caldera software package, and a good place (the software company said) to start practicing before going on to the more involved simulations. The program which the tutorial coached you in writing was one that described in maddening detail the way the virtual environment running it was supposed to act, so that you would put out your hand and feel hard, cold brass or polished wood instead of air or fog that just *looked* like brass or wood, and so that the article you created in virtuality would act like a real thing, obeying real rules of science, and reacting appropriately to whatever you did to it.

That was the theory, anyway. Unfortunately, Charlie had so far managed only a steam engine that looked like brass but felt like rubber, and which produced something that looked like steam, but was actually just cold vapor. He got up from the floor, walked around the engine, looked at it one more time.

'OK,' he said to the air. 'Main program, routine five . . .'

A 'window' opened in the air near him, showing the first of the lines and lines of code he had written so far, coached by the tutorial. Somewhere in here there was a statement that was wrong but the debugging routine hadn't found, and that the program thought was a genuine and valid instruction. *And it would be*, Charlie thought, annoyed, *if people built rubber steam engines.*

'Scroll down three,' Charlie said. 'Scroll down one. Scroll down one.' He stared for several moments at that particular screenful of text, chewing his lip. After a moment, he said, 'Line sixty. Change statement. Old statement: "vis 15 hardness 80 spong 12". New statement: "vis 15 hardness 120 spong 12." '

'What the heck is a spong?' someone said out of the air behind him.

Charlie looked over his shoulder. Nick Melchior was there, one of his best friends from school, if not the best. There was something about Nick's sense of humor that meshed well with Charlie's, and besides, Nick seemed never to have seen anything even slightly funny about the idea that a kid from as painful and hopeless a background as Charlie's should be unswervingly set on becoming a doctor. Charlie, for his own part, was always amazed that anyone from as unsettled and insecure a background as Nick's should have been able to do as well at school and be as generally good-natured and good-tempered as he was, when at any moment his dad or the whole family might be uprooted and sent off to some distant foreign place to do virtcam work for one of the major news services.

Nick leaned against the mahogany railing around the 'operating floor' and stared at the engine.

'I could try to explain what a spong is,' Charlie said, 'but I'd just confuse myself. I'm not sure *I* know all of what it is yet. It has to do with the way this thing reflects light. At least, that's all I can make of it so far.'

Nick pushed away from the railing and walked around the sim, eyeing it. He was fair-haired, green-eyed, biggish across the shoulders, though not one of the taller kids in Charlie's year – unusual when half the juniors in the class seemed to be shooting up like trees, having hit some weird kind of sympathetic growth spurt. Nick seemed stuck at about five four, and for Charlie, who was stuck at five two and was beginning to wonder morbidly whether he had some obscure glandular disorder, it was pleasant to have the company of someone who didn't look down at him as if from a great height and inquire sardonically as to why he didn't go out for basketball. 'It looks good,' Nick said.

'Yeah, well, if you put some chest rub in it, it'd make somebody a great cold vaporizer,' Charlie muttered. 'Go ahead, give it a kick.'

'Huh?'

'Go on, kick it. Hard as you can.'

The steam engine had four handsome, brass-trimmed wheels with iron tires. Nick walked over to one of them, looked it over, and kicked it, hard. Then he started jumping around. '*Ow!* Sonofa— Wha'd you tell me to do *that* for?'

Charlie stared, dumfounded. 'Buddha on a bike,' he said, 'did I fix it?' He went over to the next wheel and kicked it too, quite hard, disbelieving, then joined Nick briefly in the dance. 'Oh, *crud!*'

'Thanks loads, Charlie, like I don't have *enough* problems today, now I'm lamed for life, too!' Nick was now holding the injured foot and staring at it as if he could see through his boot to tell if something was broken.

'Ow, look, I'm sorry. I fixed it! I guess I must have fixed it, anyway. The train was soft, before, like rubber.' Charlie leaned against the railing near Nick, rubbing his own foot and then bearing weight on it gingerly. 'Sorry!' He stared at the engine. 'What the frack did I fix? I wasn't working on the hardness.'

'You're asking the wrong expert, expert. What you *can* do, oh mighty medical talent, is tell me whether my foot's going to be this sore when I come out of virt.'

'Dummy,' Charlie said. 'No. It won't hurt long here,

either; you know pain can't be turned up even as high as in real life in here. Just as well. What's your problem, anyway?'

'My foot, clueless one, is—'

'Your *other* problem. Whatever you were yapping about when you came in.'

'Oh. Just my dad.'

'Are they sending him somewhere weird again?' Charlie boosted himself up to sit on the railing, morosely studying the steam engine.

'No. No, it's just Net stuff.'

Charlie blinked. 'What?'

'You remember Joey Bane's domain?'

'Oh, yeah. Death-o-rama or whatever.'

'Deathworld.'

'Yeah.' Charlie had been through one of its upper levels briefly with Nick a couple of months back, but hadn't gone back. It was one of the more expensive domains to spend time in, and besides, he wasn't a big shadow jazz fan. His musical tastes ran more to hopflight, because of the rhythms, and terzia rizz, which was experiencing something of a comeback after four centuries of neglect. 'So what's the problem?' Charlie said. 'Bills getting too high?'

'Yeah, but that's not most of it. Mostly my mom and dad think it's corrupting me or something.' Nick's good-natured face was twisted somewhat out of its usual placid shape, and as he hoisted himself up beside Charlie, the look lingered.

'You?' Charlie blew out an amused breath. 'Nothing there to corrupt.'

'Thanks loads, Doctor Genius. No, they're just freaked out by the news stories.'

'I missed the news today,' Charlie said. 'It's Saturday. This is the day I take off from the world, theoretically.'

'To spend on really important things.'

'James Watt thought so,' Charlie said, he hoped not too sharply. 'I like retrotech. So splash me. Meanwhile, what happened?'

'Somebody killed himself.'

'Someone who'd been doing a lot of Deathworld?'

'Something like that.' Nick rolled his eyes expressively, then paused, briefly distracted by the fresco on the ceiling: Apollo was receiving Aesculapius into heaven while a lot of other gods in togas leaned in to observe, and possibly to pass private remarks on the newcomer's snappy cane with the snakes wrapped around it. 'Who *are* all those people?'

'I'll tell you some other time, if I can ever get you to stop interrupting yourself!'

Nick rolled his eyes again. 'Some guy in Iowa,' he said. 'A seventh-circler, apparently. He hanged himself. At least that's what the police were saying.'

'Did they say anything else about whether he'd been depressed, or something like that?' Charlie said.

Nick shook his head. 'Not that I heard. From the story I heard, it sounded like they were in a hurry to get him buried.' He grimaced. 'And as soon as my folks heard about it, they went completely voidside. They don't want me going in there, blah, blah, blah . . .'

Charlie leaned back a little and looked over at his friend with some concern. He had heard about the other suicides, but he hadn't really thought of them as anything significant. Oh, obviously they were tragic for the people involved, and the people left behind, but a certain number of people suicided every year due to misuse or overuse of virtual services of one kind or another, and mostly the psychiatrists figured that these were people who would have found some other reason to do away with themselves if the Net had not existed. Still, it was a little creepy. 'This is how many suicides of people associated with Deathworld, now?'

'Six, I think they said.'

Charlie looked at the steam engine thoughtfully. 'Seems like kind of a lot.'

Nick plopped himself down on one of the front-row benches and shrugged a don't-care kind of shrug. 'Aw, c'mon, Charlie, don't you side with them, too! You know the world is full of idiots looking for a chance to pop themselves, and any excuse would do. It can't be Deathworld's fault that they found their way down there at one point or another. If it were, the government would have found out about it and shut them down.'

'Well . . .' Charlie got up with a sigh, walked around the back of the steam engine and had a look at the coalbox, which had somehow started to look a little transparent. He touched it. At least it was solid, which it hadn't been until just now. 'Net Force *is* supposed to inspect and certify anything that looks like it might be dangerous to users,' he said.

'So since they haven't shut it down, it must be OK,' Nick said. He sighed. 'Not that my dad is going to care one way or another.'

Charlie kicked the coalbox experimentally. It buckled under the kick; he looked at the half-circle dent and moaned softly. 'I am *never* gonna get the hang of this,' he said, and went to sit down by Nick and stare at the steam engine. 'Main program, routine six . . .'

Another window opened up, showing the beginning of the code that 'built' the coalbox. 'Scroll down twenty,' he said. 'Repeat. Repeat. Scroll down one. Line ninety-three. Change statement. Old statement: "vis 15 hardness 120 spong 12". New statement: "vis 15 hardness 90 spong 12." '

The code readjusted itself. 'I don't get it,' Nick said. 'You're going to go to medical school, do the doctor thing like your dad, you said.'

'Yup.' *And then go into Net Force*, Charlie added

silently, but this was not something he discussed with anyone, not even with Nick. There was so much competition to get into that elite force, so many people who were also trying to get in . . . and it was not in Charlie's nature to want to have to say to anyone later, 'I wanted to get in, but I couldn't make it.' When he made it, when he started working for them in criminology or forensics after he got his MD and his specialty, *that* would be the time to discuss it. Then he would have the ID in his wallet for anyone to see, his ticket to the cutting edge, to the most exciting work on Earth. Until that day came, though, Charlie had resolved to keep his intentions to himself. If his life had taught him anything up until now, it was caution.

'So what do you need this stuff for?'

'Modeling nervous systems,' Charlie said. 'And other things. Solid in-bone surgical prostheses, temporary replacement organs, stuff like that.'

Nick gave him a wry look. 'It looks like *this* system's making *you* nervous, all right,' he said, 'but that's about all. You should lose this stuff and get out and get yourself some fresh air.'

Charlie sighed and leaned back on the bench, for the moment unwilling to go over and kick the coalbox again, for fear of what he'd find. 'Been listening to your folks too much, Nick? I bet they say the same thing.'

'Yeah, well . . .' Nick gave him an amused look. 'I can't help it. I can't get excited about baseball the way my dad can.'

'Neither can I.' The two of them laughed with approximately equal levels of irony. Once a week or so, all through the spring and summer, Charlie found himself wondering how his dad, a doctor of incredible intelligence and (usually) of good sense and taste, could go out, regular as clockwork, every Saturday when the weather was right and he wasn't on call, to play sandlot softball with the GWU med-surg team. Then, for the rest of the week, he would spend at least half an hour every morning mulling over the box scores of the most recent Braves games. He would periodically try to get Charlie interested as well, had even tried getting him interested in virtual Little League baseball. Charlie's dad would then routinely talk himself out of this idea halfway through each new effort, muttering that the virtual form of the sport was a 'poor second best.' Charlie just nodded and put up with it, this being easier than arguing the point anew every week, or trying to explain one more time to his father that right now he was a whole lot more interested in modeling than in any sport yet invented.

'Seriously, though,' Charlie said. 'You should consider taking a couple of weeks off from Deathworld, just to get your folks off your case. If they're really worried, it might be the kindest thing. Besides, once they were sure you weren't hooked on it or anything, or about to hang yourself from the shower-curtain rail as soon as they turned their backs, they might ease off a little.'

Nick shook his head vigorously. 'I've tried that before with other things,' he said. 'My mom doesn't even notice. My dad . . .' He sighed. 'You let him win one, when it's something that matters, and he starts bearing down harder on everything else. Pretty soon I wouldn't have a life left, or at least no life that didn't look like what he thought it should look like. Besides, I'm finally getting somewhere down there. If I drop the momentum now, the system'll notice and stop fast-tracking me. I've been racking up enough points that I'm gonna get somewhere significant over the next month or so. I might finally get into the Dark Artificer's Keep and get a listen to the really good music.' He shook his head. 'My dad's just gonna have to lump it for the time being.'

Charlie got up and went over to the coalbox again, nudging it cautiously with one toe. The dent he had made in it abruptly sprang out. The coalbox went almost completely transparent, except for the coal, which 'hung' there in midair as if sitting in some kind of wheeled plastic basket, like the ones in the 'grocery stores' of old. 'Frack,' Charlie said, with feeling. 'Frack, *frack*—'

'You oughta take a break from this,' Nick said. 'You're getting stressed out. Since when do you use language like that?'

Charlie looked with mild annoyance at Nick, but he had to admit that his friend had a point. 'Program, quick save,' Charlie said. 'Then close program.'

'Saved. Closing,' said the computer, folding up the various open windows. The steam engine vanished, leaving them alone in the big wood-panelled hall, with squares of sunlight from the high windows now tracking along the floor.

'Must be noontime. Probably I should get something to eat anyway,' Charlie said. 'Look, you wanna come over in the flesh later? We can make some burgers or something. Nobody at home has anything planned for today.' It was one of those moderately rare times when both his mother and his father had Saturday off.

'Thanks, but I'm busy this afternoon,' Nick said. 'They're offering a discount for Saturday Deathworld access between noon and six. Apparently that's a slow time at the moment, with the summer coming on. Look, why don't you come with me? I can "sub" you in on my account, and you can watch me get into the Keep.' Nick grinned with excitement.

Charlie thought about it, then shook his head. 'No, you go ahead, it's not my cuppa. But when you get out, drop by and let me know how it went. They let you make "tapes"?'

'Nope, the content is all copyright. They control that pretty tightly. You try to copy an experience and show it outside of their protected routines and there'll be lawyers on your doorstep five minutes later. But I can save the experience inside the "realm", and you can see it some other time.'

'That sounds good. You do that, OK?'

'OK.' Nick headed for the stairs that led up to the door, then paused. 'You *sure*? This is gonna be one for the ages.'

'Nope, you go ahead. But thanks.'

'Your loss,' Nick said. 'See you, doc.'

'Later, Mr Nick,' Charlie said.

His friend vanished. Charlie sat there a moment more, staring at where the steam engine had been, then said to the computer, 'Secure the space, please.'

'Workspace secured,' said the program that managed it, 'all files confirmed saved; backup to SafeHouse remote facility accomplished.'

Charlie closed his eyes and performed the specific slight muscle-twitch that deactivated his implant.

The world went dark. He opened his eyes, glanced around.

Sunshine was coming through the Venetian blinds of the back window of the den. Charlie got up and stretched. No matter what claims the implant-chair people made, the built-in massage and muscle-toning programs never left you completely unstiff after a prolonged session on the Net. *I really should try to do something about that sometime*, he thought, shaking his arms to get the blood moving again as he climbed out of the chair. *Tweak the programming a little . . .*

Then again, Charlie thought, *if I have as much luck with that programming as I'm having with Caldera at the moment, maybe I'd better leave well enough alone. I'd probably come out of a session with my arms and legs tied in knots.*

He walked over to the window and looked down. The back windows faced south. About twenty feet below him was their little pocket garden, a square of grass with a smaller square of paving slabs inside it, and various potted plants sitting around in it, mostly herbs for his mother's cooking. Behind the yard was another house and its yard, and to the left and right the view was much the same.

Charlie yawned and went out of the den, heading down the stairs to the first floor and the kitchen level. The house was a two-century-old 'brownstone' on 16 and W, a place which Charlie's father routinely referred to as 'the Money Pit.' The family had moved into it when it was only partly renovated. For their first year there, when Charlie had been eleven and then twelve, the place had been in a constant state of uproar involving inescapable plaster dust, thick, paint-daubed plastic sheeting, piles of demolished brick being saved for recycling, and endless crews of workmen barging in and out at unpredictable intervals. Finally, sick of the delays and the expense, Charlie's father had thrown the workmen out (having first allowed them to finish the second floor and the basement) and had announced his intention to finish the third floor and the attic himself, in his spare time.

Charlie still snickered every time he heard the phrase, since his father, like any other doctor, had a tendency to come home from the hospital and spend what little spare time he had snoring. When his dad *did* get it together to work on 'the upstairs,' Charlie and his mom inevitably got dragged into the act as well. Charlie could now mix plaster with the best of them, and his dad had announced that he was ready to be taught how to lay a hardwood floor. This had not happened yet – the new semester had begun, and in a teaching hospital like the one at George Washington University, that meant a lot less spare time for the doctors of middle seniority, like Charlie's dad. But Charlie didn't waste much time worrying about it. The house was comfortable enough as it was at present: three bedrooms and an office where one of the implant chairs lived, a kitchen and two bathrooms, and a den that housed the other implant chair, the main Net server, and a busy, messy library. The new master bedroom and private living area which his father was planning for The Upstairs would happen someday, but for the moment, Charlie tended to treat it like anything else – safely distant in the realm of myth.

Now Charlie headed down the stairs and made for the kitchen, which was in the back of the building, with doors opening out onto the little garden. He got himself a cup of coffee from the coffeemaker, which was always full night and day. He stood there for a moment, getting used to reality again, gazing out into the sunlight on the paving and the grass.

There were still times when Charlie woke up, very early in the morning, and felt bizarrely dislocated, as if his mind was comparing the shining new surroundings, the polished floor and pastel or stripped-brick walls, with some other reality, older, grittier, more basic. Floors that were not polished wood, but cracked linoleum, worn and dirty, scattered with garbage; walls that were not newly plastered and painted and hung with prints, but grimy, peeling, splotched with damp, holed where someone had punched them. The memory of someone shouting incomprehensible words of rage, someone else weeping: the memory of a face that should have been beautiful but was instead swollen and vague, blue with bruising. The smell of unwashed bodies, the smell of something burning; the too-clear image of a match under a spoon, a spray injector, a syringe—

'Hey, son, what's new in the world today?'

Charlie turned, swallowed, and the proper world came back, and with it his dad, lumbering into the kitchen, a big, broad-shouldered, dark-skinned man in a polo shirt and jeans, high-cheekboned, with thoughtful eyes and a mouth that spent most of its time grinning. Now, those dark eyes were unusually thoughtful as they took in the look on Charlie's face.

'Nothing much,' Charlie said.

'How's that steam engine?'

'Malfunctioning,' Charlie said, moving aside to let his dad at the coffee. His father tossed the morning paper onto the big table in the middle of the kitchen and went to the cupboard for the gigantic coffee cup that said YOU DON'T HAVE TO BE CRAZY TO WORK HERE BUT IT HELPS.

'Never trust retrotech,' his father murmured, emptying what seemed to be about half the contents of the coffee-maker into his cup, then going over to the fridge and opening the door. He reached in, then started rooting around. 'Kenmore, where the heck's the milk?'

'No milk today,' said the fridge.

'Well, I can *see* that, you dumb contraption, why didn't you order any?'

'Error 3033 Server Busy,' said the refrigerator, somehow managing to sound a little sullen.

'Well, you just keep trying, Kenny, or we'll trade you in for a better model before you can say "two percent low fat". See that,' his father said, shutting the refrigerator with a wounded air and heading back to the cupboard for dry coffee creamer, 'I told you, never trust modern technology.'

'You said never trust retrotech,' Charlie said as his father sat down and grabbed the *Washington Post*. It started unfolding and unfolding itself across the flowered tablecloth to the default display size.

'That either,' Charlie's father said. 'No I'll have to go

out and get milk before the game, or your mother'll be on my case.'

'I can go get it, Dad.'

'Would you?' His father looked up as if astonished by his son's kindness. It was a look Charlie had gotten used to over time, the expression of a man who has almost forgotten what free time is like, and is astonished to find that other people have any.

'No problem.' *In fact, if I get out right now, I can escape before he asks me to—*

'You know, son,' his father said, as the main sports page resolved itself in color and motion in front of him, showing a batter swinging and missing very conclusively at a 3–2 pitch, 'a nice day like this, a boy your age should be out getting some fresh air with other kids. Now if you felt like coming down to the park with me, after the game's over some of the other dads and I . . .'

'Y'know,' Charlie said, 'I just realized what I'm doing wrong with that steam engine.' *Not working on it, among other things!* He headed out of the kitchen and down the hallway toward the 'airlock' front hall where his bike sat. 'Later, Dad. I'll get that milk first.'

His father was chuckling softly behind him. As Charlie pushed the front door open, wheeled the bike out it, closed the door again and spoke it locked, he began to wonder if he had been manipulated into getting the milk a touch more quickly than he would have done otherwise.

Nonetheless Charlie grinned a little as he got up on his bike. His mother and father – his foster mother and foster father, actually, though they were working to adopt him formally, really – were the world's best. A little manipulation, in the greater scheme of things, didn't matter in the slightest. He looked up at the stripped brick of the outside of the building and saw, as if overlaying it faintly even in the bright Saturday morning sunlight, that older, darker memory: dimly lit hallways, echoing with laughter bitter or abandoned, the sounds of pain, abuse and loss. That was all gone now. Nick and Adelie Davis had come and taken him away from all that, into a world where life had a purpose besides getting high, and a meaning besides bare survival, and hope as opposed to none. When those old memories came hunting Charlie, they never caused him anything but pain. But he knew it would be stupid to deny them, or try to escape them. If he was ever going to be fully himself, they were going to have to be part of the equation.

But right now that could wait. Sunlight dissolved the shadows, and Charlie pedaled off down to the nearby convenience store to get some milk, while turning over in his mind the problem of a rubbery steam engine. *Shame I can't get Nick interested in this. He'd be a help.* But Nick plainly had other things on his mind. *Guess that means I'd better get busy.*

Chapter Three

Nick stood by the Lake of Boiling Blood, gazing idly across its blooping, heaving depths, and decided that it looked a lot like spaghetti sauce.

He sighed. All around him the scalded screeches of various media figures of past and present – movie stars, singers, reporters, producers, directors – could be heard as they noisily repented their various overindulgences and infractions against taste, style and veracity, while various demons pushed the Damned back into the boiling blood as they tried to escape, or pulled them out again (to give them a chance to recover, so that throwing them in again later would hurt more). The lake in which all the Violent-Against-Truth were imprisoned had numerous little fjords, pools and lakelets winding up among the towering dark cliffs that embraced it on all sides, and from these could be heard particularly piercing shrieks and howls of anger and pain. Nick had stopped reacting to these now, having made the rounds of all the 'specialty' areas in his search for clues about the way down to the Seventh Circle. He had seen and spent hours in the worst of them all, the giant boiling-magma Jacuzzi in which former talk-show hosts and literary critics held one another under, tearing at each other whenever anyone managed to struggle to the surface. Even from that awful scene he had come away more or less unscathed. The other, lesser torments on this level held no more terrors for Nick now. Even the stink of the lake that boiled but never burned was beginning to become a commonplace, and he was busily trying to work out the details of where he should be heading next. The Seventh Circle was beckoning.

Over everything ran the savage rhythms of the new 'unpublished' tracks from *Forlorn Voices*; right now it was 'Slasher's Surprise' playing, with Joey Bane's voice unusually soft in the leadup to the second verse, almost as if enticing you to lean in close and have your brain fried when the chorus began screaming in your ears.

'It never seems to have occurred to you
that if I cut you *you* would bleed . . .
but then it also never seems to have occurred
that I might follow your own nasty lead:
Might get the strop out, might hone the edge down,
might put the blade in deep:
maybe tonight's little pain will teach you
to look before you leap!'

And then the shriek of sound, Camiun singing out like both tormented and tormentor alternately, and Joey Bane's sardonic scream:

'Surprise, surprise, see the blood flow,
Mister Do-unto-others-and-run!
Hey, what's the hurry, don't leave, don't go,
I'm up for more of your kind of fun—'

'Surprise, surprise,' Nick sang softly to himself, as he wandered along the lakeshore, looking casually for any spot he might have missed. He was getting ready to move on shortly, though, for he thought he had all the clues he needed. And Six was getting old, anyway. At first, Six had seemed 'seriously cool,' to use his dad's ancient and hoary term. But now it had palled. In fact, at first Nick had been surprised to see how soon he had gotten used to it, how very *soon* it had all seemed slightly passé. Added to that, things had not happened in the order he had expected. He had thought that once he hit Six, the Keep of the Dark Artificer would be waiting for him. But when he reached the spot in the Ashen Plain where rumor said it was supposed to stand, he had found nothing but a big rough sign spray-painted on permanently smoldering plywood, and stuck in the ground: GONE FISHING ON LEVEL 8. SUCKER!

At first Nick had been absolutely outraged at this, and had turned to leave, infuriated at the waste of time and money. But then he thought again, distracted for the moment by the initial sight of the lake, and the smell of it, which was horrifying enough to a nose not used to it, to strike almost anyone still, or sick. He had controlled his heaves, and his initial reaction, and then it occurred to him: *Of course. It's a test. If everything stinks, why shouldn't everything stink here too? Joey never said it would be otherwise.*

So Nick had sighed, and coughed, and started hiking around the shallow Lake, looking for clues as to what was the best way down to Eight. This took him a long while, since the only source of clues was those people trapped in the blood, being pushed into it or scrambling out again. You had to talk to them, find out who they were and what they were doing here, and try to draw them out on the subject. Not that they would necessarily cooperate. Not all of them would stand near the edge of the Lake and talk to you, either. There were big gaggles and parties of them out in the hotter part of the lake, and they would stand or float there, alternately screaming

45

and looking back toward shore, scornfully, like people at a cocktail party who're in with the crowd that really matters and have no inclination to move around and meet anyone less important.

Nick had spent a long time wandering around the edges of the lake, trying to overhear something that would be useful to him. This had made him pretty annoyed after a little while. *It feels like my life,* he had thought. *I'm supposed to be here escaping from reality, not getting stuck with more of the same!*

But there was no choice, for the only other sources of clues were the other players – and they were a closemouthed bunch. None of them that Nick approached would talk to him, and finally he gave up trying. *Probably they figure they've spent good money to find out what they know so far,* Nick thought, *and they're not going to give it away to anyone for free.* Realizing this didn't make Nick feel any better, though, and eventually, after he had spent something like eight hours of 'peak time' without any result, he had sat down with his back against a sullenly hot boulder and taken what he considered would be his last long look at the place.

Then, off his guard, lost in his fury and unfocused, he saw the answer. He saw one of the gameplayers, not a demon, look over her shoulder as if concerned that she was being watched. Then, after a moment of apparently seeing no one nearby, she actually waded into the boiling blood and headed out toward one particular group. Nick's mouth dropped right open.

If she can do that, I can do that!

Nick got up and made for the edge of the lake. There, for a moment, he hesitated, for the stuff looked deadly. *But she did it!*

Gingerly, he put a foot in. He didn't feel anything. Confused, Nick bent down and held his hand over the boiling blood. He could feel the heat, and it felt bad. But after a moment's hesitation he stuck his finger in.

To his astonishment, it didn't particularly hurt. The 'boiling blood' was only about as hot as a really hot bath. And he alternately laughed and cursed himself all the way across the lake as he got right in and waded or swam toward one of the big 'get-togethers' in the middle of the lava, a whole bunch of scalded, burnt people – or former people, all of whom looked like they had been guests at a particularly interactive barbecue – who were standing around and laughing more than they were screaming. Nick felt dumb, in retrospect. He knew perfectly well that you couldn't suffer pain in Net-based experience, or at least not pain bad enough to hurt you. The implant embedded in you was designed specifically to filter that kind of thing out. And it didn't necessarily follow that what hurt the Damned would necessarily hurt you. After all, they were supposed to suffer here. It struck Nick as likely enough that even in a real Hell, the torments wouldn't hurt someone who wasn't entitled to them.

Possibly there's a message there somewhere. In any case, Nick had learned to stop taking the physical images of things here at face value, as he would have in the real world. *Maybe that's the message, too. That nothing is what it seems. That nothing can really be trusted.*

It was a message that sank in deep. Nick put it aside for that moment, though, and got busy talking to the people out in the lake. In between torments, he found them a voluble enough bunch. In fact it was hard to get them to *stop* talking, especially about their favorite topic: themselves. What was harder still was to get them to say anything about Deathworld itself, its structure and the way around it. Not that they seemed to be inhibited against this specifically. They were just so utterly self-centered that even the torment of the boiling blood served only as a momentary distraction from their recitations of the important things they'd done, all the books they'd written and the money they'd made, the millions of people they'd influenced, the trends they'd set. Nick started to find this very choice when he paired their endless effusions against the fact that he only knew who a few of them were, out of hundreds he talked to. That week he did get a very thorough grounding in the faded pop culture of the last fifty years, and an increasingly clear sense of how very little of human endeavour lasts for any real length of time, whether it's worthwhile or not.

Finally, though, Nick learned by observation that if you asked questions while the demons were actually torturing the Damned, or when they'd just been splashed by the boiling blood, you could get straight answers for a few seconds. The pain, it seemed, cleared their minds and turned them away from themselves, however briefly. Nick quickly established a short list of questions to fire at them while it wasn't in their power to give him anything but a straight answer. After many hours of this, and a lot of slogging around, Nick now had the information he needed. The exit to Seven was actually down in that lake of blood itself, right down at the bottom of it, that being how the Power that ran this place kept the Damned from escaping it. For while wholly immersed in the lava-blood, then and only then were their minds cleared to the truth of how little difference they had made in the world when they were still breathing, and how in the present time, so soon after their deaths, they were either completely forgotten or about to be so. Indeed, it was an irony which hadn't escaped Nick's notice that only here, in this virtual torment, were any of these people still even slightly famous anymore. Only the users of Deathworld, working their

way down through this level, were impelled to say,
'Just who *was* that guy?' before checking the history
sources on the Net to find out. One of the very few
exceptions to this rule, and a deeper irony still, was
the image of the old, old newscaster who had been
alive until very recently, but while still alive had as a
joke privately given the Deathworld designers permission to place him here among so many of his lesser
contemporaries. He did not deserve to be here, and as
a result he sat in something of a place of honor, off in
his own little hot-tub full of the burning lava of
Truth, looking like a wrinkled old Buddha with his
mustache on fire, and refusing to say anything to
anyone except, with a grin, 'That's the way it is . . .'

Nick had been lost in admiration when he got the
joke. *This is a great place*, Nick thought. *Better than
anyplace else on the Net. I don't care how long it takes, or
how much it costs. I'm going to solve it.* And indeed he
had been in here every day, for every waking hour he
could, for days now. It was a lot of use, he knew, a lot
of time when he should have been doing other things,
maybe. Schoolwork, or stuff around the house . . . But
those images seemed to have less power than usual to
bother him, which suited Nick fine. *Because they're not
important. They can wait. This matters more. And if
anyone doesn't like it, well, the world stinks, doesn't it? Let
them just get used to it.*

From where Nick stood now, looking out over the
lake and up at the cliffs, he saw something which he
had missed in earlier visits, but which he had now
learned to enjoy, since it never happened the same way
twice. One of the demons, a little batwinged guy who
reminded him strangely of his science teacher from
seventh grade – a round, small, jolly man – materialized
up at the top of the highest of the cliffs around the
Lake. It had a long, long projection of stone sticking

out over the lake, that cliff, and sometimes this narrow finger-like projection was almost completely hidden in the miasma of brown-black smoke that rose from the lake. For the moment it was clear, though, and the little dumpy figure walked out to the very end of that narrow pier of stone, held its arms out in front of it, yelled 'Geronimooooooo!' and jumped off. It twisted and turned any number of times as it fell through what seemed about a mile of air from that high promontory, tumbling, straightening again, spinning, finally tucking itself into a cannonball shape, then straightening out and hitting the surface in a perfect dive, striking into it like a spear and vanishing in a tremendous splash that threw burning, smoking liquid in every direction. All around, the Damned who were hit by the splash screamed in anguish. From the side of the lake, a group of six demons who had been sitting and watching the dive now stood up and held up little pairs of cards with numbers on them, one card in each claw: 5.4, 5.2, 5.1, 5.2, 4.8, 5.9. Then five out of six of them dropped their cards to the ground, and started whapping the demon who had given the diver a 4.8 over his head.

I really have to find out who the heck "Geronimo" is, Nick thought. *It might be a clue.*

He stood there for a moment more, and then thought, *OK. No use putting it off any longer. Let's put this to the test, and see if I'm right.*

He looked over his shoulder to see if anyone real, any of the gameplayers, were nearby to see what he was doing. It was a relatively quiet time. Nobody was nearby. Nick stepped off the edge of the lakeshore and started wading through the lake.

The Damned drew away from Nick a little, and some of them stopped laughing when they saw where he was headed: that deepest part, where none of them went by choice. 'Surprise, surprise,' he sang softly in chorus with the great cry of rage filling the air above him,

> 'Never thought it'd happen,
> Never thought you'd be the one!
> Surprise, surprise,
> 'Cause here comes the moment,
> I'll shave you to the bone 'fore we're done!
> Surprise, surprise—'

Nick knew he was on the verge of the deepest place. He ducked under the lava—

And everything went black.

And in the darkness there burned nothing but two great words written in blazing red fire:

SERVICE SUSPENDED

'WHAT?!' Nick screamed.

He blinked, blinked hard. There was light again, but it was just daylight, easing out of afternoon toward evening. It was the light that came through the translucence of the shades in the spare bedroom of the apartment where he lived with his folks, the room where the implant chair sat.

His father stood there with the hand commlink in his hand. 'Yes,' he was saying to someone at the other end. 'Thanks, it just went on. Yeah. Thanks.' He folded up the hand phone and looked at Nick with an expression too flat and controlled to bode well for anyone.

'Well?' he said.

'What's the matter?' Nick cried. 'What happened? Call the provider, something's wrong with the Net link!'

'I've just been talking with the provider,' Nick's father said, in a voice carefully kept as expressionless as his face, 'and there's nothing wrong with the link, nothing that hasn't just been fixed, anyway.'

'But it went off while I was in the middle of—' *Uh oh.*
'—something important.'

His father held out an envelope for him to look at. It
had their Net service provider's logo on it. In the spare
room doorway, his mother suddenly materialized,
looking grim.

'I thought I told you,' his father said, 'to stay out of
that Deathworld place.'

Nick realized that this was not a time to attempt
explanations. He said nothing.

'I thought we discussed it rationally,' his father said.
'You agreed to do as I said. Didn't you?'

'Dad, I—'

'Or I thought you had. I see now that I was mistaken.
Eight hundred dollars–' the hand with the envelope in it
was shaking now– 'eight hundred *dollars* in prime-service
charges in the last two weeks alone! Son, are you *nuts*?
Did you seriously think I wouldn't find out about this?
Did you think it was just going to go away, or that it
didn't matter? Do you know what this is going to do to
household finances for the next month, while we pay this
off out of money that was intended for other things? Like
spending money for our summer vacation?'

Nick gulped, and looked at the floor.

His father stopped, too angry to say anything else for
the moment. 'Nicky, half your spending money is going
to be docked weekly until you pay back this last bill,'
Nick's mother said. 'It would be real smart for you to
see about getting yourself some kind of parttime job for
the summer, so you can get it paid off in less time. As
regards any further Net access, you're grounded. If you
want it, you can go down to the Square and rent a
booth out of your own money, since you've proved you
can't be trusted to use the Net responsibly at home.
After the bill's paid off, we'll look at whether you're

ready to have your own service restored.'

Nick said nothing, just stood there with his ears burning.

'And assuming we give you your service back some day, if you ever pull a stunt like this again, we're going to have the thing pulled out,' his father said. 'I don't care if you think you need it for school, or because all your friends have it, or whatever. You can get up off your butt and walk to the library to do your research, the way I did when dinosaurs walked the earth. It didn't kill me. It won't kill you either. And what your friends think isn't important compared to pulling your weight in this family and behaving like the money we work hard for actually means something, instead of you throwing it out the window in handfuls.'

His father handed him the envelope and turned and went out. His mother stood there and looked at him for a moment, her expression not softening in the slightest.

'I left you some supper in the 'vector,'' she said. 'Dad and I have to go out and run a couple of errands. Have your dinner and then get your homework done on the laptop. I had the provider copy all your school files to it before they blocked your workspace.'

'Mom—'

'Now's not the time, Nicky,' she said, the anger showing in her voice for the first time. 'You have a lot of apologies to make, but not now. It sounds too easy now. Maybe in the next couple of days your dad and I can take what you have to say more seriously.'

She went out. A moment later Nick heard the apartment door shut.

He stood there with the envelope in his hands, trembling, first with embarrassment – *oh God, what will everybody say? What will they think? This is the end!* – and then, with something more familiar, something peculiarly more bearable, more acceptable: rage.

This stinks.

But then everything *stinks!*

He was right. Joey was absolutely right!

The only question is, am I going to take this lying down? Or am I going to let them see that I'm not going to just take what they dish out?

There was only one possible answer to the question for someone who had been down as far as Seven in Deathworld, only one possibly answer for a Banie.

Surprise, surprise . . . Nick sang softly, and headed out of the room to have his supper and start laying his plans.

Charlie came down the stairs from his bedroom early that Friday morning, still rubbing his eyes a little despite having been showered and dressed for half an hour. He'd been up late putting final touches on a physics paper that was due today, and he was pleased with his efforts, even if he did feel like he wanted to turn right around and go straight back up the stairs to bed.

Charlie headed for the coffeemaker and was astounded to find it empty. He opened the cupboard above it, got out another drip-pak, slapped it into the holder, filled the brewing reservoir again and got the brew cycle started. The coffeemaker promptly began making the noise which both his father and mother referred to as 'Cheyne-Stokes respirations,' a horrific gurgling gasp followed by a long 'breath' outward that sounded more like a death rattle than anything else.

'Urgh,' Charlie said to the coffeemaker, 'you sound like I feel.'

He went back to the table and glanced at the paper which his dad had left still folded there. Charlie hit the 'go' corner and it started to unfold itself in the usual manner. At that point his dad came down the stairs with his white doctor's overcoat on and his stethoscope doubled up around his neck. 'Did you start the coffee?'

'Yup. *Some*body drank it all.'

'Speak to your mother.' Charlie's dad sat down and looked the paper over, regarding the front page with his usual mild interest before paging through to the part that really mattered. Charlie watched this process, secretly amused that his dad was managing to stay away from the sports pages for even this long. Then he caught sight of a headline on the first of the local news pages.

DOUBLE SUICIDE STUNS VA, MD PARENTS

Charlie leaned in closer over his dad's shoulder.

Arlington, May 7, 2025 – Two families in the Arlington and Fairfax areas were grieving today for a son and a daughter who were found dead early Tuesday in what appeared to be a bizarre suicide pact. The bodies of Jeannine Metz, 18, and Malcolm Dwyer, 17, were discovered in a room in a hotel in Arlington, Virginia last night, after relatives received timed e-mail messages from both teens. The messages contained slightly different versions of the same suicide note.

Police were called to the scene at 1:03 AM on Tuesday by hotel management at the Arlington Radisson-Hilton Towers, who opened the room after being alerted by Net messages from the pair's concerned parents. Shortly thereafter the police on the scene notified staff from the County Coroner's office and secured the room for investigation as a possible crime scene, but by morning the Coroner said that there was no initial indication of murder or other 'foul play' as a factor. Further statements, he said, would have to await the processing of initial tissue sample tests and a full autopsy. The Corner's office declined to comment on details of the suicide method.

Dwyer and Metz were taken to Arlington Hospital, where they were identified by their parents. 'I can't understand it,' Metz's mother, Quinne Ryan Metz said when interviewed Monday morning by local media. 'She was such a normal girl, she did well at school, there weren't any family problems, we were very close . . .' Relatives of Malcolm Dwyer declined to speak to reporters.

Police investigating the suicides had no initial comment. They would not confirm or deny the suggestion that both teens had been regular users of the controversial 'Deathworld' Net environment run by morbo-jazz star Joey Bane. Calls to Joey Bane Enterprises were not immediately returned Tuesday, but a Netted template press release from the firm's public relations department, issued to the media on Tuesday evening, stated that the managers of the Deathworld environment, because of privacy issues, do not comment on user information unless specifically required to by subpoena or other court order according to the guidelines established by the Protection of Personal Data Bill.

Charlie's dad looked up at him, momentarily distracted by his son's interest. 'What?' he said.

Charlie gulped. 'Nothing,' he said. 'I gotta go get ready for school . . .'

He headed out, but not upstairs, where his books and the take-to-school computer were. He headed for the den and swung into the implant chair. He closed his eyes, twitched the implant awake. It lined up with the Net server and activated. Things went dark . . .

A moment later Charlie was in his workspace, down

by the big worktable in the shining wooden-benched operating theater. The sun was already high there, pouring in the windows. It was noon in London.

'Nick?'

No answer. Charlie was a little surprised by that. He and Nick had for a long time maintained a 'live shout' link between their two workspaces: when one of them said just the other's name by itself, while working, the computer would open up a portal between the two spaces without further fuss. *If he was going to change that, he would have told me.*

'Main routine,' Charlie said.

'Here.'

'Link to Nick Melchior's main Net address.'

'Linking now.'

Suddenly the air around him went bright, and a sign appeared in it, hanging in front of him: SERVICE SUSPENDED. *Now that's weird,* Charlie thought, until abruptly that sign flickered, to be replaced by another: FORWARDING.

Has the family changed its master Net address or something? Charlie wondered. It did happen. People changed providers from time to time if they didn't like the service they were getting, but Nick hadn't mentioned anything like that.

There was another flicker, and then Charlie found himself looking at Nick, who was sitting in a bare, white space, in an Eames chair, reading his mail in the form of the usual various floating icons, little colored or flashing cubes and spheres and pyramids and other isometric three-dimensional solids hovering around him in the air. 'Nick?' Charlie said.

Nick looked up. 'Oh, hi. Come on in.'

'What's the blast?' Charlie looked around him with some bemusement. 'Where's your workspace? You get tired of Castle Dracula?'

Nick grinned. 'Mr Tact. Nope, my folks pulled the plug on me. Sorry if it's a little bare in here . . . I haven't had time to refurnish yet. I was mostly occupied with getting the forwarding routine installed around the service block my folks had the provider put in.'

Charlie's eyes went wide. 'Well, at least you're still online.'

'Yeah. It's just a public-terminal account at the 24-hour printing and mailbox place down in the Square, though. I can't spend as much time as I would usually. I have to sneak out to use it. Listen,' Nick said as Charlie opened his mouth to say something. 'I can't be with you long, I have to get back into Deathworld soonest. I'm on the verge of going Seventh-Circle, but my last save didn't take and I'm having to recreate a lot of stuff in off-peak.'

'I won't keep you,' Charlie said. 'But listen, did you hear about those two new suicides?'

'Yeah.' Nick actually shrugged. 'The usual. They got tired of it all. The world stank, and they ditched it. And who could blame them? Anyway, they got a little media exposure on the way out. And they're probably better off. I mean, they couldn't be *worse* off than to be alive in this world . . .'

This was so astonishing an assessment, and so utterly unlike anything Nick would normally say, that Charlie's mouth simply hung open for a moment. Finally he managed to say, 'What about your folks? What happened to make them yank your boards?'

'My dad got the last Net bill a couple of days ago and pitched a real extinction-level fit,' Nick said, and shrugged again. 'You know me, though, I can't let it get me down. Got too much to do in the real world. I'm working my way down through the dark, down to the real stuff.' He grinned. 'You should hear some of the lifts I found down there! The best Bane stuff isn't out on open release, not by a long shot. He's been saving the best for his own people, for us Banies. You really should come down with me and have a listen for yourself.'

'Uh, maybe over the weekend. Look, I gotta head out, it's school in an hour. Wanna have lunch?'

'Can't today. I've got to get off-campus and make the most of that access time. It's the only time of day when my folks don't really have a clue what I'm up to. Mornings and evenings, they may have their suspicions, but at lunch I'm free. Look, I gotta go, the system's ready for me.'

'Yeah, OK, I—'

Nick's image vanished.

Charlie stood there for a moment and hardly knew what to think. *It's like the pod people came to visit and took my buddy Nick. Who the heck was* that?

For a moment more he stood there, irresolute. 'Seven AM,' said the clock in the corner.

'Thanks,' Charlie said. He was distracted, though. *This is just too weird. But . . . Deathworld. And then . . . these two kids.*

He started to worry.

After a moment he tried to be reasonable, to talk himself out of it. Nick was sensible, Nick was perfectly sane, Nick would never try anything like killing himself.

The normal Nick wouldn't, Charlie thought.

He stood there and sweated. Unlike most of his classmates at Bradford, Charlie knew what death looked like. There were some awful memories from his very early childhood that were not shadows. They were all too solid, and he did not access them willingly. But they were stirring now. And he didn't like the idea of possibly having that kind of memory about one of his best friends.

He's not suicidal, though!

Yet, said the skeptical part of his mind, the part that his mom said was capable of 'Olympic-level worrying.'

But what the frack can I do? Charlie thought about that for a moment. Then something occurred to him, an idea which he rejected, and then considered again.

'What time is it again?' he said.

'Seven oh two.'

'Thanks.' *And now the question is . . . would he be in the office this early? Well, I could always leave a message. Either way, it's worth a try.*

'Main routine,' Charlie said. 'Address book.'

'What address, please?'

'James Winters, Net Force.'

'Trying that commcode for you now.'

Charlie swallowed. All Net Force Explorers had a commcode for Winters, as their 'head honcho' and liaison to the main organization. But relatively few of them ever used it – mostly because it was understood that, except in an emergency or a situation involving the safety or security of people using the Net, if anyone misused it, he or she would shortly be out of the Net Force Explorers on his or her ear. Charlie had been contacted by Winters once before – with no bad results. And he'd contacted Winters once before on his own recognizance, and hadn't gotten in trouble, but those calls had involved much more important business. Now, even as he waited, Charlie was beginning to have major reservations over whether Winters would consider this situation anywhere near as important. *If he starts thinking I'm taking advantage or something . . .*

Nonetheless, Charlie stood still and waited.

'Winters,' said the voice almost before the virtuality settled in around Charlie. Winters' office, as it revealed itself a blink later, was relentlessly plain. There was a metal desk with neat piles of papers, printouts and datascrips, a pen stand with a US Marine insignia on it, a couple of file cabinets, one of which at least, Charlie suspected, was actually a Net data storage facility in disguise, dusty Venetian blinds, and outside of them an uninspiring view of a parking lot. The only soft touch about the place was the seethrough bird feeder outside the window, which was filled with peanuts, though theoretically you were supposed to stop feeding birds after the first of April. The window, the walls and the filing cabinets, maybe, were real. Everything else Charlie saw was virtual, an expression of Winters' own work-space, or as much of it as he wanted you to see. Behind the desk sat the man himself: tall, lean and hard-faced, with his trademark buzz cut looking even buzzier and shorter than usual. Winters must just have had a haircut. He did not look like someone whose time it would be smart to waste. But all the same, his gray eyes were friendly and interested, even at this hour of the morning.

'Charlie,' said James Winters, looking him up and down. 'Been a while since we touched base. You're up early.'

'Uh, so are you.'

Winters shrugged. 'Occupational hazard,' he replied. 'One of the few times of the day when the link doesn't go off every five minutes.'

'I wanted to catch you before I had to go out to class, if you have a few minutes,' Charlie said.

'No problem at all. Come in, take a seat.'

Charlie walked 'in,' sat down.

'How're your mother and father doing?' Winters said.

'Uh, they're fine. Dad's getting ready for some kind of in-service presentation on spinal surgery. Mom's doing a continuing education unit, something about the new nurse practitioner requirements.'

'And you? You're coming up on end-of-term time,' Winters said, leaning back in his chair. 'How's the accelerated program coming along? Any problems?'

'Nothing serious,' Charlie said. He did not feel this was the time to mention his personal feelings about calculus, or the fact that his accelerated program required that he take it, or the fact that he had never heard of any doctor needing it.

'That's not what your calc instructor says,' Winters said, casting an eye over a glowing 'text window' hanging in the air near his desk. That window looked transparent to Charlie, but he was certain it didn't look that way to Winters.

'I passed the test the second time,' Charlie said, instantly breaking out in a sweat.

'I see that. Aced it, too,' Winters said with a small smile. 'Better than I did the second time. Or the third, or the fourth. Relax . . . you're doing OK.' That window vanished. 'But this doesn't have anything to do with school, I take it.'

'Not exactly,' Charlie said. 'I'm following up on something I'm curious about.'

'Oh?'

'Deathworld.'

Winters' eyebrows went up and he folded his arms. 'Saw that in the news, did you?'

'That last double suicide, yes,' Charlie said.

'No connection has been established,' Winters said, 'between the suicides and the virtual operation.'

'Net Force checked it out, I guess.'

'Very completely, after the first two.' His eyes rested thoughtfully on Charlie for a moment. 'No reason for you not to be given a few details, I suppose. Computer? Insight investigations. Deathworld.' Another window opened, and Winters glanced at it. Text scrolled down and through it, and though Charlie could see it this time, it was still reversed.

'The first one was in April of 2023,' he said. 'A young man, aged eighteen, then a young woman aged

sixteen, about three weeks later, in early May. While
little notice was taken of the first suicide, the second
one began to raise concerns that something untoward
might be happening. So an investigation was started.
At about the same time, the two sets of parents began
to demand that Deathworld be shut down and Joey
Bane be taken to court for reckless endangerment,
corruption of youth – you name it. They felt sure that
the site was feeding its users subliminal content of
some kind, concealed messages that caused their
children to kill themselves.'

Winters raised his eyebrows. 'Anyway, the investigation went forward. Six Net Force undercover operatives
were dispatched to check out the Deathworld operation
from the inside. Another four overt agents examined the
company's books, programming, and physical plant,
and did a guided analysis of the virtual operation's code
with the "SysWatch" code sifter.' He scanned down a
little more of the text, shook his head, sat back again.

'And they didn't find anything?' Charlie said.

'Nothing whatsoever. Clean bill of health,' Winters
said. 'The place may look dysfunctional or even amoral
to some people, but it's clean. Queasy-making, but
clean.'

'What did the kids' parents do?' Charlie said.

Winters sighed. 'They continued to agitate for
something to be done about the site – preferably to
get it shut down. One of them, the mother of the first
suicide, the boy, tried to get her Senator and local
congressman to put special bills through the House
and Senate to that effect. That didn't come to
anything, which is no surprise. To start with, the
congressional calendar doesn't have time for all the
things on it. The other parents did the talk-show
circuit, gave a lot of interviews to the tabloid press;
they still send out periodic press releases to the

various Netcasters and news agencies.' He shook his head again. 'Not that it's had much effect on Death-world, or Joey Bane. If anything, it's publicity that increases usage. And truly, without any evidence to suggest that the site really is doing anything to unbalance people . . .'

Winters turned to look out for a moment at the morning sun beginning to come in through his blinds. Then he glanced back at Charlie. 'What brings this up right now?' he said.

'I've got a friend who's all of a sudden interested in the place,' Charlie said. '*Real* interested. In fact, lately he doesn't seem able to talk about much else.'

'I take it this isn't normal for him.'

'No,' Charlie said. 'And with these new suicides . . .'

Winters leaned forward with his elbows on his desk. 'When you have the volume of people using Net-based facilities that we routinely have these days,' he said, 'the trouble is that almost any death, no matter how it looks, can genuinely be random.' He touched a spot on his desk, and another window, a smaller one, opened itself in the air. It had nothing in it, as far as Charlie could see, but one long string of digits. 'Here's today's bonus question,' Winters said. 'How many people are on the Net right now?'

Charlie tried to catch a glimpse of that long row of digits, but the problem was that almost all the numbers were changing so fast they were a blur. 'Worldwide, or just nationally?'

Winters grinned. 'Always the right question, with you. Worldwide.'

Charlie tried to remember the last set of figures he'd heard. 'A quarter of a billion?'

'Try five times that,' Winters said, and flicked a finger at the window he'd been watching. It spun so that Charlie could read it. Most of the numbers were still bright blurs, but Charlie could see the numbers 1,263 . . . and then two more sets of three digits each after that, all impossible to read.

'One point two billion and change,' Winters said, 'just at the moment. It's a function of the time of day. Australia's having its after-dinner entertainment, but most of Greater Asia is still at work. Europe and Africa and Russia are on their lunch breaks, mostly, but they'll be back to work shortly. And the East Coast is up checking the news before it heads into the office.'

He leaned back and looked at the numbers. 'The "tide" ebbs and flows as the Earth turns and the terminator moves,' he said, 'but the number where the wave "crests", at the time of greatest usage, rarely drops below nine hundred million anymore. And it grows all the time as the Netted-in population grows. So, with this information in hand . . . a question. How many of those people are dying right now, while they're on the Net?'

Charlie opened his mouth and then closed it.

'You see the problem?' Winters said. 'Let me whittle it down a little, since our viewpoint at the moment should probably stay strictly jurisdictional.' The number in the window changed, grew smaller. 'On this continent alone, there are a hundred and eighty million people using the Net right this moment. So, consider the statistics. Do you know how often someone dies in North America? Whether they're on the Net or not? From all causes.'

'I'm not sure.'

'Nineteen per minute,' Winters said. 'That's an average, of course. You get statistical clusters when there are a lot more deaths than that, and statistical "dry spots" when there are many fewer. On the same average, about fifteen children are born per minute . . . with the same kind of "real time" variation on the average. But considering that at peak times maybe half the total population might be on the Net, when their particular moment to die comes along . . .' He raised his eyebrows. 'You can see how we get small clusters of numbers that seem to mean something, but don't necessarily. It tends to make us cautious about chasing patterns that almost inevitably turn out not to be patterns at all. And when you extend the statistical sampling to include the rest of the planet you see how deceptive the numbers can become.

Charlie nodded.

Winters sighed and leaned back again. 'We only have so big a budget,' he said. 'And there are a lot of people who watch very carefully how we use it. So Net Force has to be very careful how we chase after data. Granted, we provide an important service. But no one likes a government agency that starts thinking itself too import- ant to use its budget wisely. The day we stop producing results to match our output of funds . . .' He shrugged. 'That day we, and the whole Net environment in our jurisdiction, are in big trouble.'

'I see,' Charlie said.

Winters paused as a small knocking sound came from the window, where a small brown bird had just alighted on the peanut feeder. This in itself was nothing unusual, but the bird immediately picked up a peanut from the feeder, dropped it four stories, then picked up another one, and dropped that, and picked up another one, and dropped that . . .

'Now stop that,' Winters said. He turned, pulled up the Venetian blinds, and tapped sharply on the window. 'These guys, you give them all the food they can use, and what happens? They start to get picky. You! Yeah, it's you I'm talking to! Cut it out!'

He tapped on the window a few more times. The bird pointedly picked out two more peanuts, dropped them, and finally selected a third and flew away with it.

'I swear,' Winters muttered, 'they think I'm a charity.' He sighed and turned back to Charlie.

'All right,' he said. 'If you find anything worth our attention, you'll let me know, of course. But you really should examine the possibility that your friend has something else going on in his life at this point which is making Deathworld look like an attractive alternative to physical reality. There are enough things on the Net that people find useful for that kind of purpose.'

Charlie nodded. 'I'm looking into it,' he said. 'But I really don't think that's it.'

Winters regarded him with an expression that was hard for Charlie to understand, until he spoke. 'Certainty,' he said, and the tone was approving . . . in a way. 'It's a wonderful thing to be so sure of your results that you'll discuss them with a superior before you produce the goods.'

Charlie swallowed, and hoped it didn't show. 'I'm pretty sure,' Charlie said.

Winters sat quiet for a moment. 'Good,' he said. 'Then go do some discovery, and report to me when you think you've found out everything you're going to find. If nothing else, what you turned up, if it's anything germane, can be appended to our master file. Data is always good, even if it's just deep background.'

'All right,' Charlie said. He got up.

Winters stopped him in his tracks with a dark look. 'And Charlie – one thing. Any evidence you find that suggests *anything* like conspiracy, or anything else obviously illegal, I want to hear about it pronto. Don't get in over your head.'

'Right, Mr Winters,' Charlie said, sweating again.

'Right. So get out of here and get to class.'

Charlie started to get.

'Oh, and Charlie . . .'

He stopped and looked over his shoulder. Winters was half turned to bang on the window glass again, for the brown bird was back, chucking peanuts out of it, four stories down, at about a peanut per second. 'One of the better uses for calculus, I'm told, is in the design of custom in-bone surgical prostheses. Check it out.'

Charlie grinned. *Does that man read minds? Or just faces?*

He headed back to his workspace in a hurry to get ready for school though school was now the last thing on his mind.

Chapter Four

That afternoon at Bradford Academy, Charlie saw Nick at lunch, long enough to sit down next to him and spend twenty minutes or so there but not long enough to have any decent conversation with him, for Nick was surrounded at his table by other kids who knew him, all of them plying him with questions about Deathworld and the Seventh Circle. Nick was positively smirking with glee, telling them about it in hints and riddles mostly, and pausing to play the occasional scrap of a legally 'lifted' audio track from the virtual experience on his pocket HardBard.

Charlie wasn't all that interested in the music. It sounded too much like unadulterated screaming to him, the vocals shrieking so relentlessly that it was hard even to make out the instrumentals, mostly blaring stuff in electrohorn and amplified lute so riddled with feedback that you could hardly tell what key it was in. What did concern him was Nick. His buddy was absolutely holding centercourt and plainly enjoying it. A lot of the other students had heard about the suicides; many of their parents had told them to stay out of Deathworld. A few, whose parents hadn't been concerned, had ventured in and then become seriously frustrated by the challenges of just the first level. All of them were pumping Nick for information about level one, or asking him if he knew any of the kids who'd killed themselves, or if he wasn't worried about getting in more trouble. Nick was laughing it all off as if it was minor stuff.

Finally the crowd thinned briefly, and Charlie, who had actually had to stand and wait with his lunch tray until a seat opened up a few spaces down the table, was finally able to lean over and say, 'Nick, you OK?'

'Huh?' Nick looked at him strangely. 'Why wouldn't I be?'

'Your folks just yanked your circuitry,' Charlie said. 'Most of us might find that a little annoying.'

Nick frowned. 'It won't last forever,' he said. 'Besides, I'm getting a job lined up for over the summer. I'll be able to pay for my own access time and they won't be able to stand over me and say what I should do and what I shouldn't.'

This made Charlie blink slightly. Nick was not exactly someone he would have categorized as the rebellious type but all of a sudden all kinds of personality quirks that Charlie hadn't noticed before seemed to be popping out. *Could it just be some developmental thing?* Charlie wondered. *Kind of a stage? People get those . . .*

'Besides,' Nick said to him, looking a little ways across the room, 'there's no point in assuming my folks are going to just let this drop, even after I've paid the bill off.' And abruptly he looked depressed. His whole face sagged out of shape. 'They stink, just like everything else, and if they don't give me trouble about this, they'll find something else pretty quick. About time I started pulling back a little, letting them realize that they don't get to say what kinds of things I enjoy, or get to run my whole life until there's none of it that feels worth living. Soon enough they won't be able to run any of my life, anyhow.'

Charlie opened his mouth to say that whatever Nick's

folks did, they didn't particularly stink. They were certainly no worse than his. There was something slightly unnerving about the phrasing of that last line, when it came out of somebody wearing that profoundly depressed expression. But then Nick's face brightened up again, just as if someone had thrown a switch, and he said, 'Anyway, did you hear the lifts I got?'

'Uh, it was hard not to hear them. The guy's voice is, uh—'

'Staggering, isn't it? Wait till you hear the stuff I bring back later in the week. I'm gonna make Seventh in a matter of hours, and there's a whole bunch of new stuff down there, really hard-edged.' Nick grinned, a rather feral look. 'And I already got a hint about some of it.' He nudged Charlie conspiratorially with one elbow. 'You know what the theme is down there?'

'No.'

' "Strung Out." '

'Oh.'

Nick laughed, a laugh that almost sounded like his usual self. 'Charlie, you're so deadpan sometimes, they could make coffins out of you. "Strung—" get it?' And he made a gesture above his head like someone pulling a noose tight, and crossed his eyes and stuck his tongue out, and made a 'gack' noise.

Charlie blinked.

'Hey, Nicky,' one of the other kids said from the group gathered around his HardBard. 'The thing's stopped playing.'

'Huh? Oh, that's the copy-defeat, it wants me touching it every so often.'

He scrambled up from the table and went over to them, leaving Charlie staring, somewhat bemused, at a cold cheeseburger. Then the 'tone' sounded, a siren-bleat that was a five-minute warning of the approach of the next class period. Nick vanished, with everyone else.

Charlie got up, ditched his tray in the recycler, and went off to his physics class. He got 97 percent on the physics paper he had turned in that morning, an occurrence that normally would have caused him to either do handstands or call the media. But by then, and even several hours later as he waited for the light-rail tram home from school, Charlie was feeling rather grim.

There was no sign of Nick although it was the time they usually met there to share the first part of their respective rides home. *He might have caught an earlier one*, Charlie reasoned. *Or else he's gone a different way. Maybe caught the bus around the corner, up to the Square, where his new access is.*

Doesn't mean anything's really wrong.

But Charlie was finding that hard to believe.

And what if the problem's actually at my *end?* Charlie thought, as the tram swung around the corner toward the little plaza that was nearest his house. It wasn't a pleasant idea. *Could it be that I just don't know my best friend as well as I thought I did?*

Charlie got off the tram at his stop, plodded down the street, for once completely unmoved by the scents drifting out of the neighborhood pizzeria, and turned the corner into his street. *And maybe I'm overreacting. Maybe it's nothing. He's been stressed. I've been real busy . . .*

But that sudden look of depression that had taken possession of Nick's face was like nothing Charlie had seen before. He couldn't get it out of his head, nor could he stop thinking about the way it had come and gone like something turned on and off with a switch. As Charlie went up the front steps and let himself in, he realized he was more worried now than he had been before he talked to Winters.

His folks were out, as he'd known they would be. His

mom was going to be coming in later than usual because of her in-service, and his dad was still at the slipped-disc seminar. Charlie rooted around in the freezer for a burrito, put it in the oven, waited thirty seconds for the 'ding', put the thing on a plate and ingested it at high speed, thinking. *You need to get a handle on this,* he told himself sternly. *You need to put Nick aside and concentrate on your research. Yeah, sure.*

Nonetheless, Charlie sat down at the table, where the 'newspaper' still sat, and pulled over a pencil and a scratchpad. 'Whether you're going to crack someone's chest or paint a wall,' his father always said – the last time, ruefully scraping the last teaspoonful out of a container of spackle – 'always make a plan. It saves you time, it breeds more useful ideas, and it keeps you from looking stupid later.'

Charlie scribbled on the pad for a few minutes. Having filled one page of it, he paused, wondering one more time if all this was overreaction. *Might be able to get through to him now . . .*

He dropped his pencil and trotted upstairs to the den, sat down in the implant chair, lined up his implant with the server, and closed his eyes. A little shiver down the nerves, like a shiver of cold, but without having anything to do with temperature, and Charlie was standing in his workspace. Gaslights were lit around the walls of the oval room, producing the usual faint smoky/chemical smell. It was ten in the evening in London, and outside he could hear people making their way to the opera through the crowded eighteenth-century streets.

Charlie stood there looking around him. There were virtmails hanging there in the air over the worktable, bobbing gently up and down, but none of them were vibrating or bouncing around in the way Charlie had programmed his system to use when a message was urgent. He went over to the worktable, touched one of the messages. The air lit with its transmission information and source. *MAJ GREEN*. Nice to hear from her but it could wait. He touched another of the little spheres floating there and it lit from within with a blue glow. Next to it a man appeared, saying, 'Tired of fast food? Looking for something better in regional cuisine? Come to Georgetown's newest—'

Charlie grimaced, grabbed the spammy little mailsphere out of the air, dropped it on the floor and stepped on it. It vanished with a satisfying crunch, and the man vanished as well, making a digitally strangled noise.

He sighed, looked around him. 'Nick?' Charlie said.

'Making that connection for you now,' Charlie's system said. 'Access is open.'

'All right.' He went over to the doorway that he used for access and stuck his head through. But on the other side was nothing but the plain, glowing whiteness he had seen before. There, sitting in the middle of it, was the Eames chair, and some mail-solids spinning unanswered in the air, but no sign of Nick.

He went back into his own space, and said to his workspace, 'Conditional instruction.'

'Ready,' the workspace maintenance program said. 'State the conditions.'

'If Nick Melchior calls, e-mails, or shouts for me,' Charlie said, 'call the house comms number until 2300 hours. Implement immediately.'

'Conditional instruction saved. Implementing now.'

'Thanks.'

Charlie closed his eyes and told his link through the implant to undo itself. With that slight shiver he was back in afternoon light, in the den again.

With a frown, Charlie went downstairs, sat down at

the table, and once more started making notes on the scratchpad. Soon he'd filled a page, and then another. He was more worried about Nick than he had been on the way home. Afternoon was shading toward dusk when he looked up again at a sound from down the hall.

'Charlie?'

'Down here, Mom,' he said, looking with surprise at the pages of notes. His mom – small and dark and petite in her 'formal' whites, which she didn't normally wear at work when doing psych – came strolling in, dropped some textbooks and her computer/workpad on the table, and draped her pink sweater over the chair at the table's other end. 'You have anything to eat, sweetheart?' she said.

'Uh, yeah.'

She opened the fridge and rooted around for a moment, coming up with a jug of iced tea. 'I wish,' his mother said, sloshing it thoughtfully, 'that someone would explain to me why this always goes cloudy in here.'

He thought about that. 'Microparticulate matter?' Charlie said. 'Tea's not really an infusion when you make it out of teabags. It's a suspension. The characteristics of the suspension change when you chill it.'

His mom shut the fridge and went to the cupboard for a glass, then came back to get some ice out of the freezer. 'Sounds good to me.'

'It's a theory,' Charlie said. 'I'll ask my physics teacher tomorrow.'

'Why? Sounds like you're on the right track.' She sat down at the table on his right, glancing idly at the newspaper.

As she did so, her eye fell on the headline about the two suicides. Charlie saw her look. He sighed and pushed away the notes he was making. 'Mom . . .' He glanced up, trying to find a way to begin to explain it all to her.

'Charlie,' she said, 'what is it? You look like you've lost your best friend.'

'Uh, not quite.' He found himself wondering whether the phrase, as she was using it, was intended simply as a cliché. It could be a slightly unnerving experience, having a psychiatric nurse as a mother. Not that she could read your mind or anything . . . In fact, her normal disclaimer was, 'I don't *have* to read minds. Faces are more than enough.' *Maybe in my case,* Charlie thought, *it's more than usually true. She sees my face every day.* 'Suicide,' Charlie said.

'Hmm,' she said. 'Are we coming at this as a general subject, or for a specific reason?'

He swallowed. 'I'm worried about somebody.'

'Who?'

Charlie shook his head. 'Uh, I want to be clear about my facts first. How do you tell for sure if someone's going to kill themselves?'

'For sure?' his mother said, raising her eyebrows as she sat down. 'You don't ever, for sure. I wish . . . Oh, there are various signs. Personality changes . . . changes in behavior, inability to concentrate or do business or school work, for example . . . changes in the way someone sleeps or eats, feelings of worthlessness or hopelessness. Also, a lot of talk about suicide coming up suddenly can be significant. Or gestures like suddenly giving prized possessions away . . .' She turned her glass around on the table. 'You have to look to see how many of these signs are there at once, how serious they seem – *and* look hard to make sure that the person isn't doing these things for some other reason.'

Charlie sat back in his chair. 'Did you hear about these suicides in the "Deathworld" virtual environment?'

She raised her eyebrows. 'Matter of fact, I have. There was a mention of them in an article in one of the psychiatric journals last month.'

'Did the article say anything about what might have caused them?'

His mother thought for a moment. 'Nothing concrete,' she said. 'The authors talked briefly about the details of the people who had suicided, but the article didn't go into a lot of depth. Mostly it was investigating the possibility that this was a "artefactual suicide cluster," a situation in which there are an unusually high number of suicides in a given area or set of circumstances, but none of the deaths exhibit any affiliation to the others – any identifiable common cause. A statistical fluke, in other words.'

'You mean the article couldn't find any linkage among the suicides, except for the fact that they had all been in Deathworld.'

'That's right.' His mother shifted in her chair. 'But bear in mind, honey, that this was just a short article and it was thin on detail.'

Charlie thought about that for a moment. 'OK,' he said. 'Then tell me something else. Have you ever heard of someone committing suicide because of some kind of implanted suggestion?'

She looked thoughtfully at him for several seconds before replying. 'While such things can be done,' his mom said, 'they take a lot of doing. A whole lot. The human mind is committed to keeping itself going, at any cost, even under what looks like intolerable pressure to the outside world. Sometimes it copes by going crazy. Even though that may not seem like a particularly wonderful option to you or me, it satisfies the mind's basic need – to keep on going. It takes a considerable intervention, a very noticeable level of interference, to subvert a mind sufficiently to make it completely give up that commitment to survive.'

'Like they used to say that you couldn't be hypnotized into doing something you wouldn't normally do?'

'Nothing important, no.' His mother leaned back in the chair again. 'Let's put it this way. Your whole life is a series of conditioning experiences. Your early life, for example, is about teaching you how to behave in human society, everything from "thou shalt not put they feet up on the furniture" to "thou shalt not kill".' Charlie hurriedly took his feet off the chair nearest to him. His mother smiled. 'And your training, the conditioning you get from your parents, your teachers, your friends, slowly slots everything more or less into "order of importance" in your unconscious, your id, whatever you want to call the part of your brain that reacts before you really have time to think about it. You learn, ideally, which instructions are really important and which ones aren't. So someone who hypnotized you might not have too much trouble getting you to put your feet up on a chair. On the scale of "important," that's pretty low. But if they tried to tell you to kill yourself?' She shook her head. 'You wouldn't do it. Not unless you had been conditioned all your life to believe your own survival wasn't particularly important . . . or unless you were deranged already.'

'What about subliminal stuff, then?'

She stretched. 'That has some effect, yes. But they've been arguing about it for a century now, and no one's sure how much. Again, the question has to be taken case by case. Some people are more susceptible to subliminals than others . . . and not necessarily people who are stressed or have psychiatric problems, either. Some environments are more conducive to the admin-istration of subliminals than others, and suggestions which produce strong results in one format or medium will fail completely in another.' She shrugged. 'Use of subliminals in public communications is illegal, of course. Not to say there's not ongoing suspicion that they're occasionally used. But as for making someone kill themselves?' She shook her head. 'I very much doubt it.'

'What if someone found a new way to do it – more strongly, or in some way that couldn't be detected?'

'New things are happening all the time, honey,' Charlie's mother said. 'But what can't be changed is the principle on which such a technique would have to operate. To be subliminal, a command has to affect a mind without that mind noticing. A healthy mind tends to notice when something tries to tell it to stop its own function.'

Charlie sighed. 'OK.'

'Now are you going to tell me what this is about?' she said. 'Somehow I don't think this is for some report for school. Are you concerned about one of your friends?'

He hesitated. 'Yeah,' he said. 'But, Mom, I can't tell you any more about it yet. I'm not sure I'm not completely off course.'

She gave him a long, considering look. 'Funny,' she said. 'Part of me wants to jump on the table and demand that you tell me everything right now. But that other part reminds me that if you're being careful about your conclusions, that's probably something you picked up from your dad and me over time.' She smiled, the expression rather rueful.

She put the iced-tea glass cup down. 'OK,' she said. 'You tell me when you're ready. But, Charlie, if this starts to look like real trouble with your friend, whether you're ready or not, I want you to tell me then. Right?'

'Right,' he said.

She got up and took her glass over to the sink, rinsed it out and stuck it in the dishwasher. Charlie got up and stretched too. 'I feel silly,' he said.

'Why, honey?'

'I feel like I should have known all this stuff. When it's explained, it sounds like common sense.'

His mother chuckled. 'Your father said the same kind of thing,' she said, 'when he and I first started talking about the human mind, all those years ago. No matter how medical schools swear they're going to pay more attention to the psych side of things, it never really happens. So I married your dad to make sure we would both have plenty of time for me to educate him.'

Then she grinned. 'Of course,' she added, 'he thinks the same about *me*. So I suppose we're even.' Her smiled got more wicked. 'But then, doctors always do think they can teach nurses things. Far be it from us to dissuade them. Speaking of which, let me get changed out of this uniform before he gets home . . .'

She headed out of the kitchen.

Charlie looked at his notes, then gathered them together and went up the stairs to go back online.

He spent the next three hours or so in his workspace, pulling off the Net every reference to the suicides that he could find. Shortly his space was full of scraps of virtual paper floating in the air, both those copied from his original notes and those sourced elsewhere on the Net. He had little windows screening video clips of police statements, too, and local Net and live-media reporters, and scraps of text burning in the air by themselves; stories chained together by little associational lines of light, and here and there a virtual report or reporter, with a genuine piece of landscape, or a person or persons talking. It was very crowded in Charlie's workspace, more so even than the time he called in Sir Isaac Newton and the whole Royal Academy to find out why it took them so long to get the Longitude Problem straightened out.

The images of the suicides were, by and large, not much use to him, and the stories routinely gave him information on everything except what he wanted to know. *What* caused *them*? No one seemed to have the slightest idea.

About *how* they happened, there was more information. One suicide had been in the kid's own bedroom, another had been in the living room while the parents were away. The third had been like the most recent one, in a hotel room not so far from the suicide's home. A fourth had been in a park. A fifth had been in a car in a public parking garage. Maine, New York City, the D.C. area, a suburb of Atlanta . . . *All east coast*, Charlie thought, *except this one in the garage. Colorado. Fort Collins – a college town.*

All of them, actually, were in or near college towns, even the suicide in Maine, in a suburb of Bangor. *But that would be Deathworld's target age, anyway*, Charlie thought. *Eighteen to twenty-five.* The age spread of the victims varied: nineteen, several eighteen-year-olds, a twenty-one-year-old, another who was sixteen.

But that matches the stats, Charlie thought. After talking to his mother, one of the first things he had done online was to pull up stuff on suicide. The age spread of all these suicides generally matched the stats, too. There seemed to be a tendency toward suicide in the late teens and early twenties, for reasons that none of the authorities seemed able to agree on.

Charlie walked among the scraps of information hanging in the air around him, peering at them, trying to find a pattern. None was obvious, except for one or two mentions of how the suicides had happened. *Maybe there really isn't a pattern, no matter what I'd like to believe*, Charlie thought. *The cops must have looked at all this stuff and decided there was no connection.*

But for whatever reason, Charlie couldn't bring himself to believe this. There was something about all these deaths that bothered him.

Partly it had to do with what had been said in the two news accounts which were even slightly specific about methods. What they implied matched uncomfortably to something Nick had mentioned. *'Strung out . . .'* From what Charlie could find out from random mentions in the chat groups dedicated to Bane and the Banies, there was a lot of this kind of hanging symbolism in the 'lower circles.' Mostly it was seen there as a good way to punish criminals, especially murderers.

Charlie turned to look at one of the displays, a virtual 'snap' taken with a digital handheld sampler. It was a tabloid picture, obviously taken from a distance, against the law enforcement agency's wishes, using a heat-assisted imager and looking through a window that had carelessly been left open for a moment. It still raised the small hairs on the back of Charlie's neck. It looked, at first glance, like someone hadn't really thought things through. You wouldn't normally think that trying to do yourself in from a coat hook would be all that effective. But in this case it had worked entirely too well. And the face . . .

Charlie was not willing to spend too much time looking at it. The face told him very little. But the awkwardly splayed out body troubled him more. The sight of it made him gulp, and then he was ashamed of himself, embarrassed, even though there was no one to know about his reaction. But it was going to take a long time to get rid of that initial wash of nervousness at seeing someone lying in that position. He remembered seeing people like that in his first home, the home he preferred not to think about anymore. When those scenes surfaced from memory later in his life, when he was old enough to understand, Charlie had realized that those people had all either been stoned, or dead.

He gulped again. He was eventually going to have to come to terms with the worst of those memories, he knew. But it was hard.

For the moment, Charlie went back to studying the news story that went with the image. It told him little about the cause of death that he didn't already know. Hanging, obviously. But nothing about the details surrounding the death. No autopsy information. None of the follow-up stories had given anything like that, especially not this virtual tabloid. It was the horror of the death itself that the tab was interested in selling.

I wonder, though. Are the police purposely having the news services withhold information? It made sense. They might be waiting for someone to reveal information about the crime that only they knew, that they didn't want the general public to have access to.

Good for them. But it doesn't help me any. He kept flashing on Nick saying, with glee, 'Strung out—'

Charlie shook his head and looked back at the 'window' in which he had the salient details of the deaths set out. There was something which had briefly attracted his attention earlier, and to which he now returned: the dates. The first suicides were in May and July of the year before last. The third and fourth had been in May and October of 2024 . . . and now here were the fifth and sixth, both in May as well. He remembered Winters' caution about the accidental aspects of this kind of thing. *But at the same time, could May mean something in particular to Deathworld people?* 'What's Joey Bane's birthday?' he said to the computer.

'August 8, 1996.'

Charlie sighed. 'So much for that theory,' he muttered. 'Have we got the *Encyclopaedia Retica* capsule on Bane?'

'Displaying it now.'

It spilled out in front of Charlie in two different windows: the text version, with a discography of the man's music and various analyses of his style by various critics, most of them surprisingly supportive. Clearly Bane was thought by his peers to be a genuine talent, even if Charlie wasn't impressed. The other window had a sound-and-motion record consisting of snippets of various concert performances and interviews.

One of these, which appeared in the capsule only as a soundbyte over some stills – Bane's voice saying, 'My goal is to get Hell to pay me royalties' – caught Charlie's attention, if only because it was a quote he had heard several times recently, in the brief flow of news following the most recent double suicide, and never in context. He got up, went over to the window and poked the still then showing with his finger. The computer said, 'Holding. What would you like me to do?'

'Expand that audio clip. Is there imagery to go with it?'

'Yes. Expanding.'

Shortly Charlie found himself looking at a full-virtual version of the infamous Josh Billings interview on CCNet. There Joey Bane sat, at ease and dressed all in black, in the well-known and instantly recognizable minimalist set, looking amused as the famous interviewer tried, unsuccessfully, to get him to say something self-incriminating. Charlie stood a few feet away, his arms folded, and watched it.

'Look,' Bane was saying to Billings' shocked face, 'you should stop being so hypocritical about it. There's not a being on this planet who hasn't reflected on the cruelty and pain of life, the unfairness of it. Some of the greatest literature of every age has dwelt on the problem. But nowadays if we give any consideration to it at all, we're so terrified of confronting the issue directly that we do it in secret. There's no consensus that it's all right to think these kind of thoughts anymore. In fact, nowadays if you talk about death or pain, people almost immediately start to think you're morbid, and if you talk about it *frequently*, they're likely to try to have you hospitalized. Is that fair? Is that sensible? We raise our kids on fairytales from two centuries ago, for pity's sake, and suggest to them during the most impressionable part of their lives that the most they're going to have to worry about in life is wolves trying to steal their picnic baskets. When they come to you with their real concerns – that people suffer and die unfairly, that the whole *world* is essentially cruel and unfair, that living in it hurts – we try to pretend it isn't so, we get uncomfortable, we turn away and do anything we can to avoid the subject. We don't have answers. Neither do our kids. If they're lucky they'll grow up and find some answers that we haven't seen. But *not* telling them the truth about the world, the Bad News, in my opinion predisposes them to the kind of despair that causes people to check out early. In my site, at least, kids get told the truth. *Yes,* the world stinks! What you do about it, that's *your* business. But at least there's a place for them to express their anger, which is a luxury a lot of them don't have anymore in our increasingly nicey-nice culture, where expressing an antisocial idea "inappropriately," or in front of the wrong people, can get you taken away from your parents indefinitely by some meddling social worker. In my place kids can *see* the truth, see the pain, and also see what happens to those who don't handle that anger right, who seal it over until it breaks out. You think I condone violence or crime or hatred? No way. But there's a lot of all those things out there and pretending they're not isn't going to make them go away. I think we help kids by at least *preparing* them for the idea that the world stinks, so that when their folks finally let them out of the overprotected hothouse environment that the modern home has become, they're ready for what they're going to see when they're on their own. When mommy and daddy aren't holding their hands anymore. And that's where a lot of the resistance to our site is coming from, from outraged mommies and daddies who're ticked because we're telling their little darlings the truth they never had the nerve or the brains to tell them themselves.'

It went on like that, nearly half an hour during which poor Billings barely had room to get a word in edgewise. Perhaps when he offered Bane the interview time, he hadn't thought what it would mean to offer virt-time to a man with the aerobic advantages produced by spending hours every night screaming and singing nonstop on stages real or virtual all around the planet. Only once did Bane pause, when Billings managed to say, 'And over your gates, where it says "Abandon hope . . ." isn't *that* crime? Plagiarism?'

'Nope,' Bane said cheerfully. 'It was lying around in the public domain, and no one was using it. I trademarked it. My goal is to make Hell pay me royalties.'

Having come to the soundbyte itself, the image froze on the confident, arrogant face, and Charlie sat there looking at it for a while, thinking.

The folks accusing this guy of being evil, he thought, *are wrong. He's not, really. Or at least I don't think he is. Still, something's going on at his site to cause it to act as a "core" for these suicides.*

Now all I want to know is: what?

Charlie stood there and brooded for a moment. The man himself might not mean anyone any harm but there was always the possibility that someone in his organization did. That someone was either trying to sabotage Deathworld by causing these suicides, or perhaps was running some other agenda, something a lot more obscure.

After a moment, Charlie sighed. If that was the case, the odds of him ever finding out about it were minuscule. *Besides,* he thought, *remember "Occam's Razor." Don't go introducing possibilities into the equation out of nowhere. Deal with the ones you have evidence for, before making things up.*

Charlie turned away from Joey Bane, frozen in his chair, and frowned at the polished wood floor of the old operating theater as he walked among the 'exhibits.' *And evidence is the problem. I don't have enough to come to any conclusions. For a good diagnosis, you need data – clinical data – on what happened to these people.*

I could ask Captain Winters . . . But the information Charlie needed was medical. If it was in the Net Force files at all – which it might not be – it was almost certainly inaccessible under seal of confidentiality.

If there were some other way to get at it . . .

He thought about that. *Violating confidentiality . . . But that's not what I would be doing if I just looked at data like that illegally,* Charlie thought. *If I told anyone else about what I found, yes, then it would be. But this isn't about spreading the information around. It's about finding out what really happened. Because I don't think anyone else has yet . . .*

Charlie sat down on one of the 'ringside' benches and looked across at the frozen image of Joey Bane. *If someone doesn't find out what did happen, it leaves us wide open for it to happen all over again.*

He swallowed, thinking of Nick. Granted, Nick wasn't showing any signs of being suicidal that Charlie could detect. *But then neither were these other kids,* he thought. He got up and walked over to the various windows showing the excerpted stories of the earlier suicides, hanging there in the air. He poked a finger into one window, then another, starting their text scrolling by. The second one had a history of depression. But all the rest of them seemed to take everybody by surprise.

'News alert.'

Charlie glanced up at that. 'Whatcha got?' he said to the workspace management system.

'You asked to be alerted of any news story containing the following term: Deathworld.'

'Got something new? Yeah, play it.'

Off to one side, in the few open spaces of floor left down in the 'pit' at the moment, a newsman sitting behind a desk appeared, with his mouth open, frozen. 'Playing content,' the program said. 'Source: FTNet nightly Net-business news bulletin, today, 1810 GMT.'

The clip started moving. '—ther news, Net host provider SourceStream today published weekly stats which are good news for shareholders, if a little on the macabre side,' said the newsman. 'Net access and revenue figures for the controversial Net environment "Deathworld", which hosts at SourceStream, are up nearly twenty percent from the last half-month report-ing period. SourceStream spokesperson Wik Nellis declined to speculate on the sudden leap in the site's popularity, but other industry sources suspect that the cause is the spate of recent suicides which have attracted unwelcome attention from Net-content watchdog groups and law enforcement agencies in various jurisdictions. Walkthroughs at the "morbo-jazz" site are up sharply, with SourceStream again declining to confirm the exact numbers, but industry rivals suggest that the publicity may have attracted as many as five million new users to the site, with a potential revenue injection of as much as twenty million dollars in the past two weeks. Meanwhile, the merger of BBC with WOLTime has been—'

The clip froze again. Charlie stood there looking at it, slightly disgusted. 'Sick,' he said softly. *That these people should be making more money off the fact that their users had been killing themselves* . . .

Charlie made a face. Then he sighed. It probably wasn't their fault. But it annoyed him nonetheless.

'Save that,' he said to the computer.

'Done,' it said, as he turned his back on the clip and looked at the other pieces of information littering the place. He strolled among them, trying to think. Suddenly a most paranoid idea occurred to him, so awful that it stopped him dead in his tracks. Supposing that people at Deathworld were causing people to kill themselves in order to drive the user stats and revenue up?

He shivered. *Oh, that's a sick idea. This is making me morbid. Besides, you would need evidence that they were able to make people do something like that . . . and you don't have any.*

Charlie sighed. *Just paranoia,* he thought, walking among the 'exhibits' for a few moments more. *Too many clues, not enough hard data for a real theory. For any kind of theory.*

I need harder data. I need those autopsy reports. He sat down on one of the benches and looked out across the Pit. *But how am I going to get them?*

He sat there thinking for a long time, while outside, eighteenth-century London started (finally) to go to bed, and the sky showing high up in the Royal Society's windows started to pale toward dawn.

And suddenly Charlie sat up straight. *Mark!*

'Time check,' Charlie said.

'Twenty twenty-nine.'

'I want to make a virtcall,' he said. 'Mark Gridley.'

'Trying that connection for you now . . .'

In another part of the virtual realm entirely, it was raining fire, and Nick was standing under an asbestos golf umbrella and wondering just where to go from here.

The patter of ash and live cinder on the umbrella over his head would have been strangely soothing had it not been for the brimstone smell in the air and the shrieks and wails of those in torment. All the cries were word-less, here. The Damned in this circle had been deprived of the only thing which had marked them as human while they lived on earth, the gift of speech. In all other ways that matter they were judged to have abandoned their humanity, and so they ran forever under the fiery rain, with demons scourging them through the black, blasted, ash-strewn landscape. In the distance, on the lowering horizon, a volcano was erupting, belching ash and fumes and fountains of lava into the air, and the ground rumbled constantly, crevasses always ready to open up and swallow the Damned as they ran.

Nick started forward cautiously. It was difficult to see where you were going, and those crevasses were very much on his mind. Naturally you couldn't really get hurt down here but until you knew what the crevasses entailed in terms of gameplay, it was wise to be cautious.

'Going somewhere?' someone said from behind him.

Nick turned and saw a shadow of someone about his height standing there and watching him, with folded arms. At least he thought they were folded. She was more a silhouette against the deeper darkness than anything else, apparently wearing a long, dark 'shellcoat' with its three draped layers. The hood was pushed back to show a head with shoulder-length hair, held at what looked like a somewhat arrogant angle. She was eyeing him, finding him amusing.

'Are you real?' Nick said. Down here, it was a fair question.

'I'm another Banie, if that's what you mean,' she said, tossing her hair out of her eyes, flicking away a couple of burning ashes. 'You just get here?'

'Uh, yeah.'

'Come on, then, and I'll get you oriented. You know where you're going?'

Nick pointed toward the only light he could see, the volcano.

'Mount Glede,' she said, 'that's the spot. Come on, it's a bit of a walk.'

She set out, and Nick went after her. 'Not used to doing this with a friendly guide,' he said.

'Don't mistake me for anything friendly,' said the dark shape, sounding annoyed. 'I'd as soon leave you to your own devices. But that's not how this circle works. We have to help each other.' The expression in the girl's eyes was sullen and bored, as if she thought Nick was a waste of her time.

The opinion was mutual but Nick had come far enough by now, and spent enough time and money in Deathworld, that he wasn't going to let mere bad temper, hers or his, interfere with his conquest of this environment. 'You never did tell me what to call you,' he said.

She didn't quite grit her teeth, and Nick could just hear her thinking, *I didn't intend to.* But finally, 'Call me Shade,' she said.

He smiled slightly, though he turned away so she wouldn't see it. Every Banie knew that Joey himself, or the surrogates of him which were part of the program, sometimes walked the circles in disguise, pretending to be just another Banie, and if you mistreated someone else who was working their way down, or went against the House Rules, the House could very well use it against you. Chances that might otherwise have been offered to you would be withheld; luck wouldn't go your way.

'So what do we do now?' he said.

'You didn't tell me your name, either,' Shade said, eyeing him.

'Nick,' he said. It was how the system knew him. He didn't see any point in establishing a handle just now.

'Well, Nick, mostly we head for the Mountain, and try to keep from getting distracted, or falling into any crevasses. That's gonna be a fulltime job, so stay close and don't go running off after the inmates.'

He followed her as she set off. It was difficult going until your eyes got used to it. The constant fall of ash produced an effect like black snow, a dead, soft, soot black with no highlights, no features. You put your feet down without any real sense of when they would hit anything solid. The only light was that dim red glow from the volcano, the swift-fading glimmer of the flakes of burning ash as they fell, and the burning whips of the demons that chased the Damned across the plain through the shin-high, fluffy blackness.

'Look,' Nick said a he struggled to keep up with her, 'Shade, aren't we supposed to ask these guys here anything?'

She laughed at him. 'Not much point in that,' Shade said. 'They can't do anything but scream. They could speak once, but that was taken away from them after they became murderers and wound up down here. According to Joey, they're no better than animals.'

Nick opened his mouth, but she flung her hand out to stop him. 'There,' she said, and pointed right down in front of them. Slowly, softly and silently, the earth was yawning open. He would have missed it until it was too late, and would already have been falling down into what he could just now make out as a dim, red, angry glare.

'Uh,' Nick said, swallowing.

'Yeah, "uh",' Shade said, scornful. 'Game over, if you fall into one of those. Big waste of time. No recall from that, either. No "save" from a crevasse. So watch yourself.'

Together they sidetracked a long way to their left to get to the point where the crevasse narrowed enough to be stepped over. 'I was going to say,' Nick said, 'if they can't talk, what's the point of them being here?'

Shade looked at him with amusement. 'It's not like seeing the guilty get punished for murder isn't worth something by itself. Wouldn't you say?'

Far away across the dark landscape, Nick thought he could hear something like an electrolute tuning up. His heart leapt. 'That's a new "lift"!'

Shade sighed. 'Yeah, it's the warmup for "Strange Fruit." Not a bad cut, that one.'

' "Strange Fruit?" '

'It's a cover,' Shade said. 'Joey doesn't do many covers. A lot of people down here think it's a tribute to the Angels of the Pit.'

Nick shook his head, confused.

'You really haven't *talked* to a lot of people down here, have you, Shade said.

'Uh, no.'

There was another long sigh. 'I guess it's understandable,' she said, rather more softly, as they went forward. 'The upper circles aren't much about talking to real people. The "Angels of the Pit" – those are the kids who died after being down here.'

'The ones who committed suicide?'

'We don't usually put it that way,' Shade said, pausing again as another crevasse started to open up in front of them, then leading Nick off to the right this time. ' "Death wears many faces . . ." That's what the song says. They left us before they were finished. Whatever made them do it, they're gone now, but we remember them.'

This was so unlike what Nick had been thinking about the suicides that he was startled. 'Didn't any of them make it, you know, all the way down?'

Shade shook her head. 'No way. No one who's ever made it down into the heart of the Ninth has done anything like that. There are things that happen down on Nine . . .' Her voice trailed off.

'Like what?' Nick was eager. He had almost never heard even a scrap of rumor about Nine before.

Shade laughed at him then. 'You're asking me?' she said. 'You think I've been down there? As if I'd still be slumming around up here if I had.' She sounded scornful again. 'No, some of them just come back and help a few newbies before they go on. I've got a ways to go yet.'

They went on in silence for a while, following the faint tune-up notes of Camiun across the darkling plain. It was hard to judge distances, but Nick thought it would have been something like a mile in the 'real' world. A Damned person ran by them, howling, in battle fatigues, and behind him came a couple of winged demons, their whips aflame, every stroke burning a white-hot slit through the big, burly man's combat jacket as he fled from them. Nick slowed down to watch him go.

'Some gangster,' Shade said, bored. 'We get a lot of them down here. Little tin-pot dictators and their paramilitary hangers-on. While they're in power they think they're invulnerable, that they can kill anybody they like. But sooner or later it catches up with them. Their henchmen learn their bosses' lesson too well, that you don't have to treat anybody with pity, or compassion. Eventually the henchmen turn right around, shoot their bosses and take their jobs. Not that they last long.' She chuckled.

Ahead of them, the volcano seemed to be getting closer, and Nick squinted at it. There was something odd about the shadows at its base. He was distracted though. The darkness, the ash and the screams, they all seemed to press in strangely, and Camiun's tinkly, tuning cadences seemed unusually distant. 'Kind of depressing down here,' Nick said.

Shade looked at him thoughtfully as she jumped over a small narrow crevasse that opened up in front of them. 'You feel that way?' she said.

Nick nodded. 'Sometimes. But it's worse up at home – a whole 'nother story.'

'Problems?'

Nick made a face. 'The usual. My folks think I'm wasting money down here. Even some of my friends think I'm wasting time. None of them seem to think I'm capable of figuring out what I really want. "You're too young to really know," "you'll get over this, it's just a fad . . ." ' He sighed, glanced up at her. 'What about you?'

Shade laughed. 'Yeah, I've heard the same kind of thing. I ignore it. And my folks and my friends don't know anything about down here . . . so I ignore them, too. They're all so concerned, like it's going to affect my mind somehow. But, I mean, what's down here that could possibly be more depressing than real life?' And she gave Nick a look that, even in this dim light, was extremely ironic. 'Not enough money to do the things you want to, not enough time to do them if you had the money, not enough life to do everything you'd like to even if you had the time – what could be worse than that? This is just dark. And for us, not even painful. Not as painful as The Real World.' She pronounced the words with profound disdain. 'A day job you can never afford to give up until you're too old to remember what you would have done with your days if they'd been yours to spend, when you were young. What's a little fire and brimstone to that?'

She looked closely at Nick as they walked, almost as if there was some response she was expecting. 'I don't know,' Nick said. 'Life stinks, yeah, but I don't know if it stinks *that* much!'

'You *are* young yet,' Shade said. 'Just wait a while. You probably have all these great ideas about how wonderful it'll be when you get out on your own, how you'll have all this terrific freedom. Wait till you do it, and see how hard you have to work just to keep a roof over your head and enough food inside you to keep your stomach from waltzing with your backbone every night. While the people you're interested in take themselves out of your life, one by one.' She laughed. 'After too much life spent that way I can understand why some people might want to . . . *you know*. Do what *they* did. The Pit Angels . . .'

Nick had no immediate answer to that, for what Shade was saying had abruptly struck him with surprising force. It had never occurred to him that he *wouldn't* find life better after he finally left home, that there might be a *bad* side to freedom. But now, hearing it from someone down here, the possibility occurred to him that he might be making a mistake.

Yet at the same time, if I don't make that mistake, I'm trapped . . . Trapped with an angry mom and dad, in an apartment that was too small and where they watched his every move to see whether they would approve of it. And if he kept going the way he had been going, before this most recent blowup, what would follow? College, but if he didn't manage to get a scholarship to someplace far enough away that he would have to live on campus, it would just be the same thing all over again. Except it would be even more intolerable, because he would be *college age* and still having to obey his parents' dumb rules. Everyone would laugh at him, and the whole point of college, getting away and exercising some independence, would be lost.

Yet Nick was pretty sure that he wasn't going to be in line for any scholarships. His grades hadn't been perfect. He was holding his own at Bradford and was not in danger of failing, but the grades he had at the moment weren't going to get him into anything but the state college or one of the community colleges in the area. He could just hear his folks: *Why spend money on boarding at someplace that's only twenty miles away? You'll stay here with us.*

. . . Where they can keep me under their thumb.

Suddenly it all seemed very hopeless. Nick just stopped where he was and gazed ahead in the blackness as Shade kept going. Suddenly he could understand it. Not wanting to go on, not seeing the point. Past college, what would there be for him? He wasn't even particularly sure what he wanted to do in the world. Or that there *was* anything for him to do in the world. For the past couple years now he had been surrounded by kids working hard, full of plans and goals, and he had laughed at them busting their guts as if they were adults working at something that really counted. Now here he was, without any plans or goals, and suddenly Nick suspected that the other kids had, all along, known something he hadn't. Now they were heading toward lives, busy lives full of interesting things to do, even if the work was hard. *And here I am,* Nick thought, *with nothing. Nothing.*

Except parents who're going to remind me of it every chance they get, for the foreseeable future.

Suddenly Nick could understand how nice it might be for it all just to stop. *Like going to sleep and not waking up.* The sudden desire for it to be that way, just quiet, just no more trouble, came down on him, darker and stranger than the surroundings. Nick shivered.

Shade stopped, looked back at him. 'Nick. Come on, what's the matter?'

'Uh, nothing.'

That feeling was gone now, but it had been . . . weird. Nick went after her, shaking the umbrella a little to get the excess ash off it. The dark shape up ahead of them, in the shadow of the mountain, was a little better defined now, starting to look like a building. 'Uh oh, watch out for this one,' Shade said, stopping very suddenly.

Nick stopped and looked down, stepping back

hurriedly as the growing crevasse shot out arms in several directions, one of them stitching along right in front of his feet, the ash in front of him tipping down into it, faint flakes of darkness against the quickly revealed dull-red glow of the flow of lava, away down there. In the air above them, Camiun's tuning-up paused and then segued into a low minor-key strumming. 'So strange,' Joey Bane's voice sang, 'so strange . . .'

They made their way around the new crevasse and kept walking. A shadow reared out of the air near them as they walked. Nick stopped and stared at what was swinging there. Two shapes. It wasn't a tree of any kind. It was some sort of metal framework, and a man and a woman were hanging upside down from it. 'Mussolini,' Shade said. 'You know, Italy . . . last century? They caught up with him, eventually'. She raised her eyebrows, just visible in the light of the nearby volcano. 'There are plenty more like that around here if you care to investigate . . .'

'Thanks, no.' Nick gulped, sickened by the image swinging gently in front of him. Then he looked past Shade, still unnerved by that odd feeling that had come down on him, and saw something more to the point. Past the tall metal frame, at the foot of the volcano, was something that interested him a whole lot more. A faint shimmer of light, something genuinely reflective in all that dead matte-black – a wide, dark sheet of water. It was the Lake of Tears, and beyond it, reflecting darkly, rose the Keep of the Dark Artificer at last, all gleaming black towers and walkways, and high up in one tower, a single light.

'That's really it,' Nick whispered. 'Finally . . .'

'Yup,' Shade said, looking at the Keep. To Nick's eye she looked astonishingly blasé about something which, in its way, was the heart of Deathworld. 'Bigger than it looks,' she said. 'Don't be fooled by it.'

He nodded then turned back to Shade. There was something about her voice, something sad. 'Are *you* OK?' Nick said.

She looked at him in surprise. 'Why shouldn't I be?' The answer was defensive, flip, a little sarcastic.

Why wouldn't I be? He'd said to Charlie, and laughed at him. And Charlie had genuinely been concerned. Nick bit his lip. 'Just asking,' he said.

'Yeah, well, thanks.' She tossed her hair back, a shadow in her greater shadow. 'So what are you waiting for? You pass. You might as well go on in and see what's waiting.'

' "Pass?" ' Nick was bemused. 'But I didn't do anything.'

Shade gave him that scornful look again. 'You asked the right question,' she said, and began to fade away in the volcano's feverish light.

'But which one?'

She grinned. 'If you have to ask,' Shade said, 'I can't explain it. Go on, go ahead and see if you get anywhere in the Keep. The way to Nine is through the Keep, they say. If you can figure it out. But I wouldn't hold out a lot of hope.'

She vanished completely.

Nick turned to look at the huge doors of the Keep. Slowly, hauled open by troops of demons singing *yo-yo-heave-ho* and pulling on giant bronze ropes, the massive doors swung open before him. Nick stood there feeling a great flush of triumph as Camiun's voice cried out in feedback-fuzzed ecstatic arpeggios all up and down the scale.

The demons stood waiting, standing at attention.

Nick, though, stood still there, thinking.

The way to Nine is through the Keep, they say.

. . .If you can figure it out.

Nick stood there, considering, for a while then deliberately turned his back on the Keep and started to kick his way back through the downfalling ash, back the way he had come.

'Hey,' yelled one of the demons down by the door. 'Where ya goin'?'

'Back to help some people,' Nick said, and scuffed off into the darkness, toward the edge of the Eighth Circle again.

From the shadow of the doors, a tall, dark form, not a demon, faded back into existence, watching him go . . . and smiled.

Chapter Five

Mark Gridley's workspace this week looked like the old Vehicle Assembly Building down at Cape Canaveral. This was a new one on Charlie though it didn't exactly surprise him. On earlier visits he had seen it looking like an underground cave full of stalactites and stalagmites, like a single gigantic floor of an office building towering over the Singapore skyline, like the entrance hall of the Museum of Natural History in New York, like the salt flats outside Bonneville, Utah, and like the surface of the Moon in an area not far from the Lunar Appennines, where some astronauts had left their moon buggy. In his own version of that empty, arid place, Mark had constructed a garage for the buggy, one which had also quizzically sheltered a beatup lawnmower and a folded-up Ping-Pong table. Charlie had come to believe, both at the sight of those workspaces and during some of the events later associated with his visits to them, that it was entirely possible Mark Gridley might have a hinge loose somewhere.

But whether he did or not, there was no ignoring the fact that Mark was possibly the single most dangerous person on the planet, at least as far as the Net was concerned. Whether heredity had anything to do with it, Charlie wasn't sure. Having the head of Net Force for your father and a talented computer tech/heavy-duty philosopher for your mother could certainly predispose you to think more about the Net than most people did. But just thinking about it a lot couldn't possibly endow anybody with the kind of talents Mark had with computers in general and the Net in particular. He was a genius at getting into any kind of computer system *and* exploiting it while there. Maj Green had remarked once to Charlie that the Net Fairy had plainly been present at Mark's christening. Charlie wasn't so sure about that but there was no keeping Mark out of any system he was interested in. And he was interested in everything.

At least, he always had been before. Today Charlie was banking on the idea that nothing had changed.

Charlie headed across the vast concrete floor of the VAB, looking for signs of life. He didn't see any. The huge space, thirty stories tall, was empty. This by itself wasn't so odd: in the real world it had been a long time since spacecraft had been built there, and mostly the building was kept for its history as the assembly area for the first rockets to take man to the Moon, and because demolishing the VAB would have upset the colonies of pygmy Cape buzzards that nested there and worked the little 'pocket' weather system inside the building.

Off in one corner, though, about a quarter-mile away, Charlie saw where a beam of sunlight came in through the movable cowling in the roof, and shone down on what looked like a conversation area. There were various chairs arranged in something like a circle, with a big low hardwood desk off to one side. Charlie made his way toward this, listening to the creaks and cheeps of the buzzards above him as they circled in a mini-updraft near the roof.

'WHO DISTURBS THE GREAT AND POWERFUL OZ?' thundered a huge voice all through the VAB. The buzzards squeaked in protest and flapped over to the sides of the building, perching and shaking their heads at the noise.

'It is I,' Charlie said, rolling his eyes. 'I mean, it's me, Squirt. Lay off the "great and powerful" trip before I choke myself laughing.'

'I don't think you take me seriously enough,' said a much more normal voice, that of a thirteen-year-old kid again. It echoed in the huge space, but didn't roar as it had a moment before. Mark came into sight now from somewhere behind the 'conversation circle,' his arms full of virt-mail images. He was wearing swimtrunks and a MoldToYou T-shirt which was presently showing, one phrase at a time, in bold white letters on black, the message SPACE IS BIG / SPACE IS DARK / IT'S HARD TO FIND / A PLACE TO PARK / BURMA SHAVE.

Charlie blinked at that. Mark was part Thai but Charlie still wasn't sure what Burma had to do with anything. 'How is it possible to take you anything *but* seriously,' he said. 'You busy?'

'Nothing important,' Mark said, dumping the load of virt-mails onto his desk of the moment. They scrambled around on the surface of the desk, putting themselves in some prearranged order, then ascended gently into the air and hovered there, like well-trained bubbles. 'Just trying to get down to the bottom of the Inbox before the end of the week.'

'Why? What's the end of the week?'

Mark snickered and brushed his dark hair out of his eyes. He was due for a haircut, or maybe this was just some new style he was trying out. 'My dad's been threatening to take me surf-fishing for about the last year. Well, the stars or whatever must be propitious, because we're going away for the weekend, up to some place on the Jersey shore. Or so he claims.' Mark gave Charlie a knowing grin. 'I'm betting you something'll come up Saturday morning and it'll all be off. But I can't absolutely count on it, so . . .'

'*WAAAH*,' said something nearby, a raspy upscaling voice that vaguely suggested a soul in torment.

Mark looked over his shoulder. 'Yeah, yeah, it'll be dinnertime soon,' he said to someone Charlie couldn't see.

'What was that?' Charlie said, looking around. It didn't sound like a buzzard.

'The cat. Theo,' Mark said. 'Or, as we call him, The Gut Who Walks.' Another piercing Siamese-cat shout filled the air, suggesting either that Theo didn't appreciate the characterization, or that this conversation wasn't producing food, or that he was testing the acoustics. 'So look, what brings you by? Not that I don't think it's entirely social.'

Charlie grinned. Mark had taken some ribbing from the older Net Force Explorers about his age, and his size – he was short and light even for a thirteen-year-old – until they started to discover that the area in which Mark was decidedly no lightweight was his brain, and that he could outthink, and sometimes outmove, any of them. Those who had christened him The Squirt as a joke had since turned it into a title of honor, and kids five or six years older than him had soon learned not to treat Mark as if he were too young to be taken seriously. Charlie had never been one of these. He knew entirely too much about what it was like to have people decide because of your background that you weren't worth their time.

'Got a problem, Squirt,' Charlie said.

Mark looked surprised, and eyed him curiously. 'Yeah, you do, don't you?'

'Does it show?'

'You look bothered. What's the matter? Trouble with your folks?'

'*Me?* No.' Charlie laughed, but he wasn't surprised

that the sound didn't come out sounding particularly humorous. 'Look, I have to ask you something.'

'Blaze away.'

'I'm not sure it's not illegal.'

Mark raised his eyebrows. 'Oh? Not your usual mode of operation, Mr Straight Arrow.'

'Don't remind me. I need to get at some information.'

'You interest me strangely.'

Mark's suddenly delighted expression made Charlie laugh. 'Nothing real involved. I need to get at some medical records.'

Mark looked bemused. 'Thought you'd usually ask your dad about that kind of thing.'

'Not just general information. I need to get at some County Coroners' files.'

'*Aha!*' Mark said, and leaned back in his chair. 'Not public files, then.'

'Nope. Autopsies.'

'Wow, truly disgusting,' Mark said, not sounding disgusted in the slightest. 'I wanna see, too.'

'Not sure it would be good for you to see this stuff,' Charlie said, uneasy. 'Heck, I don't really even want to see it.'

'You're gonna have a hard time getting at it in the first place without me,' Mark said, sounding all too matter-of-fact. 'Come on, Charlie, I'm not going to look over your shoulder if you're really worried. But it'd make me feel a lot better if you'd tell me what was going on.'

Charlie didn't see that he had any choice. He sat down on one of the chairs pulled into the circle and told Mark the basics of his problem, without mentioning any names.

When he was finished, Mark folded his arms, thinking. 'Been a lot of attention on Deathworld, hasn't there?' he said. 'Since the last couple of suicides . . .'

'Yeah.'

'But you don't need me to break in there, I take it.'

'Nope. It's just this medical stuff I'm after.'

Mark sighed. 'Pity,' he said. 'Deathworld would have been a challenge . . . But as for this other stuff, we can do it this evening, if you like.'

'Really?'

'Shoot, we can do it now.'

Mark opened a drawer in his desk, looked at the virtmail 'solids' floating around above the desk. 'OK, everybody in . . .'

One after another the icons dropped into the drawer, all but one, a recalcitrant sphere that hung bobbing in the air over the desk and wouldn't budge. 'Yes, you too, get in there!'

'You promised you would deal with this today,' said the virtmail, in Jay Gridley's voice.

Charlie's eyebrows went up. Mark flushed pink and grabbed the mail out of the air, stuffing it in his pocket. 'No rest for the weary,' he said. 'Never mind.'

Mark dusted his hands off, knocked the drawer shut with his hip. 'OK,' he said, 'let's see what you've got.'

Charlie fished around in his own pocket and came up with a notepad, the icon for a little file full of bureau names that he was carrying with him. He handed it to Mark. Mark tossed it onto the desk, and a window appeared in the air in front of them and displayed the list.

'Mmm,' Mark said. 'Bangor County Coroner's Office, Collins County Police Coroner, Arlington City Coroner's Department . . .' There were six offices matched with six victims. The paired suicide, the most recent one, was being handled by two different coroners' offices: the kids had lived in two different jurisdictions.

Mark stood there with his arms folded, thinking for a

moment. 'Let's do the county systems first,' he said. 'Then the police ones. The cops are likely to have better security, and they might take us a little longer.'

'You don't think they're likely to alert each other that someone's going after data on the suicides?' Charlie said, beginning to get nervous. He was feeling guilty already.

'I doubt it,' said Mark. 'There isn't nearly as much cooperation between police forces as there should be if they really want to make their systems secure. Especially regionally. Too much rivalry.' He grinned slightly. 'Old habits die hard. Besides, these people don't seem to have been comparing notes in the first place, do they? I mean, just from what you told me now, all the suicides seem to involve a hanging of one kind or another and no one seems to have picked up on that. At least nothing's been mentioned about it on the news.'

'They might be hiding that information,' Charlie said, uncertain.

'If they were coordinating, yeah. But we don't have any proof that they are. So let's stir around a little and see what we find. If any of the data you're interested in is tripwired, or has associational links to similar data in some other police department's network, then that might indicate that they're talking to each other privately about this stuff. Meanwhile . . .' He looked at the list. 'Let's start with Bangor.'

Mark looked around him. 'OK,' he said to his workspace, 'strike the set.'

The VAB, the sunlight, the little flickery shadows of the buzzards away up high all vanished away in a blink, leaving them in a peculiar sort of darkness in which the two of them were illuminated, but nothing else was. The only other thing visible was the window with the names of the agencies Charlie wanted to raid for information. 'Bring up the advanced-level penetration utility,' Mark said.

The floor of Mark's workspace suddenly became visible. More than visible. It was transparent, so that Charlie could see down into it, for what looked like maybe a thousand meters. The space below their feet was full of light, light of every color, columns and lines and pillars of it, some horizontal but mostly vertical, interwoven, sometimes even interpenetrating. This was an expression of a program that Mark had designed for getting into other programs. 'What language did you write *this* in?' Charlie said, very impressed.

'Digamma, it's called. Nasty stuff.'

'I believe you.' Charlie knew in a general sort of way that every line of the light he saw reaching down to limitless depths beneath him was a statement in computer code of some kind, but there his knowledge stopped. 'Man, I'm just getting the hang of Caldera. I thought *that* was complicated!'

'Yeah, you wouldn't want to mess with Digamma unless you were seriously unbalanced,' Mark said. He looked down into the abyss of light, and the whole deep panorama began moving with great speed underneath him, slipping sideways. Then it was as if the floor on which they stood plunged downward like an elevator, though they weren't actually moving at all. Rather, the graphic expression of the 'penetration' program was pouring itself up past the two of them into the air around them as ghosts of structures of light. It paused, then poured sideways again as the program sorted for some specific spot that Mark had in mind. After a moment it stopped, which was a good thing, because Charlie's stomach was bouncing around inside him as if he was on a rollercoaster.

' "Unbalanced," ' Charlie said, trying to get control

of himself. 'This suggests certain possibilities about you, Mr Gridley.'

'Don't it just,' Mark said, sounding distracted for a moment. 'Necessary, though. Lot of the Net Force master computers' routines are running in Digamma. You want to work with those, you have to learn it eventually. My dad started teaching it to me when I was seven. I'm just now really getting the hang of it.' He interlaced his fingers, cracked his knuckles. 'OK, now watch this.'

He beckoned over the window in which Charlie's 'addresses' were written, and poked the first one with his finger. 'Identify,' he said to his program, 'and locate.'

They stood there in the bright silence for a moment, and suddenly a string of letters and numbers which meant nothing whatsoever to Charlie strung themselves out in the air in front of them in a blaze of crimson. Around them the colors of the penetration program went mostly to blues and greens.

'Good,' Mark said. 'That's the raw Net address. It tells me a little about their security, which frankly, needs to be looked at. These guys must think they're safe from intrusion.' He smiled slightly. 'Well . . .'

'Can you get in?' Charlie said.

'In? We're in already.' Mark glanced around him. 'At least, we're in their system. Now we have to crack their security, preferably without them noticing, and go hunting. Look, the information you want, it'd probably be easier for you to identify as images, yeah?'

'That's the best way for me.'

'OK. Home system. Go graphic.'

Everything went dark, then filled with light again, and the two of them found themselves looking at a wall. It reared up as high above them as they could see, and ran off to what seemed infinity in both directions. It appeared to be made of red brick, and some wit had posted up on it a neatly lettered sign that said: FIRE-WALL.

'Everybody's a comedian,' Mark said, walking alongside the wall for a little way, examining it. 'Let's see what we've got here. C^3? Caldera? Levolor?' He patted the wall, felt one of the bricks. 'Nope, it's Fomalhaut. One of the lousiest programming languages of the decade. *Why* in the world did they use Fomalhaut for this?'

Charlie stood watching Mark kick the wall once or twice in an experimental kind of way. 'What's the matter with the language?'

'Terrible structure,' Mark muttered. 'You have to really like doing things over and over to use Fomalhaut. Look at this.' He glanced up and down the length of the wall. 'In any normal virtual programming language, a wall like this would be set up with one command that you then told to repeat itself however many times, and then you would tell it where to stop, or to seal itself up. In Fomalhaut, you have to do every single command separately.' Mark shook his head. 'Each of these – ' he kicked another brick – 'represents a separate command. Really dumb.'

'So why would they have used it, then?'

Mark shrugged. 'Oh, some people might think it was better for security. More trouble, they would think, to have to disassemble a "wall" brick by brick; you couldn't just subvert one. But plainly it didn't occur to them that sooner or later, a more sophisticated way to deal with this protocol might come along. Or that someone else who knew the language really, really well . . .'

Mark reached out behind him, plucked something out of the empty air. It was a crowbar.

Charlie had to laugh. ' "More sophisticated"?'

'Yeah, don't laugh. You'll see. Meanwhile . . .' Mark

stood there and touched one brick. It lit from within, revealing what looked like a little churning square of boiling alphabet soup, all letters and numbers. 'Right.' Mark said. 'And this one.' He touched another brick, further down the wall. It revealed another oblong full of soup. 'Uh huh. One more.'

The third brick revealed the same contents. Mark stood there for a moment. 'Someone here,' he said with satisfaction, 'got real sloppy.' These aren't all separately written instructions. They've been cloned from a single one. Jeez, a *lazy* Fomalhaut programmer. What's the point? Why use an obsessive-compulsive language, and then not obsess?'

Mark shouldered the crowbar and grinned at Charlie. 'Never mind,' he said, 'we're in business.'

He put two fingers in his mouth and whistled.

From some distance away came a tiny sound, like a faraway screech of surprise. 'Aha,' Mark said, cheerful. 'Come on, that's what we're after.'

He started to jog to their left, down the wall. Charlie followed him. 'Look,' he said, 'what are our chances of getting caught in here?'

Mark grinned as he trotted along. 'No better than one in a hundred at the moment.' Charlie instantly broke out in a sweat. He preferred *much* longer odds. 'I mean, think about it, Charlie! Programmers are a spoiled bunch these days. They work what they used to call "banker's hours." Nobody in the coroner's office in some little county building in Maine is going to be hanging over their terminal at eight thirty in the evening waiting to see if someone breaks in or not! *If* the system is even housed in the same building, which isn't necessarily the case. And their automatic system security is junk. I know, because I broke through it five minutes ago. I pretended to be its system administrator, and my penetration manager gave it a nice set of circular instructions to play with, based on its own check cycle. Right now it's doing the machine equivalent of staring in the mirror and telling itself that everything is fine. And here we are.'

Mark stopped and pointed at a brick high up in the wall. 'See that?'

That particular 'brick' was glowing red hot. 'Kind of hard to miss,' Charlie said.

'That's the instruction all these other ones were cloned from. Now then.' Mark started to walk up the air as if there were stairs there. With the crowbar, he pried out that particular brick, and caught it in one hand as it fell.

The wall started to crumble. Charlie jumped back, out of reflex, but as the wall tottered outward toward him, the bricks began to fade: by the time they reached the 'floor,' they were vanishing like fog in sunlight. A moment later he and Mark were looking out across a vast hall full of thousands of beige filing cabinets.

'Wow, imaginative,' Mark said, sounding unusually dry. 'Somebody in the data processing department here really gets off on their work.'

He walked down out of the air again, tossing the single glowing red brick in his hand as he did. 'We'll hang on to this,' Mark said. 'We'll want it to put things back the way we found them when we're ready to go.' He shoved the brick into the air between them. It vanished.

Charlie started walking among the lines and lines of filing cabinets. 'This is the visual paradigm the people who work here have been using?' he said.

'The default, yeah,' Mark said. 'It may make it easier for you to search. The clerking staff'll probably have left some markers for themselves, to make it easier to find things. But boy, oh boy – ' Mark chuckled – 'at times like this, do I ever get seized with the desire to redecorate.'

'Please *don't*,' Charlie said, walking among the filing

cabinets and looking at the little cards inserted in their drawer-fronts.

'Oh, come on, Charlie. Let me just leave a potted palm in here somewhere. I'll even tie a big red ribbon around it.'

'No!' *2004–2005*, said one cabinet: *2005–2006*. Charlie walked along the line of cabinets, looking for *2024*.

'Just kidding,' Mark said. Charlie wondered about that. 'Aha,' he said, and grinned at himself. Mark's turn of phrase was catching. '2020.'

The 2024 cabinet was the fourth one down. Charlie pulled its top drawer open, and suddenly there were five other cabinets standing next to that one. 'January through May,' he said.

He headed for May, opened that cabinet up and started riffling through the files there. *Delano*, he thought. *Richard Delano. May third.*

The file was there, a plain manila folder. Charlie pulled it out.

Instantly the air around him and Mark was full of windows. One of them showed a file structure 'tree,' full of files all of whose names began with DELANO. Another few windows showed pictures: crime scene shots, pictures of someone's house, probably Delano's. Then one more window said STATE PATHOLOGIST'S REPORT.

'Yes, indeed,' Charlie said softly. 'Mark, can I copy these into your workspace?'

'You can copy them right back to yours, if you like. I've still got a link open.'

'Both, then. I want to make sure the data's safe.'

'Consider it done.' A big bright gold hoop appeared in the air, and set itself on fire. 'Chuck anything you want copied through that: it'll make copies both places and then refile itself.'

'Good.' Charlie glanced at the ring, amused, then

reached out and, with one finger, poked the window with the pathologist's report. It opened out into a series of still more windows, with screenfuls and screenfuls of text, and in one window, images of the body at autopsy. Charlie looked at this somberly, then turned his attention to the text.

'He looked real young,' Mark said, from behind him, softly.

'Yeah. This was the sixteen-year-old,' Charlie said as he read hurriedly down through the report, skimming it, and finding the words he had suspected he would find: *Strangulation. Self-inflicted.*

'Right,' Charlie said, and folded the window down small, and chucked it through the ring. The ring flared. The window vanished. Charlie gathered all the information together again which had come out of the original file, and threw it, too, through the ring. Then he closed the file drawer.

'That it?' Mark said. 'You sure you don't need anything else?'

'Not from here. But we've got five other places to hit, still.'

'Gonna be a short, dull night for me at this rate,' Mark said, sounding disappointed. 'Never mind.' They walked away from the filing cabinets again to the point where they had first entered, and Mark plucked that red brick out of its hiding place in the air. 'Be fruitful and multiply,' he told it, and dropped it on the floor.

A moment later there were two of it, and then four, and eight, sixteen, thirty-two, sixty-four. Within about thirty seconds the wall had completely rebuilt itself, even to the sign that said FIREWALL. 'Mark—' Charlie said warningly, for the sign was now upside down.

'Oh, come on, Charlie! I was real good. I didn't even leave them a potted palm.'

'Mark!'

'Oh, all right. Spoilsport.'

The sign righted itself. A moment later they were back in Mark's space, where a stack of what appeared to be manila files was floating in midair, and Mark was referencing the 'list' window again. 'Next.'

The lines and columns and pillars of light dived and swooped around them again, and Charlie closed his eyes after a few seconds, since his stomach really did *not* like this. 'Here we are,' Mark said, and they found themselves in another walled area, but this time they were inside the painted concrete walls, not outside them.

'Hmm,' Mark said. Charlie gulped, wanting to say a lot more than that, for the walls were moving in on them, like something out of an ancient 2D horror flick . . . except that these walls were in 3D, and, as they watched, were slowly sprouting long, cruel, inward-pointing iron spikes.

'Interesting,' Mark said. 'Those would pin us here, and ID us to the local system administrator, and lock a trace onto my system and any other one affiliated with this search. *If* we left them.' He snapped his fingers, and the pale tracery of his own Digamma routines became more visible around the two of them inside the rapidly shrinking space.

'And we're not gonna let them do that,' Charlie said, sweating hard, 'are we?'

'Not a chance. Hush up now, I have to think.'

Charlie started to sweat harder, and closed his eyes again as once more the Digamma framework around them did its zoom-and-swoosh rollercoaster number.

'They're a little paranoid here,' Mark said matter-of-factly. 'I wonder if they've had a break-in recently?'

Charlie opened his eyes again. The disorienting slide and swoop of colors had stopped, and Mark was holding in his arms what appeared to be a wide pipe of pure glowing yellow, as thick as the trunk of a tree. He was wedging one end of it against the inward-pushing wall on the lefthand side, and as Charlie watched Mark picked up the other end of the branchless yellow 'tree trunk' and began to pull on it. It lengthened as he pulled, until it came right up against the wall on the righthand side. The walls pushed against it. The 'tree trunk' glowed briefly brighter, bent a little, then braced itself still, bending no more.

'There,' Mark said. He watched the walls keep trying to push, but they were making no headway. 'Automatic system,' Mark said. 'No one's watching it. Banker's hours, as I said. Or else someone's gone for coffee.'

'Any way to tell which?' Charlie said, looking around them for a way out.

'Not without taking a chance that they might notice,' said Mark. 'Come on, let's find you what you need.' He walked over to the wall, brushed his fingers along it in the same testing sort of gesture he had used with the last one. 'Huh,' he said. 'Thought so. Just Caldera, this time. Here, watch this.'

Charlie went over to him, looked over his shoulder. 'See this?' Mark said, and pushed his hand right into the 'wall.' 'You can manipulate the programming directly without separate instructions, if you know where to grab each line. And you can exploit the holographic nature of the program.'

Charlie didn't know whether or not he should be relieved that he didn't have the slightest idea what Mark was talking about. A second after Mark thrust his hand into the wall, he pulled it out again, holding a doorknob. 'And as I thought,' Mark said, 'the programmer left herself a nice tidy way back into the main programming space for when she was finished testing this.' A door outlined itself in the wall: Mark used the doorknob to open it, and stepped through. 'Mind your step, here.'

' "She"?' Charlie said, stepping through after him. They appeared to be in a dimly lit office that stretched for miles in all directions. 'You sure about that?'

'Ninety percent,' Mark said, walking through the office and looking around him. 'Just something about the feel of it. Uh, oh. Somebody's in here. No, don't panic!'

Charlie froze and looked around him. Far off to his right, at what looked like about a mile's distance across this absurdly huge spread of carpeting and desks and office furniture and dividers, he could see a light shining over a desk.

'Just somebody looking at a file, somewhere else in the system,' Mark said. 'Possibly halfway across the city from where this facility is based. The odds of whoever it is being able to see us, or even being authorized to see us, are minuscule. Don't sweat it, just come on and let's see what the paradigm is.'

It took them only a few minutes to find it. Some of the desks had old-fashioned computer terminals on them, and Mark stopped by one of these and poked at it, a rounded, eggy-looking thing done partly in a rather retro turquoise, partly in a translucent white plastic. 'Somebody here has a sense of humor,' Mark said, 'or nice taste in antiques.' He bent over to tap at the keyboard. 'What's your victim's name in Colorado?'

'Velasquez.'

'First initial?'

'J. Jaime.'

'Which year?'

' '23.'

'Right.' A moment later a large pile of square virtual datascrips appeared on the desk in front of them, and Mark glanced at them. 'Copy again?'

Charlie looked through them. Each scrip, as he

picked it up, showed him on its surface what it contained. AUTOPSY SYNOPSIS, Charlie read, RAW DATA, ORGAN ANALYSES, TOXICOLOGY. 'Yeah.'

Mark tapped at the console again. The datascrips vanished out of Charlie's hands. 'Done. Let's beat it and hit the next one.'

They got out of there, Mark carefully removing his 'tree trunk' and allowing the squashing walls to start coming together again, while at the same time wiping out any evidence of his and Charlie's intrusion.

Then they hit the third facility, the coroner's office in Arlington. It had rather more effective security than the first two, so that Mark had to spend five minutes or so breaking in and making sure they wouldn't leave any trace of their entry behind, but the result was the same as in Bangor and Fort Collins.

The fourth Net-based system, at the coroner's offices in DeKalb County just east of Atlanta, to the astonishment of both of them had no security precautions installed around it whatsoever. Mark was practically dancing with frustration at such careless-ness while Charlie raided it for the information he needed. It was only with the greatest difficulty that Charlie kept Mark from building a security barrier around that system and then locking the DeKalb County staff out of it. Nothing Charlie could do, however, could keep Mark from putting up a big virtual billboard that said KILROY WAS HERE in front of the space.

'Somebody I should know?' Charlie said as he made sure the files were copied back to his space.

'Probably not,' Mark said, disgusted, 'and probably they won't, either.'

'There won't be any trace that it was *you* doing that, will there?' Charlie said, nervous.

'Are you kidding? Of course not. You think I want my

dad to . . .' Mark gave Charlie a look. 'Never mind. Come on. Two more.'

They next hit the data storage system for the coroner's office in Queens. The City of New York system was surrounded with a set of nested security barriers so arcane that they actually kept Mark and Charlie away from the target data for a whole hour. Mark spent the whole time sweating and swearing – first in English, in language that Charlie wouldn't have thought Mark knew, and then in Thai, with great vehemence – as he dealt with the barriers, which in this implementation looked like layer after layer of barbed-wire fences, with long stretches of bare ground between them. But finally they fell, and the two of them found themselves making their way into a virtual domain that exactly duplicated the coroner's clerk's offices, right down to the potted plants and the baby pictures. The records Charlie found there were more complete than they had been anywhere else they had raided, and Charlie began thinking that they could have saved time by just raiding this one. *But how would we have known? And I need all that other data to make sure the case is watertight.*

Charlie was taking a moment to look more closely at one of the files he was carrying while Mark chucked other records one by one through his ring-of-fire 'copying' routine. He turned a page, and a great spill of organic-chemistry imaging and visualizations poured out into the air around them, long-chain molecules and imaging of translucent platelets and ribbony blood fractions. 'Just look at this toxicology report,' Charlie said, overcome with admiration. 'Somebody here is a real professional.'

'Yeah, well, so are their DP people,' Mark said, sounding actively nervous for the first time. 'Let's make it quick, huh?'

Charlie started to fold the file up preparatory to

tossing it into the ring. This particular file was going to be useful for him. Most of the other coroners' blood and tox results had had rather minimal information about the dead person's blood chemistry. This one listed blood fractions that Charlie had only heard of in his most recent study. Whoever was working tox here was seriously interested in genetic microfractions, as well as . . .

Charlie stopped and looked curiously at one molecule that was hanging in the air off to one side. It looked familiar. He put the main file aside and went over to it, plucked it out of the air, turned it several different ways, looking at it. 'Mark, hang on a minute.'

'OK, but no more than that. Whatcha got?'

'This looks familiar.'

'It looks like Tinkertoys,' Mark said. 'Thought you were a little old for this kind of thing.'

Charlie upended the molecule, tried looking at it from another angle. It didn't help. 'Squirt, don't push your luck. Home system.'

'Online.'

'Let me see this as golfballs.'

'Processing.'

The construct in his hands changed, got bulkier, and the 'sticks' between the colored balls vanished, the chemical bonds now expressing themselves as spots where the balls squashed together. This was the method that his physics teacher had trained him to prefer, almost against Charlie's will, but it did work better than sticks and Ping-Pong balls for him. He turned the molecule over in his hands again, trying to find the best way to hold it. The benzene ring at one end suddenly triggered a memory, and so did the bromate structure sticking out of the middle of it.

'Charlie,' Mark said, 'you should save this for later. We really oughta get out of here.'

Mark, getting nervous? It was worth seeing, though Charlie wasn't willing to linger – under the circumstances. Nonetheless, he grinned to himself briefly. 'Right. But one thing first. Home system.'

'Ready.'

'Orthodox name for the compound.'

'Scorbutal cohydrobromate.'

Charlie's eyes narrowed. *Oh, no. Oh, no.* 'I hate this,' he growled.

Mark looked up at him. Charlie refused to repeat himself. 'Come on,' he said, folding up the file and chucking it through Mark's copying ring. It vanished along with the ring. 'Let's get the heck out of here.'

They hurriedly backtracked the way they had come, through a shortcut Mark had 'wire-cut' to the outer security perimeter. He had to stop to reweave the wire, patching his cuts, but it didn't take him too long. Which was as well, for far away, inside the 'blockhouse' away inside the wire, Charlie thought he could hear sirens wailing. 'Company?' he said.

'No kidding. Their security program woke up. Took it long enough.' The implementation was getting louder, as if closing in on them, and Charlie had no desire to see what form it was going to take when it finally appeared in their neighborhood. The last hole chopped into the outermost fence rewove itself. 'Kill it!' Mark said to his penetration program, and then he and Charlie were once more standing in the darkness of his own workspace, surrounded by the light-forest of the Digamma penetration program.

Mark let out a long breath, and suddenly looked very thirteen. 'These guys had it a little more on the ball than the others,' he said.

Charlie grinned. 'Not necessarily a bad thing. But Mark, you're not afraid of getting *caught*, are you?'

'Not much. I mean, no, of course not. It's just that, you know . . .'

'That that one was closer than you like to get.' Charlie looked at him. 'You want to call it quits?'

'No. Let's finish.'

'Good,' Charlie said, because they were shy only one set of information now, and it would be a shame to have to stop without it. There would always be that nagging doubt that some single important thing had been missed, the one piece of data which would have clinched the case.

But Charlie rather thought it was clinched already. It would only be a matter of taking all this information home, sitting down with it and comparing everything very carefully. All he needed was the data from their last stop, the coroner's clerk's office in Forestville, Maryland. There the security was almost as nonexistent as it had been in Atlanta, and Charlie picked up and copied the set of records belonging to the second kid involved in the recent 'double' suicide. They were nowhere near as complete as the New York records had been but they would have to do. The final raid took them fifteen minutes. At fifteen minutes and ten seconds they were standing in Mark's workspace again, with the forest of light sinking into the virtual floor under their feet. Mark let out a long breath of relief.

'Mark,' Charlie said, 'you're a hero.'

'I'm modest, too,' Mark said, wiping his forehead. 'Ask me about it sometime.' He plopped down in one of the chairs. 'Lights!' he said to his workspace, and the VAB reasserted itself, the angle of the sun having changed slightly but everything else as it had been before. From high up in the air, the creaky voices of buzzards could be heard, and beside Charlie, piled up on the floor, was a stack of manila files nearly as tall as he was. 'It's all there,' Mark said. 'I'll keep copies secure for you, if you like.'

'I'd appreciate it,' Charlie said.

'No problem. But just what was that you found back in New York?'

Charlie shook his head. 'Bad stuff,' he said softly. 'Ask me later.'

'Mark?' a man's voice said from out of the air around them.

'Ohmigosh, get out of here, it's my dad,' Mark said hurriedly. 'Probably with a brain full of bait.' He leapt for the pile of files, scooped them up and started stuffing them into one of his desk drawers. 'These are encrypting. But I need to wipe my logs of these, and you, before he comes in. Go on, blast out of here!'

Charlie hurriedly headed for his doorway into Mark's space, which appeared a few feet away. 'Mark, thanks!'

'Yeah, yeah, thank me later. When I get back, gimme a shout and tell me what you find!'

'I will!'

Mark vanished. Charlie was left standing in his workspace with a pile of files.

'Son,' he heard his father say from outside in the real world. 'You've been in there for an elephant's age. Want a sandwich?'

'Absolutely,' Charlie muttered. He checked to make sure that the files were saved, then closed down his workspace and returned to the real world, where his stomach was growling fiercely. But not so much that it drowned out the nervous muttering in his head.

Scorbutal hydrobromate.

Were these really suicides . . .?

Late the next afternoon, Nick stood out in the softly falling ash and held very still, listening for something beside the screams of the Damned. He didn't immediately hear the sound he was waiting for but he was willing to wait for a good while. If there was anything he had been learning in the last couple of days, it was patience.

He was in no hurry to get back to the spot he had finally reached during the session before last, the first 'sub-basement' of the Dark Artificer's Keep. Even though his money was getting close to running out, even though his folks were getting increasingly interested in 'sitting down and having a talk' with him. Nick had the secrets of the Eighth Circle seriously on his mind, for he was beginning to suspect that there was more to play for, a lot more, than just lifts of new songs and the possibility that you might meet one of the clone-Banes down here.

Nick had decided to follow a hunch. He had gone back to do what Shade told him she'd been doing: to talk to others he found wandering around the ashy wilderness on the far side of the Lake of Tears, and guide them through. At first he wondered whether this had been such a great idea, for the environment responded badly to it. It was as if the crevasses started to target Nick, going out of their way to stitch themselves straight at him as he made his way through the knee-deep ash. He had had a couple of extremely close calls over the first few hours, as the ground stubbornly, even maliciously, opened again and again under his feet. Once, if this had been reality, he would have left the skin of the palms of both hands on the jagged outcropping of rock that was all that kept him from plunging into the lava-filled abyss below. But Nick kept doing what he had decided to do. It was sheer stubbornness, at first. If the environment was going to target him, he was going to outlast it.

After five or six hours of this, things got a little better. The environment started getting less dangerous – or perhaps Nick just got better at anticipating it. He also stopped noticing quite so acutely what it was doing, for he started getting interested in the conversations he was having with the people he was guiding through. Their responses to the situation in which they suddenly found themselves varied from complete confusion to annoyance that they were no longer in control of their path through the darkness. But one way or another, they were all glad of the help, though a few plainly would have choked rather than admit it. Some of them were wearing virtual 'seemings' that were meant to make them look very impressive and self-sufficient indeed – tall shapes cowled in darkness, like the image of Joey Bane in the 'front door' to the *Orpheus, Don't Look Back!* virteo collection, or barbarian heroes, or statuesque women wearing space-babe slicktights and toting projectile weapons the size of their upper bodies, or giant snarling beasts slinking along through the fiery night and trying to look independently deadly. Some of them protested at being saved from falling into a hole in the ground by a skinny high-school kid in neodenims and a beatup Mets batting helmet. Most of them 'forgot' to thank him. But none of them, Nick noticed, told him to go away while he was actually helping them out.

At the end of his last session Nick had gone home exhausted and collapsed into bed too weary to even be annoyed with his mother, who had been waiting up for him. He had taken care of his homework before he'd left, so he wasn't sure why she was waiting. She gave him an odd look as he passed through the front room on his way to bed.

'Honey,' she said, in an unusually neutral tone of voice for her, 'your friend Charlie called earlier.'

'Yeah?'

'He was asking about something called a "walk-through." Would you know what he wanted?'

'Huh? Oh, yeah, I'll take care of it tomorrow.' That caught Nick a little by surprise. Charlie wasn't much of a gamer, preferring to do 'solid construction' sims, the more concrete kind of virtual experience. *All the same, if he's getting interested . . .*

Nick looked for Charlie the next day at school, but didn't see him. Either he'd had to swap his lunch periods to take care of some study commitment, or something else had happened to throw their schedules out of synch. Nick went through the day more or less on automatic, as he had done for the last couple of days since things started to get really interesting back in Deathworld.

That afternoon he headed back into the WorldBooths public Net-access center down at the Square in an unusually good mood, despite the fact that his money was getting so short. At the end of the week he would have some more allowance coming and he'd be able to really get back into the swing of Deathworld over the weekend.

For now Nick had spent the day getting ahead of schedule on his homework, which his folks had been checking with unusual care. They'd have no excuse to bother him for two whole days.

And after that, when the money does run out . . .? Two full days of gameplay would exhaust what he had.

Nick sighed, paid at the cashier's booth in front, took his recharged cashcard, and headed back to his usual booth right at the rear. He locked himself in and settling into the implant chair, slapping the card into it. *Have to deal with that when it happens,* Nick thought and blinked his workspace into being around him.

It was still bare. He hadn't felt like spending the time to get his redecorating done. But off to one side, standing there, was a simulacrum of Charlie, in end-of-the-day shinesweats, arms folded, smiling that wry smile he wore sometimes, an expression that suggested he was feeling foolish about something.

'Go,' Nick said to the simulacrum.

'Sorry I missed you,' it said immediately, in Charlie's voice. 'I was up late last night doing some research. Look, all work and no play, you know the drill . . . I was wondering if you had any walkthroughs of Deathworld. I wanted to have a look but I don't want to spend six weeks dragging around in the upper levels. You have something that can get me about halfway down? Give me a yell or leave me a message.'

The image froze again. Nick was caught between two impulses – to catch Charlie 'live' right now, if possible, and take him down into Deathworld himself, or to leave him a message. The second impulse won.

'System,' Nick said, 'record reply.'

'Ready,' the system said in its plain-vanilla voice. Nick raised his eyebrows. He really should get some Bane audio in here, if nothing else.

'Charlie, sorry I missed you too,' he said, getting up out of the 'chair' on the virtual side and going over to the doorway where his files were stored at the moment. He opened it, and looked in. 'File access. Deathworld,' he said, 'press material, walkthrough. Yeah, that one. Transfer to Charlie Davis' machine.'

He turned back to the simulacrum of Charlie. 'Here,' he said. 'This one came out of the "Last Train Out" review environment about a month and a half ago. The data for the first three levels is still good, as far as I know. The company's been swapping in new material from about Four down, to defeat the older walkthroughs that're out there, but this should still be a help. Let me know if you have any problems. I'll talk to you later.'

The simulacrum, having been answered, vanished. Nick breathed out, then closed the door and opened the second one, his automated login gateway to Deathworld.

He had implemented a 'shortcut' entry that let him in to pick up where he had left off. The Deathworld system still showed him the copyright statement burning crimson in the air for a few seconds – there was no getting away from that, no matter how many times a day you might come in here – and then Nick walked through into the darkness awaiting him on the other side.

Falling ash, the volcano in the distance . . . Nick reached up into the air and recreated the 'asbestos' golf umbrella he normally carried, then started making his way toward the Keep, to see who he might meet along the way. As he looked, he was a little surprised by how few players seemed to be around. This was an unusually quiet period for this time of day. Normally Deathworld started to get noticeably busier around the time that high school and college classes let out in North America, though obviously there would have been plenty of Europeans and Asians in over the earlier part of the day.

Nick shrugged and made his way along through the black ash 'snow,' keeping an eye open for crevasses. For the moment they seemed to be avoiding him, though he saw what looked like a huge one opening away across the plain. Faintly he thought he heard some yells of surprise from that direction. It was a little too far for him to do any good. By the time he got there, everybody involved would either have saved themselves and each other, or fallen in.

He kept going, making for the Keep of the Dark Artificer. Shade's warning about the size of the place had been a useful one. Its interior was, Nick thought, probably bigger than the whole gigantic plain that surrounded it. This posed problems of topology that he didn't bother his head about, for the attraction of the Keep lay in the music that was in there, and also in the exploration of the countless dark rooms, deep caverns and hidden towers associated with it, and (most importantly, Nick thought) the solution of the great Maze at the Keep's heart. He couldn't get rid of the feeling that the access to the fabled Ninth Circle had to do with that maze. Probably nothing so simple as just getting to the middle of it. Nick was sure you needed to do more than that, or have some specific piece of information once you arrived.

Nick skirted around the Lake and headed for the doors of the Keep. The demons on guard there – little, black-leather-skinned, bat-winged guys about five feet tall, wearing ornate doormen's costumes and affable gargoyle faces – saw him coming and started pulling on the giant braided bronze ropes that opened the doors. He waved at them in what was beginning to be a ritual. 'Hey there, boys,' Nick said to the two nearest demons, 'how're things going?'

'They stink,' said the demons nearest the doors in the ritual answer. One of them, pausing from the work, wiped his forehead with a big, smudgy hanky and added, '*And* the boss turned down the union's request for the pay raise.'

Nick made *tsk tsk* noises as he passed them by, walking in over the shiny dark pavement which some beneficent agency kept clear of the ash that was always falling outside. 'Keep working on it, fellas,' he said.

The doors closed behind him, and Nick paused there in the huge 'front hall,' looking around to see who else might be there. The Keep's vast entryway, lit by a huge crystal and onyx chandelier shaped like one more stalactite hanging from the great dome of the ceiling, routinely held a surprise or two. You might hear a snatch of music here that you hadn't caught elsewhere or meet someone who would do your quest some good. At the moment, though, it was nearly as quiet inside as it had been outside. The place was practically empty. *A slack period,* Nick thought. *Coincidence.*

He walked on in, looking around at the bizarre portraiture that hung on the walls of the entryway. They were supposed to be images of gameplayers who had passed on successfully to Nine, Nick knew; normal people living in his own time. But the portraits made them all look like crazed royalty of two or three centuries back, in rococo clothes and wigs that looked like they might come alive and crawl off their wearers' heads. He wondered what his own portrait would wind up looking like if— *When. When* they did it.

Nick smiled slightly and headed toward the doorway on the far side of the entry hall. Past that door was where things got interesting. Six staircases apparently designed by Escher led off toward the roof, and six more toward the basement, though none of them felt particularly like 'up' or 'down' when you were climbing them. Somewhere in this vast pile, in which none of the normal directions mattered, the Maze was hidden, a huge tangle of paths and walkways, arched and open, covering all six of the walls of a great cube of space somewhere in the Keep. Nick had actually found it accidentally once, when he was first in here and just wandering around in the place trying to get a feel for it. Then he'd lost the Maze again while trying to work out how he'd found it to begin with. *A whim of the system,* he thought. *Never mind. Over the weekend there'll be time to start doing some proper searching.*

'Hey, Nick . . .'

He turned quickly at the sound of a slightly familiar voice. It was Shade again. In here she looked a little less like her name, but only a little less – just a young girl of maybe fifteen, in a long black outer coat, a short dark purple skirt and a black sweater, dark purple hair, and eyes that shaded from violet to almost black depending on how much light there was. Those big, dark eyes, and the somber set of her mouth, suggested some old sorrow hanging over her. She was pale. In this light, almost right under the great chandelier, Nick could see much better how frail she looked, how fragile. Not that Nick was so foolish as to be misled by appearances down here. As in most virtual environments, anyone could look like anything they pleased. For all he knew, up in The Real World, Shade was a six-foot-six, two-hundred-and-eighty-pound football player. Somehow, though, Nick doubted it. There was a brittle feel to conversations with her that made him wonder if she was either a plant from Joey Bane Enterprises, someone used to see how players treated each other, or someone who wasn't really cut out for this particular virtual experience but who was just too stubborn to give it up.

'Hey, Shade,' he said. 'You doing OK?'

She sighed. Most of her conversations seemed to start with a sigh, or contain several of them. 'I guess so,' she said. 'It's quiet today. You'd almost think everybody was scared off by something.'

Nick shrugged. 'Not me.' The whole business with the Angels of the Pit had rolled off his back pretty quickly once he got into the Keep and started working on the business of solving it.

'I don't know . . .' Shade said. 'I wonder if maybe there's something to it.'

'To what?'

She shrugged, gazing up and about her. 'What they did . . .' She turned those violet eyes on him. 'I keep wondering if it's really so terrible. When everything's going wrong . . .'

The way she trailed off, Nick had a feeling that she was about to tell him how everything was wrong for *her*, if he didn't stop her. He shook his head. 'Some people

131

might think it isn't,' he said slowly. 'I guess there are times when everything really does seem to stink. But that's not where I am at the moment.'

'Things are better for you, then, at home?'

'I don't know about better,' Nick said. 'A little quieter, maybe.' Certainly his father had been letting him alone. Whether he was unwilling to restart their fight, or not, Nick wasn't sure. Just the news that Nick had a job lined up for the summer seemed to have quieted things down somewhat. For the rest of it, it was as if his mother and father had declared a truce for the moment. The lightening of the atmosphere in the house had been noticeable. 'I'm not thinking about that right now, Shade. I'm on my way to the Maze.'

'Aren't we all?' Shade said, and laughed a little. 'But I haven't finished exploring the Keep yet. There's still a lot of ground that I haven't covered yet.'

Nick laughed. 'You sound like you enjoy rummaging around in here for its own sake. Not me! I want the music.'

'Oh, I do, too . . .'

'Well, then, come on and help me find the Maze! That's the way down to Nine, and Nine's where the good music's supposed to be, the "unknown" lifts. And Joey himself.'

Shade gave him an odd look, almost nervous. 'Oh, I don't mind hanging around up here,' she said. 'Besides, they say that once you leave Eight for Nine, you can't come back.'

That surprised him. '*Who* says?'

'Other people up here.' Shade glanced around her, although those 'other people' were not much in evidence right now. 'All the time, in the Upper Circles, you see people from as far down as Eight wandering around. Slumming, helping the newbies, or torturing them with news of the lifts you can get down lower.'

Nick nodded. He'd seen enough of this as he worked his way down. One and Two were particularly bad in this regard – a lot of the people from the circles between Three and Six seemed to enjoy coming up there and making the new Banies nuts. 'But have you noticed,' she said, 'that you never see anyone from Nine?'

Nick nodded. This might have been why rumors about Nine were very few and far between. It left another question, of course: *If nobody from there comes back to tell us what's happening, then how are there any rumors at all?* But rumors didn't need reality to get started. That was one of the things this level was about, as he had been discovering.

'You hear anything else about how to get down there?' Nick said to Shade.

She shook her head. 'Nothing that's done me any good,' she said. 'But I wish you luck.'

'Yeah,' Nick said, 'thanks. Look, I'll see you on the way out, maybe?'

'Maybe you will.'

She turned away.

'Hey, Shade . . .'

She glanced back at him.

'Thanks for helping, the other day.'

'I didn't help,' she said. 'Not really.' That faint air of sorrow seemed to come down on her again.

Shade headed for the doors, which swung back to let her out into the darkness. Nick watched her go, thinking, *Poor kid, I wonder what her problem is?* But then, if he asked her, he had the awful feeling he'd find out, and right now, he had enough problems of his own. Besides, tonight was about enjoyment – he wasn't going to be able to afford much more of it.

Nick turned and made for the door at the back, the entry to the Stairwell of Doom, to pick a stair and see where it took him.

In the doorway, a dark shape watched him for a few moments, then shrugged and turned away.

Chapter Six

That evening, Charlie was sitting once more in his workspace, with piles of files around him, in the blackest mood he'd been in for days. Part of it was because this session had been delayed. His sandwich with his father, last night, had segued into one of the more ferocious games of cut-throat 'timed chess' they'd ever had, and his father had won – an unusual outcome. Charlie had chalked it up to the fact that he was slightly distracted by his evening out with Mark. Now, though, he was in the midst of analyzing the information that Mark had helped him bring back. *That* was accounting for the rest of his dark mood.

He leaned back on the bottom-most bench in his workspace and looked into the Pit. It was full of virtual information and exhibits again, so much so that he'd had to move the worktable out of the middle of it. Now the floor of the Pit was occupied by six different sets of information, floating in the air. What bothered Charlie the most was the similarities between four of them.

They had all been strangulations, of course. That was bad enough. But in four of those suicides – the 'double' suicide of just a few days ago, and the New York and Fort Collins ones – the toxicology reports had turned up something that would have immediately struck the authorities as suspicious, Charlie thought, *if* they had bothered comparing notes. But they hadn't.

He got up, strolled over to the New York suicide. This had been Renee Milford. Charlie had been through her autopsy but he had no heart for looking at those pictures of her. He had found one that he preferred in one of the local New York virtual environments dedicated to news and current events – a family 'virtshot' of Renee sitting at the beach in a one-piece bathing suit, with the tall brick watertower of Jones Beach State Park behind her in the distance. She was blonde, and pretty, and eighteen. Her smile was sunny, she had a slight sunburn on the tops of her shoulders: she was laughing at the camera and she looked like she didn't have a worry in the world. The picture had been taken in 2023, the year before she died.

Charlie looked down at the image of Renee sitting there, her hair a little tousled by the wind, blown and glittering in the air. Next to her, hanging in the air like some kind of malevolent, multicolored, multilegged bug, was the image of the molecule the city toxicologist's analysis had found in her blood. It was scorbutal cohydrobromate.

The hydrobromates were not in the pharmacopeia, either the government's informal 'N.P.' or the official 'U.S.P.' list. They had no legitimate medical use. They were what an earlier generation had referred to as a 'designer drug,' a chemical built to get people high, and sometimes intended to perform other functions as well. In the case of the hydrobromates, the high was usually enough. But scorbutal hydrobromate, when it started to be produced in the 2010s, soon acquired a tarnished reputation even for a recreational drug. It was a mind-dulling, inhibition-loosening drug, and was used by crooks who wanted their victims to be less than clear about what was happening to them. One form of it, delivered as an aerosol spray, had briefly been used on night trains in Europe in a real-life scenario of the old urban myth about people being 'gassed' unconscious so they could be robbed in their sleeping compartments. The gangs who did this had been caught and put away but not before the drug's reputation spread, and more of it started to be made all over the place, in Europe and then in North America. 'Sco-bro' was popular, for it was cheap and relatively easy to make. It could be thrown together out of various readily available house-hold chemicals and a well-known remedy for upset stomachs. Best of all, from the criminals' point of view, it tended to metabolize quickly. It was very short-acting. Having left the brain muddled and dozy, its molecule then came apart into its component bromides in the bloodstream itself, often before the liver even had a chance to start detoxifying it.

Charlie scowled at the molecular model hovering gently in the air by the image of Renee Milford, who appeared to have strangled herself in her parents' garage. The toxicologist in Queens – who knew what she had been thinking of while she was working on this case, or what she might have suspected? – but she had run a much more thorough and expensive blood series on Renee than had strictly been required . . . and the scorbutal had turned up in it. *Luck*, Charlie thought, *or just good timing*. The drug deconstructed itself even more quickly in the rapidly acidifying bloodstream of someone who was dying or dead than it did in the blood of a live person, and in a matter of minutes there might have been none of it left at all.

He sighed and moved on to the next set of 'exhibits,' the one for Malcolm Dwyer, who had been one of the two kids to die here in the D.C. area a few days ago. Malcolm had had a big dose of the drug, so much that even after the delay in finding his and Jeannine Metz's bodies, there had still been significant amounts of it in his bloodstream. Enough, at least, to identify it by the bromide and bromate fractions pooled in the parts of his body already beginning to experience rigor. The coroner in Arlington had found it and recognized it immediately for what it was.

The problem was that, by itself, finding sco-bro in someone's bloodstream didn't mean that much. Yes, the drug was illegal, like almost all the other designer drugs. But lots of people took it anyway. And in a case like this, the nature of the crime scene would itself tend to minimize the role of any drug. After all, no drug could *make* you commit suicide . . . could it?

Charlie stood there, looking at Malcolm's image – another virtclip, a young black guy not that much older than Charlie, tall, good looking, cheerful. And dead now. Charlie's mother had been pretty certain that you couldn't cause anyone to commit suicide if they weren't already suicidal. But even she had been willing to admit that new ways of doing things were being invented every day.

And how do I know this isn't a coincidence, anyway? Granted, it would have to be a huge one . . .

Charlie walked around to the third set of data that had shown the drug. This was Jaime Velasquez, from Fort Collins. He was little, dark-haired, dark-eyed, built sort of like Mark Gridley, but older, and with a much more innocent face. The picture Charlie had of him was of a guy almost completely muffled up in ski clothes, grinning past a ski mask which a friend just out of shot in the same virtclip had just pulled down, waving his ski poles at the camera, then falling down in the snow as the same out-of-shot friend hooked a ski behind one of Jaime's knees and knocked him sprawling backwards into the powder. In Jaime's bloodstream – either because he had had a very slight dose, or had lived long enough to detoxify it, or had been too long dead before they had found him – there had been almost none of the whole sco-bro molecule left at all. The toxicologist had either missed the bromide fragments in the post-mortem blood samples, or had seen them and assumed they had come from some other source. Perhaps he had simply dismissed them as unimportant. Either way, they hadn't been mentioned in his dictated text report.

All the same, the drug had been there. Charlie heaved a big sigh of frustration. If the coroner in Colorado had known about the findings of his associates in New York and Maryland, he might have been able to get his own police force to examine the crime scene more carefully for signs that anyone else had been there. But it hadn't happened. There had been no comparison of data.

Charlie scowled as he walked around to the next set of exhibits. Some of it had to do with what Mark had described: separate states' failure to contribute information to a common pool, intrastate authorities' unwillingness to cooperate with one another. But there could have been other causes as well. *Coroners who saw what they wanted to see,* Charlie thought. *Or what they were convinced that they should be seeing. Just another suicide. Nothing unusual . . .*

But then each of them was looking at a separate case . . . not at one case as part of a group or set of cases. It's not their fault they didn't realize what they were looking at.

But here I am, Charlie thought, *and I think I know what I'm looking at.*

Murder.

The minute you find anything . . . said James Winters' voice in the back of his head.

Charlie opened his mouth to tell his system to place a call . . .

. . . then closed his mouth again, thinking.

You know what he's going to say, said something in the back of Charlie's mind.

He sat down on his bench again and looked out at the exhibits.

There were very few things that Charlie hated more than drugs. He had seen them ruin people's lives, had seen them ruin the life of his birthmother, the one person he had loved more than anyone else in the world. They'd killed her, slowly, by hours and inches. That memory was one that he didn't often examine closely. He was not up for looking very hard at it right this minute, either. But the moment he called James Winters and started to present this data to him, that painful old history was going to be held up in front of him by that careful and thorough man. Winters would say to him, *Are you sure this isn't clouding your judgment a little, Charlie? You know how you feel about drugs. I understand it completely. It makes perfect sense to me that you would want to keep other people from suffering the same kind of loss that you have.*

But you shouldn't let it make you see losses like that where there aren't any.

And he would remind Charlie once again about the huge numbers of people on the Net, and the incidence of accident and circumstance among those people, and the way they impacted on mortality statistics.

But it wouldn't matter. I know what I'm seeing here. These people did not commit suicide. They were "helped" to die.

Charlie looked over at the New York data again. Here, unfortunately, the investigation into Renee's death had been less wonderful. The coroner had been conscientious but the police had not, and they had done very little work on the actual area where she had been found dead. Up in Maine, though, in Bangor, someone had been suspicious. Or just not certain of what they were seeing. And there were some odd findings at the scene.

Charlie went around to Richard Delano's exhibit and looked at what was spread out there. There was a virtclip of Richard, a short, well-muscled guy, blond, gray-eyed, in baggies and a hot-weather vest, walloping someone's fast ball in a softball game on some unnamed summer afternoon, then taking off around the bases, leaving a cloud of dust behind him. And there, spread out next to the clip, was the Bangor police department's own virtual version of the crime scene, the living room of the house where Richard had been found. They had gone right around the room and virtsnapped everything, in both macro and micro. They had come up with some odd fiber evidence: bits of cotton fluff that were found nowhere else in the house but in this one room, the living room. And they were on the 'top' of the rug, not old, not trodden in as they might have been expected to be, but something new. And not native to any of the suicide's clothes. Charlie looked at the fibers, enlarged and hanging in the air like tangled white ropes.

A friend? Maybe. But a friend who had never been in the house before? Or in any part of it except the living room? That was a little weird. *Someone the person didn't know?* But there was no sign of forced entry. Whoever that person was, Richard Delano had let him or her in.

It was very odd, and Charlie didn't know what to make of it. Neither did the Bangor police. They had not been able to confirm any other person being in the apartment around the time of death. Unfortunately the entrance to Delano's house had been hidden by shrubbery from the other houses in the street. The outside light had come on and gone off again within a minute or so, as it might have no matter how many people were entering the house. That was all anyone had noticed. Finally, after days of investigation, the police had listed their concerns about the crime scene as 'inconclusive' and had moved on to other issues. If they had noticed scorbutal cohydrobromate in the body, they might have thought otherwise, but they hadn't.

Charlie looked over at the other two sets of evidence. They were inconclusive, too, lacking either any suggestion of other persons being in the area, or any detection of sco-bro in the victims. His case was not at all complete. James Winters would not be convinced.

This'll all have been for nothing.

He put his head in his hands, depressed. Nick was still somewhere in the middle of Deathworld, and Charlie felt sure in his bones that someone else was there too, stalking the place, looking for another victim. *If I don't convince Winters that I'm right about what I've found, someone else is gonna get killed. Maybe not Nick . . . maybe someone else. But it doesn't matter in the slightest. Murder's going to happen.*

Especially since it's still May. Charlie could not get rid of the idea that this meant something specific.

Anyway, it's beyond coincidence at this point. What are the odds that all these suicides should just happen to be using this drug? . . . And just happen to be in Deathworld, and just happen to kill themselves this way? Taken separately, there was always the chance. But this many coincidences, taken all together . . . suddenly they weren't coincidences anymore.

Charlie breathed in, breathed out.

But it's still *not proof of the kind that Winters is going to need. Everything I've got is circumstantial.*

Now, if I had some proof that somebody was being targeted, being followed . . .

Yeah, like who? He was in no position to go through Deathworld and start asking questions of everybody he met. Word about nosy 'strangers' and 'newbies' traveled fast in these online demesnes. The Banies were probably no different from any other kind of fans defending their territory, in this regard. Anybody who showed up and started asking a lot of questions would be identified as a stooge, maybe a cop, and isolated, within hours. *Or else just fed a lot of misinformation that would completely screw up any serious investigation.*

No, there has to be another way.

Charlie sat there for a long while as it got lighter outside in the London of two centuries ago, and the sky started to turn a pale peach color up in the high windows.

Then he sat up straight.

All right, Charlie thought. *When investigation takes you as far as it can, when the data won't support the conclusions securely enough . . . then, if you're really sure you're right, you go find the information to* make *it support them.*

By catching somebody in the act . . .

Nick stood quiet between the dark stone walls in the dripping darkness, with his eyes closed, and listened. It was the only way, down here, to tell truth from falsehood. Appearances were deceiving, as he had learned higher up in Deathworld, and there was no point in wasting your time on trying to work things out from the way they looked.

The inside of the Dark Artificer's Keep was the kingdom of fraud . . . all the different sorts of it: flattery and lies, hypocrisy and purposeful misdirection, rumors started to make trouble or destroy reputations. Counterfeiting and impersonation were punished there, and all the kinds of theft. Illegal copying was punished there, too, and theft of ideas. And since Joey Bane had suffered enough from that kind of thing in his early career, Nick was not entirely surprised to see the Thieves of Song hung up from the trees in the Black Arboretum, squawking out twisted fragments of song while the black birds picked at their tenderer bits. He had passed through there with some amusement, picking up in passing, from under a rock in the Arboretum, the clandestine lift of 'Steal From Me . . .' with all the pirated versions of other Bane songs sampled and intercut into it, Joey Bane's own convoluted joke – the audio version of a trophy wall, one that grew and grew day by day, so that every new version was a collectors' item.

The punishments down here in the stony black tunnels and passageways were all variations on a single theme. Those who had stolen others' stories and lives and taken them for their own use were now bound forever in one place, immured in the black stones themselves, and forced to listen in silence to those who actually had lives of their own. It was the living who had the key to the secrets here. Their questions, asked of the darkness, were the answers to the Keep. As elsewhere in Deathworld, some of the people you met in the Keep were real players but some were actors or 'plants,' part of the game, and to find out what they knew about the way down to the doorway into Nine, listening was the key.

At first it had seemed to Nick merely a frustration designed to weed out those who weren't really serious about finding the way down. But slowly he had begun to suspect the truth lay elsewhere. Whether he would find it in time to descend to Nine before his money ran out, and before his folks entirely lost patience, was now his main concern.

He sat down on one of the benches let into the wet, black stone wall, underneath one of the occasional torches that were fitted into iron wall-brackets, and listened. It was damp down here. He was below the level of the Lake, Nick guessed, and that warm saline body leaked and oozed through to most places on this level, trickling down walls, welling up as puddles in the narrow, close, dark stone passages. Listening was the whole art of finding your way around here, listening for the sound of water and the direction in which it ran, listening to other voices, finding your way to them, discovering what they had to say. It was not like Seven, where manipulation of the pain of the Damned was how you found out what you needed to know. Here, keeping your own mouth shut and your ears open was everything. Someone's story told in a long, soft monologue, a phrase of music heard in silence and waited for, was what would make the difference. There was always a clue, something useful.

It's a shame that listening to people in the real world isn't always this useful, Nick thought. If it could be this way with other kids at school, or with parents, or other people you met, what a difference it would make. Unfortunately they were usually intent on forcing you to come around to their way of thinking; any listening on their part was limited to checking to see whether you were agreeing with them.

Though who knows, he thought. *Maybe it would be possible to out-listen them, if you just had enough patience.*

He got up again, stretched. Last time Nick had sat there for nearly two hours before he caught that faint shimmer of music, far away in another passage, and after much feeling his way around in near-total darkness he finally found his way to the little chest set into one of the stone walls, where the lift of 'Down The Narrow Ways' had been hidden. But Nick didn't think there was any point in waiting here any longer. A certain 'feel' was missing to this tunnel/passage which the other one, where he'd found the lift, had had. So now Nick was trying to cover as much ground as possible in each session, trying to locate spots that had the same 'feel,' and which could also conceal doorways or hidden passages that might somehow lead to the Maze itself.

He turned right, then right again, down another low-ceilinged passageway, paused, and listened for sound, for that particular 'feel.' Nothing. Nick went on, trailing his hand along the wet, cold stone.

'Ow!' he said then, stopping and looking at the wall. Nothing but lumpy rock, and here and there something jutting out that might have been an elbow, a knee, frozen in the stone. Except where his hand had been there was someone's mouth, there were teeth, and half-buried in the stone, the glint of an eye, watching him.

'Sorry,' Nick said, making a resolution to watch where he put his hands in the future. He continued walking. *This could take me a long time,* Nick thought. Some of the walkthroughs claimed that the so-called 'anteroom chambers,' the approaches to the Maze itself, regenerated themselves in new and random patterns every few days, so that you would think you had learned them and then return to find them completely different. Others said that no such thing happened at all, and that the people making the claim were confused. Nick wasn't sure what to think. In his cynical moods, it struck him that randomly regenerating the pattern would be a great way to make some extra money. But somehow he didn't think Joey Bane was quite that desperate for funds.

He came to a dark opening on his right and paused, looked in. It was just a little cavelet, not much bigger than a walk-in closet, with a stone bench built into the black wall and going right around from one side to the other. The light from the burning cresset out in the main 'hallway' reached it only dimly. Nick had run into these in other parts of the 'anteroom chambers' over the past few hours, and often enough they were in places where you might hear something if you stayed there long enough. So he went in, sat down, and spent a little while more just listening.

His head turned as, down the corridor, in the direction from which he had come, he heard voices, and the sound of soft footsteps approaching. At first Nick was torn and thought about leaving . . . *Not sure I want to meet anybody right now* . . . But he was also feeling a little lazy, and a little curious, especially as the voices got closer. One was a guy, one a girl, though her voice was not that light – it had a husky sound. So far he had tended to keep to himself in Deathworld, except for a few chance encounters such as that with Shade, but maybe it would be better to start putting aside that tendency down here.

Nick stayed where he was. 'Look, forget it,' said the soft, husky voice. 'I'm not going to waste any more time arguing about it with you, either. I'm just going to find it, no matter how long it takes . . .'

Two shapes passed by the doorway, silhouetted against the cresset-light from the passage. One of them kept right on going, but the other paused to peer in, taking a moment about it, letting her eyes get used to the dark. She was about Nick's height, maybe a little younger than he was. It was hard to tell. He saw a long fall of blond hair, nearly waist length, stirring a little in the cool air running down the passageway behind her; she was dressed in light shorts and an 'infrablack' T-shirt that glowed slightly, even in this shadowy place, with the intensity of its darkness. She drew in breath sharply as she looked at him.

Nick blinked. 'Uh, sorry,' he said.

She looked at him for a moment more: Elsewhere it would have been an invasive stare, but in Deathworld you got familiar with it fairly quickly. It was the expression of someone trying to work out whether you were part of the game or not, and whether it was worth their while to stop to talk to you. Nick had to chuckle a little. 'I'm not local,' he said, that being one of the code phrases meant to indicate that you weren't a plant or a generated feature.

The girl looked at him a little less intently, but the expression was still curious. A moment later she was joined in the doorway by her companion. At first glance he looked like a football player – tall, big across the shoulders, brawny. The effect was increased by the fact that he was wearing a *plaidh mhor*, the so-called 'great kilt' which was just coming into style for guys at the moment. The kilt was patterned in infrablack and a very dark blue, the 'Armstrong Hunting' plaid. Everything else about the guy's clothes matched, from shoes to the tied-on headband. He looked like her brother, or maybe an extremely well-matched boyfriend. 'Somebody you know?' he said.

'No,' Nick said, and 'No,' the girl said, in the same breath. Then the girl laughed.

'You waiting for somebody?' she said.

'Besides Joey? Nope,' said Nick. 'Nobody here right now but us chickens.'

The guy looked at him like he was from Mars. The girl looked oddly at him too but then she laughed. 'I thought my mom was the only person on earth to say that anymore,' she said. 'Suddenly I don't feel quite so weird.'

The two of them glanced around them. Nick knew why. 'No boobytraps in here,' he said. 'It's a quiet spot.'

'We should go,' the guy said.

'Why?' said the girl, sounding annoyed. 'We haven't found anything. And we're not going to, not today, not before our nickel runs out, anyway.'

'You're looking for?' Nick said.

'The Maze,' said the guy. 'Like everyone else down here.'

'Among other things,' the girl muttered. She sighed. 'You mind if we sit down?'

Nick moved down on the bench a little. They came into the chamber and sat down, looking around the way people do when they're suddenly in a small space with someone they don't know.

'Thanks,' the girl said. 'Sometimes the quiet down here gets to me.' She sighed. 'Tires me out a little . . .' Then she gave him a slightly embarrassed look. 'Sorry,' she said. 'I'm Khasm.'

'Nick,' he said, nodding to her.

'I'm Spile,' said the guy.

'Pleased,' Nick said. To Khasm he said, 'I know what you mean, though. It's a lot quieter down here than up in the top levels. Not quite so much of the screams and yells of the tormented.'

Khasm laughed, a very brief sound, not all that humorous. 'No need,' she said. '*We're* the tormented, walking around, doing what we want, saying what we like . . . and there's nothing they can do about it.' She glanced at the wall, out of which here and there a face looked, frozen in stone, the only thing alive about them their eyes that watched, watched everything.

Nick thought about what Khasm had said. Somewhere, once, he had read someone's opinion about life: *Hell is other people*. Maybe this was the same principle. 'I wouldn't bet on them not being able to do anything,' he said. 'One of them bit me a little while ago.'

'Hope you got your shots,' Spile said, and grinned, also a rather mirthless expression. 'You find any lifts around here?'

'Not close,' Nick said. 'The last one was about, oh, half a mile back that way.' He pointed off to his left and behind him. 'Or up a little . . . or down a little. You know how this place twists.'

'What was it you found?' said the guy, fiddling with his plaid as if he wanted to get going again.

'Uh, "Down The Narrow Ways." '

The girl's eyes went wide. Nick could see it clearly even in this light. 'You did? *Where?*'

Her intensity, and the almost anguished sound of her voice, surprised him. Sure, there were a lot of people who got really worked up about Bane's music, but so far Nick hadn't met any of them. 'Uh, if you're really looking for it, I can show you. It's not too far, unless the corridors have reconfigured themselves.'

'It's not for me,' Khasm said. Nick suddenly noticed how tightly her fingers were laced together. 'I have . . . I had a friend who was looking for it.'

The sudden 'had' came down in the middle of the sentence like a boot stamping on something. The hair stood up on the back of Nick's neck. 'You . . .' He stopped, unused to being so certain about something, and uncertain just how to proceed. After a moment he said, much more softly, 'You knew one of them? One of the Angels of the Pit?'

'I *hate* that name,' growled Spile, staring at the floor.

'Two of them,' said Khasm, sounding bleak. 'Or anyway, I knew Jeannie Metz. She lived down the street from me. We went to the same school. We were buddies.' She looked over at Spile. 'He and Mal Dwyer played virtual football together.'

Nick didn't know what to say. But at the same time, he was shocked into a sudden alertness that surprised him. This was more than just some story that would help you find your way to the Maze. This was real.

He couldn't keep himself from asking. 'What made them do it?' he said softly.

Spile turned his head away, wouldn't say anything. 'I

don't know,' said Khasm, angry. 'I know *this*, though:
she *wasn't* suicidal.'

Nick wasn't going to say anything.

'I know what you're thinking!' Khasm burst out.
'That nobody knows anybody as well as they think they
do, and all that crap. I've had it up to *here* with hearing
that, the last week! From everybody. Even her mom.
She of all people should know better . . . but she really
doesn't know her either, it turns out. Not if she
seriously thinks Jeannie did any drugs.'

Nick opened his mouth, closed it. 'Oh, yeah,' Khasm
said, 'it wasn't in the news. The cops said they were
doing her family a favor by not letting it get out, said it
was tragic enough.' She scowled. 'But they told her
family that, all right. Some favor.'

'They claim,' said Spile, looking up at last, 'that it
was one of these "amnesia" drugs. Real convenient.'
He shook his head fiercely. 'And now both the families
are blaming each other's kid for getting the other one to
kill themselves. Real neat.' He glared at Nick. 'Mal was
the most normal, geekly guy you ever saw. Terrified of
doing anything illegal. He wouldn't *ever* have done
drugs, just because it would have embarrassed his folks,
and he would have hated that. Plus, he wouldn't have
seen the point anyway. He used to say to me, "Why do
I need another level of consciousness when I like the
one I have just fine?" ' He lowered his head, looking
suddenly stricken, like someone who had too accurately
reproduced someone's tone of voice, and now was
stricken to the heart by it. 'And he sure would never
have killed himself,' Spile said. 'He'd been having a
hard time of it lately, but not that hard!'

'And Jeannie hated drugs more than anything,'
Khasm said. 'Her dad died of an overdose a few years
ago. She'd *never* have done drugs, no matter how
depressed she was!'

'Uh,' Nick said. He was a little shocked to find himself edging away from them both. 'Look, I'm sorry, I didn't mean—'

They looked at him in some shock themselves. Then Khasm sagged. 'Sorry,' she said. 'I'm sorry. It's just that – you know how it is, everybody here we knew has been going around not asking the question – but you know they're thinking about it. Then when somebody does actually ask it . . .'

'It's OK,' Nick said. 'Look, I can take you to where that "lift" is.'

'That'd be nice of you,' Khasm said, sounding subdued.

'Yeah,' said Spile. 'Once we've got it, we can get out of here.'

They stood up. 'Down this way,' Nick said, and started retracing his steps through the low, dark corridors, with the other two behind him.

Neither of them said much for a while. After some minutes, Khasm said, 'The last time I saw her was a couple of weeks ago, with Mal and Bitsy and a few other friends. Down here. They loved this place.' She sniffed once, softly, like someone trying to hide it. 'She and Mal would come down here and hang out with the rest of us when things weren't going right; when we couldn't hang out together elsewhere.'

Nick thought for a moment about the best way to phrase this. 'Was there some kind of problem?'

'Oh, yeah, Jeannie and Mal had a thing going. And her mom didn't approve. Neither did his folks. They all thought they were too young to be thinking about marriage.' Another sniff. 'Both of them were angry about that, yeah, and a little depressed . . . but not *that* depressed. They were going to wait their parents out for a couple of years, let them get used to the idea. Jeannie told me so. And she told me that Mal agreed.'

Nick paused at a corner, trying to remember which way he was headed. There was something niggling at him and he felt he had to ask. He turned to Khasm. 'Look, uh . . .' There was no kindly way to ask. He gave up trying. 'You're saying she didn't *ever* mention suicide?'

'Exactly once in all the time I knew her,' said Khasm, and somewhat to Nick's surprise, she didn't sound angry this time, just tired. 'What normal person doesn't think about it every now and then? It would be sick not to admit that it happens. And dumb, when life gets nasty, not to admit that it wouldn't be nice if all the pain just stopped! But not that way. She never talked about it to *do* it. You know what I mean?'

Nick thought of that sudden rush of make-it-stop that he'd had the other day. Yet at the same time he hadn't had the slightest intention of taking the thought through to its logical conclusion.

'That was why the drug thing was so awful,' Spile said as they turned a sharp corner, left, then right again. 'But at least it didn't make the news.'

Nick thought about that. Somehow it didn't seem either accidental to him or an act of kindness. The news people were notorious for publishing anything they could get their hands on, the more scandalous the better. *I wonder. Is that something the cops are keeping secret?*

But why?

It was weirding him out. Nick saw as much pain and death and unhappiness on the Net news as anyone else did but coming up against it in terms of real people, real lives, was something else again. And there was something else going on inside him, too. His dad was a Netcam man, one of the best. That was why he kept getting sent all over the place, why they had had to keep moving around so much when Nick was younger.

Reporters fought to be assigned with his father, for he had (one of them had said once, in Nick's hearing) 'a gift for finding trouble and following up on it.' Now, unnerved, Nick was beginning to wonder whether that gift was starting to reveal itself in the next generation.

'Here,' he said, and turned the last corner. Fortunately the corridors hadn't been doing anything unusual. Right up until now everything had been where it was supposed to be, and now the wall at the far end of what otherwise looked like a featureless dead end was exactly where Nick had left it. 'Your account open?'

'Yeah,' Khasm said. Nick went down to that blank wall, bent close to it. The light wasn't great down here, and he had only found this lift's hiding place because of a stubborn tendency to touch everything. 'Here,' he said, getting down on one knee. 'See that kind of dimple there? It just caught my eye. It doesn't belong . . .'

'Yeah,' Khasm said again. She leaned down to touch it.

The rock in front of them seemed to tear itself open. A moment later they were all looking at what Nick had found earlier: a small chest carved of what appeared to be a single emerald. Down in the bottom of it was what Nick had found there before, when he opened it himself: a single eighth-note, glowing gold.

Khasm looked at it for a long moment before she reached in and touched it. The air filled with the sound of Camiun's strings being plucked slowly, one after another, more as their own small, soft poem on the air rather than any accompaniment, and then came Joey Bane's voice, sorrowful and low:

> 'I never went the way you told me to,
> I argued every word you said.
> I never thought the way you would have
>   liked,
> I never walked the way you led.

And now he's gone with you where
   I would not,
There in the dark he holds your hand;
And how I simply let you go to be with him
I'll never understand.

So now I have them all to myself, at last,
All my sorry, empty days,
And now I walk alone and self-sufficient
Down the narrow ways . . .

Nick stayed where he was, didn't move, as Khasm and Spile held still and listened to the second verse of the song. Finally the last few notes faded away, and Khasm lifted the eighth-note out of the casket and closed her hand around it. When she opened her hand again, the note was gone.

She stood up and sighed, sniffled again, and for a few moments she wouldn't say anything. 'When they release the body and let her mom bury her,' Khasm said at last, 'I'll play it at the grave for her. After the funeral, when things quiet down.'

They went out into the corridor. Nick, following her and Spile, was finding it hard to understand how he felt. Spile was a silent, glowering presence in this darkness, but there was no feeling of threat about him, only pain, and Khasm, her eyes downcast, seemed to have gotten control of herself again. But that was even worse for Nick, in a way, than the sound of her fighting with her tears had been.

'Look,' he said. 'If there's anything else I can do . . .'

Khasm shook her head. 'This,' she said, holding up the closed hand that no longer had an eighth-note in it, 'this means a lot. Uh . . . thanks.'

She went off down the corridor, and Spile started to go after her. Nick astonished himself by putting a hand on that huge arm. Spile stopped and stared at him.

'I mean it,' he said.

Spile looked at him in a kind of lowering silence, then said, 'Yeah. Thanks. I—'

'Nick Melchior,' Nick said. 'I'm in the login lists.'

'OK,' said Spile. 'I – maybe we'll get in touch.'

He went after Khasm. Nick stood there, watching them go, and then headed out into the corridor himself, in the opposite direction, slowly making his way back toward where he had been when they'd found him.

It had never occurred to him that there might have been something odd about those suicides. But Khasm and Spile had been absolutely certain. And now Nick found himself remembering that Charlie had been a little concerned about Deathworld, himself, and all the time Nick was spending there.

Was he thinking about the suicides, too?

There was no telling. But he had certainly mentioned them once . . . and Nick had brushed him off. And then Charlie had asked him for that walkthrough.

Nick had been delighted about this earlier: the idea of ranging around Deathworld with Charlie in tow would have been fun. Part of that was that Charlie was so smart about a lot of stuff. Nick didn't grudge him that. His buddy had been through hell in his time, a real hell as opposed to this rather entertaining, fake one. But this would have been one place where, for once, Nick was just a little smarter than Charlie . . . and he didn't think Charlie would grudge him that, either.

Now, though, the concept had acquired an entirely different slant, and Nick wasn't sure he liked it at all. There was something about these suicides and Deathworld that was bothering him, all of a sudden . . . something fishy. And now Charlie was going to be wandering around down there, new to the place, not knowing the ropes. Anybody could come along and tell him anything . . . possibly get him in some kind of trouble.

Oh, come on, said the 'sensible' part of Nick's brain. *It's not like the environment's dangerous, or anything. If it were, Net Force would come in and shut it down. And Charlie's not dumb! Far from it.*

But all the same . . . these suicides . . .

All of a sudden they gave him the creeps.

I've got to go see Charlie, he thought. *As soon as I finish here today . . .*

Nick headed off into the darkness.

Charlie had been up late again, the night before, sitting sideways on the lowest of the benches in his workspace with his feet up, studying the Deathworld walkthrough. It was complex but not as bad as some environments he'd played in at one time or another. A lot of the business of getting through the upper circles seemed to involve talking to the Damned. That, by itself, was interesting for Charlie. Later on, once you got down to Eight, it started to be about talking to other gameplayers. *It's as if the game designers are trying to teach people to talk to each other,* Charlie thought. *Easing them into it gradually. It starts out as sort of an entertainment, "look at all the bad people getting what's coming to them . . ." Then it changes focus.*

Charlie wasn't quite sure what to make of that. *Is this the work of some benign behind-the-scenes environment designer? Or could this be something that Bane wanted put in?*

He paused for a little while to scan through the various virtclips and text interviews with Bane that he had gathered together. In none of them did Joey Bane say much about his actual input into the environment's design. If anything, he seemed to avoid the topic, or to try to suggest (in one or two of the interviews) that he was a non-techie who didn't know much about computers or the Net.

That Charlie found hard to believe, especially in the light of the way the professional music business was these days. It had become inextricably interwoven with the Net in terms of music distribution and marketing over the last twenty years, and if there was anything Charlie was certain of as far as Joey Bane was concerned, it was that the man was expert, even inspired, in terms of marketing. He suspected that Bane was as involved in this as in anything else to which his name might be attached. But proving it . . .

Then again, there wasn't any reason to worry much about that right now. The environment itself was going to present its own challenges. *Because after Eight, after you find the way into the Maze and down into the Ninth level . . . no details.* Even the walkthroughs, which were theoretically slightly illegal and usually went out of their way to reveal such details, suddenly went dry. *It's as if it all stops there . . . or some really powerful influence is keeping people from discussing what they find there. Weird.*

The threat of lawsuits, maybe?

But then you would think that was enough to keep people from talking about the first eight levels, too. And it's not.

Charlie brooded over that for a while. *What influence was powerful enough to keep something so secret?*

If I get down there, I may find out. Meanwhile . . .

He swung up and walked around his little gallery of exhibits again. Charlie had folded away all the autopsy results, and now was left with the kids themselves, sitting on front steps, lying on beaches, hitting a softball again and again . . . Jaime and Richard. Jeannine and Malcolm. Renee and Mitch. *They could have been anybody from Bradford,* Charlie thought. *Or from any school around here. They look perfectly normal.* Except that they had all committed suicide. That was the problem, of course. A suicide looks like anybody else, until the crucial moment hits during which taking one more breath becomes just too painful.

And then there are cases like these, Charlie thought, *when there's something else going on . . .*

. . .and only one way to find out what.

He sighed, glancing up at the windows. It was fully dark in London now but it was still afternoon on the East Coast. He headed off toward the doorway that led to Mark Gridley's workspace, opened it, and put his head through.

The heat and humidity hit him like a blow. *Well, it's Florida, isn't it,* Charlie thought, and stepped into the hot sunlight and close still air inside the VAB. *But you can have a little too much reality. Mark can be such a perfectionist sometimes.* 'Mark,' Charlie shouted as he walked across the concrete, 'you in here?'

'Yeah,' Mark said, from somewhere right across that huge space, though out of sight. 'Be with you in a minute.'

Charlie made his way across to where the hardwood desk had been sitting last time. It was gone. There was one of the new Rolls-Skoda cars there, the sleek new armored number that everyone was talking about. Its hood was up; Mark was peering in at the engine.

Charlie came up beside him after a couple of minutes and looked in, too. The engine was clean enough to eat off, a complex welter of shining tubes and piping and a massive engine block which had probably been carved in one piece out of a solid cube of steel. 'Considering a purchase?' Charlie said. 'Or is your dad worried about somebody's security?'

'Huh?' Mark straightened up, dusted his hands off. 'No, it's just a sim,' he said. 'Somebody I know let me borrow it. They're having trouble with the way it runs. Keeps going nonphysical at bad moments.'

Charlie thought rather ruefully of his steam engine.

'I've been having spong troubles myself,' he said. 'But that's not what I came over for.'

'So tell me.' Mark put the Rolls's hood down and boosted himself up to sit on it. 'And what happened with all those files?'

'A lot,' Charlie said. 'But Mark, would you for cripesake turn on the air conditioning? It's like a sauna in here.'

'Nope,' Mark said. 'I'm waiting for something.' He glanced up. Charlie followed his glance, but didn't see anything but the pygmy buzzards, way up high by the huge slot in the ceiling, circling near it. 'So tell me what's up.'

Charlie shook his head in mild exasperation, but went ahead to briefly describe what he had found in the autopsy files. 'There's something going on with all these deaths that just doesn't feel right,' he said. 'And there's no way to look into it except from the inside.'

Mark gave him a thoughtful look. 'Looking into death from the inside,' he said, 'would seem to preclude you doing much of anything else.'

'Not *that* far inside,' Charlie said, with only a little annoyance. 'Mark, I need you to wire me.'

Charlie had expected to have to explain to Mark what he meant. To his surprise, he didn't. But he was also surprised to see Mark sit down on one of his folding chairs and blow out his cheeks like someone with a big problem.

'Don't need much, do you?' Mark said.

'You can do it, can't you?' Charlie said.

'*Will* I do it? Yeah, you know I'll do whatever you need done. Is it going to be easy? No, not like raiding those systems the other night.'

Mark pulled his feet up under him to sit crosslegged on the Rolls's hood. 'That was stealing-from-the-cookie-jar stuff compared to this,' he said. 'Deathworld's probably got more copy protection schemes built into it than any environment I can think of. Bane's really sensitive to having his stuff ripped off so half his technical staff keep busy inventing new and interesting ways to stop people from piping information directly out. A whole lot of stuff to have to defeat, second by second. And naturally you don't want anybody noticing what you're doing.'

'Uh, no.'

Mark sat there and brooded for a little. 'By the way, what happened to your fishing trip?' Charlie said after a moment. 'I didn't think I'd find you here.'

Mark snickered. 'Oh, I would have won. Dad has to stay home and do some classified thing.' He shrugged. 'Maybe it's just as well. He'll be out of my way for the rest of the weekend, and maybe longer . . . which is going to be good, since this is gonna need a lot of concentration.'

The two of them sat there quietly for a few moments more. Then Mark said, 'Talk to me later tonight. I'll let you know if it can be done.'

'OK,' Charlie said, getting up. 'Mark, thanks.'

'Yeah, yeah . . .' But then Mark looked up, blinking. 'You hear something?'

Charlie looked around. 'Uh, no.'

'I did, though. Mark slid down off the hood of the Rolls, and looked up. '*Hey* . . .'

Charlie followed his glance. The buzzards were suddenly crowding off to one side of the VAB's upper reaches, and all looking hurriedly for high spots on which to perch, as if on the top of a cliff. Charlie looked up and saw . . .

He opened his mouth, then closed it again, for he didn't know how to describe what he was seeing. His first thought was, *The air is thickening*. The idea seemed silly. But that was exactly what it was doing – thickening, like steam, like a thick fog, thicker, like smoke – though through it the sun poured from above, untroubled. Charlie shook his head, astounded. Clouds were forming above them, right there inside the VAB, and as Charlie watched, what looked like a thin silvery smoke seemed to start drifting down from them. He walked out into the middle of that space, not hurrying too much, for that silvery drift was taking a little time to come down, and finally he stopped, with Mark behind him, and felt, on his upturned face, the first fine drops of rain.

'Will you look at that,' Mark said, triumphant. 'It does this sometimes, the real one. I knew that if I'd really got this simulation down right, sooner or later it would happen.' He pounded Charlie on the back and laughed. 'Congratulations, Charlie, you've witnessed history!'

'Yeah,' Charlie said, 'and it's wet.' He brushed the rain off his shoulders and made for the door, smiling slightly but still thinking about that gallery of smiling faces sitting inside his own workspace, intent on finding out what had happened to them . . .

. . .without becoming one more smile.

Chapter Seven

Nick exited Deathworld into the bare white space of his public-access area. He looked around at the white walls with a faint feeling of guilt. Even if they did eventually look better once he'd got his decorating done, it wasn't going to be the same as his own space on the family's server. He felt annoyed at himself for not having been more careful with his time, and for getting his mom and dad so angry. He was beginning, much to his annoyance, to see their point.

Pretty soon I'm going to start thinking I should go apologize to them some more, Nick thought rebelliously.

But would that be such a bad idea? It might do something to change the fact that his life seemed to be completely screwed up at the moment.

You're just freaked because of this stuff Khasm and Spile told you about.

He swallowed. That was true.

And Charlie . . .

'Charlie Davis' space,' he said to the white walls around him. Nick was feeling a little ashamed of himself. He should have stopped by days ago. But he'd been busy . . .

'Trying that workspace for you now.'

That busyness had been shaken out of him, now, by his conversation with Khasm and Spile. Until now Nick had assumed that the suicides were genuine, just people who somehow couldn't cope. It had never occurred to him that something else might be going on. He still wasn't sure what, but the idea gave him the creeps.

'The space you require is accessible,' said his public space's management program.

Nick got up out of the virtual version of the implant chair and went over to the air, pulling on the doorknob sticking out of it. The door opened and he looked through into the big, circular, wood-paneled space with its portraits of doctors in frock coats and wigs, the stadium benches, and the steam engine down in the low part in the middle.

The steam engine wasn't there though. What was there was a group of 2D and 3D images of people . . . kids Nick didn't know. He walked down the stairs between two sets of bleachers, looking at them. There was no sign of Charlie. Either he was out in the real world somewhere or working on something else.

Or he's in Deathworld someplace.

Nick thought about that, then went back up the stairs and stepped back into his workspace, shutting the access to Charlie's space behind him. Then he opened the doorway he usually used to access Deathworld. Burning red, the copyright information hung there in front of him. 'Yeah, yeah, get on with it,' Nick said. 'Front door access, please.'

The long copyright warning notice hung there a few moments more, and then showed him the great front gates. Nick walked in and said, 'Deathworld utilities, please.'

In front of him appeared a huge, dark green onyx desk, piled high with ledgers, and behind the desk, a clerk-demon wearing a green eyeshade, sleeve garters and a bow-tie (though no shirt). It looked up at him with a blunt, only slightly wicked face, like that of a cartoon bulldog with the demise of some cartoon cat on its mind. 'Yeah? Oh, it's you, Nick.'

'Hi, Scorchtrap,' Nick said, strolling over to the desk. 'How's the union thing going?'

'Aah, the usual,' said the demon. 'Management says they can't budge on the last offer, we say fine, we'll strike, they say OK, they'll bring in cheaper labor . . .' The demon leaned to one side and spat brimstone into an ornately carved spittoon by the desk. Sulfurous smoke rose from it. 'Scabs, that's what they mean. It stinks more than usual, Nick. Our problem is we got no rights.'

'Well, just hang in there,' Nick said. 'You guys have personality. They'd be nuts to get rid of you.'

'From your mouth to the Boss's ear,' said Scorchtrap. 'Cheapskate that he is. He promised us that this bargaining round, he'd give us a decent profit-sharing agreement. Now he won't even give us the time of day. It's enough to make you lose your faith in market forces.' The demon grimaced. 'But enough of my problems. What can I do for you?'

'Looking for a friend of mine,' Nick said. 'Charlie Davis.'

The demon pulled up a thick scroll from behind his desk. This unrolled out across the floor and into the distance, where it vanished, like railroad tracks converging at the horizon. Scorchtrap made a disgusted face, tossing the scroll to the desk. 'Retrotech,' he said, and reached into the air, grabbing a little cord that hadn't been there a second before, pulling down a text window. 'This guy come in here recently?'

'The past day or so, I think.'

Scorchtrap studied the text that was scrolling through the window too fast for Nick to read, and finally came to the end of it. 'Nobody by that name.'

'He might be using a "nym".'

'Yeah, but if he is we can't disclose it,' Scorchtrap said, pulling on the cord again. The window rolled itself up like an old-fashioned window blind, with the same flapping noise, and vanished. 'Privacy legislation, you know how it is, Nick . . . gotta keep the nosy-bodies at bay. Even when it's in a good cause.'

'Yeah, I guess.' Nick let out a long breath. 'Listen, do this for me. Let me have a look at the login records for the last couple of days.'

Scorchtrap raised his eyebrows. 'You kidding?' he said. 'You must feel like curling up by the fire with a good book. You know how many people we get in here every day?'

'Just the newbies, Scorchtrap. There can't be that many of them.'

'You wanna bet?' The demon shook his head and reached up to pull the cord. The window came down again. 'Been busy around here the last week or so, Nick. Lotta trouble upstairs, you know what about.'

'I know,' Nick said, somber, and leaned his elbows on the desk, looking at the window.

Scorchtrap hadn't been kidding. Deathworld had experienced between five and ten thousand new user logins per hour from all over the planet during the period in which Nick was interested. Even though Nick waded through it as best he could, there was no telling what "nym" Charlie might have chosen. He was not one of the dim types who pick an anagram of their name, or their mother's maiden name, for a pseudonym.

Finally he sighed and gave up. Scorchtrap made a sympathetic *tsk tsk* noise and rolled the log window up again. 'Sorry about that, buddy,' the demon said. 'Anything else I can do for you today? Got some new "lifts" being released on Six.'

'Naah,' Nick said, 'not for me, today. I've got business on Eight.' He turned, waving at the demon. 'You take it easy,' he said.

'Yeah, you too, Nick. Hey wait a minute!'

Nick looked back. 'Yeah?'

'You check the message boards yet?'

'Uh, no! Not a bad idea. Thanks, Scorchtrap.'

'Any time, kid.' The demon opened a large ledger labeled DAMNED WITH EXTREME PREJUDICE and started leafing through it. 'And you keep your feet dry down in the Maze! You don't wanna catch anything down there.'

Nick grinned. The desk, and the demon, vanished. In Nick's opinion, the Deathworld programmers were using the demons to keep themselves amused, sometimes possibly even playing them 'live'. This amused him, too, and he wasn't above playing the game with them when the opportunity presented itself. *It might improve my game stats,* he thought, *but besides that, why shouldn't they have fun, too?*

He walked through the darkness a little way to where he knew there was a huge archway somewhat reminiscent of the main gate. This one, though, had engraved in the stones of the arch the words MARX WAS WRONG: THE OPIUM OF THE MASSES IS NEWS.

Nick headed in through the archway and found himself in a tremendous room modeled after the Beaux-Arts reading room of the 42nd Street branch of the New York Public Library, but all done in black and gray, with high, dark windows, where the original had been done in ivory, wood, and gold. He made his way past the pillared 'calls' desk. Behind which a huge white lion was standing on its hind legs and going through some card-catalog drawers on the desktop. He glanced down the length of the room. There were two lines of huge, long, dark-topped tables, each table with four shaded lamps down the middle of it.

Nick walked to the nearest of these and sat down in

the subdued light of one of the lamps.

Moving and shifting beneath the surface of the table were hundreds and hundreds of text messages, images, and 'flat' virtclips, scrolling by, never stopping, all messages from Banies to Banies, talking about Deathworld itself, or the music, or other Banies, or Joey, or any of the myriad other things that Deathworld fans could possibly think of to discuss when they weren't actually exploring the place. Nick placed a hand flat down on the table and said, 'Start a search, please.'

'Whatcha lookin' for, boss?' said the table in another demon-gruff but friendly voice.

'Uh, any message from Charlie to anybody else.'

The table emitted a sigh. 'You know how many Charlies we got in here, Nick?' it said. 'You wanna narrow that search down a little, or don't you have a life?'

Nick laughed. 'Any message from a Charlie to me, or from any Charlie to any Nick.'

'Nothing found on the first search,' the table said. 'Nothing on the second. Try something else?'

Nick thought for a moment. *If Charlie's been in here, at least he hasn't been trying to reach me.* That could be a good thing. Or might not. 'Any public message about suicide,' Nick said after a moment.

'You really *don't* have a life, do you,' said the table. 'Eighteen thousand messages about that in the last two weeks. And another six thousand went into the bit bucket between then and now. I *told* them I needed more storage, but do they listen to me, *nooooooo . . .*'

'Yeah, right,' Nick said. He leaned his head on one hand for a moment, thinking. 'Look,' he said, 'show me any message in which the words "I want to kill myself" or "I feel like killing myself" or "I want to end it all" are used.'

'You want me to be a dumb machine and sort just for

those phrases,' the table said, soundly slightly affronted, 'or can I get a little bit heuristic about this and also look for sentences that mean the same thing?'

'Uh, feel free.'

'Better sample,' the table said. 'Still pretty big. Four hundred eighty-six messages.'

'Lord,' Nick said. 'Display them.'

'You want something to drink?' the table said.

'A cola.'

A glass of it appeared next to Nick on the table. 'Statutory regulations require us to inform you that the ingestion of virtual beverages does not provide any hydration, nutrition, or other dietary benefit to your physical body,' said the table in an intensely bored tone of voice. 'Then again, there aren't any calories, either. So drink up and don't spill.'

Nick raised an eyebrow, picked up the glass, and drank, while starting to read the messages. Every time he had read enough of one, he tapped on the table and it vanished, to be replaced by another.

Pretty soon his tapping finger was getting tired. A lot of the messages were facetious. A lot of them were deadpan, in terms of composition, but when there was no video to go with the text, as often happened, there was no way to tell how serious the person leaving the message had been, or if they were serious at all. One message Nick came across, which had been left only a few hours before, was typical. WHATS THE POINT? said its subject line.

'I don't know what people are yelling about. It's only death. Death isn't so bad compared to some other things that can happen to you and when it just hurts too much you want to say all right let it all be over with. Maybe Joey is right maybe this is the time to cut the strings and have some peace and quite. Nobody would really care if I wasn't here and in fact I think I would prefer it; it would be less trouble for everybody I know, one less thing to worry about like my mom says. I don't know what life is for anyway, there's nothing that seems to be the thing I'm supposed to be for and everyone else seems to know, I'm the only one who doesn't have a clue. The sooner all this pointlessness is over for me the better I think.'

There were various replies to this, some sympathetic, some jeering, but no one seemed to be taking it very seriously, or actually dealing with the idea that this person really seemed to want to 'end it all.' No one even just came out and said 'don't!' *Because they're afraid of finding that he or she was kidding around, maybe, and they don't want to take the chance of looking stupid?*

Nick let out a breath and glanced at the sender's name 'MANTA.' Just another handle, behind which sat a real person in who knew what state of mind. At first glance it would be easy to think it was someone too depressed even to look over the text and correct it where the context filter in the Deathworld voice-to-text system had slipped up. *A yell for help?* Nick thought, glancing down at the time stamps and other system information, node locations and so forth, saved at the bottom of the message. *If it was one, how could you even find the person? This stuff is all coded, it isn't meant to help you locate them easily.* Though he had heard that there were ways to track back an original user to his virtmail account, even to his posting location, from this footer material, *if* you knew how to read it. *By the time you did, though, would the person who'd left the message even still be breathing?* And if you *did* find them, would they just laugh at you for taking their joke seriously?

Nick shook his head and went back to his reading, but after about twenty minutes he stopped, exasperated by his inability to be certain about whether the messages were genuine. 'Is there any way to tell which of these people mean it?' he said. 'Semantic analysis or something?'

'I'm a computer, not a doctor,' said the table. 'That starts getting into diagnosis. You think I want the AMA after me? Life's tough enough.'

Nick had to laugh. 'OK,' Nick said, 'forget it. But listen . . .' He thought for a moment. 'Are there any messages from any of the . . . you know. The Angels of the Pit?'

'Three remain in the database,' said the table. 'But they've been locked off, Nick. Confidentiality issues.'

Nick sat back in his seat, thinking a little more. 'OK,' he said. 'Would you do me a favor?'

'Anything within reason,' said the table.

'If any messages come for me while I'm in-environment from a Charlie – or, never mind that . . . from anybody – route them to me right away.'

'You're overriding your previously set no-bother instruction?'

'Yeah.'

'Got it. Let us know if you want it changed back at some point.'

'Right. Thanks, guy.' Nick patted the table, then got up and headed out of the reading room again.

He made his way back to his access door, back into his plain white workspace, and stood there a moment, thinking. *Do I want to comm him at home?*

Maybe not . . . it might freak his folks somehow. Or it might freak mine, if he called me back at home and let them know what it was about.

Instead, Nick made his way back into Charlie's workspace. 'Hello . . .' he said, hoping to wake up the system.

'Hi, Nick,' said the soft, woman's voice that represented Charlie's 'system manager.' 'Charlie says, "Make yourself at home and use whatever you have to." '

171

'Uh, good. I need to leave him a message.'

'I can record virtual voice, virtual image and voice, or text. Tell me what you prefer.'

'Virtual image and voice.'

'Go ahead. Stop for five seconds and then say "Finished" when you're done.'

'Charlie . . .' Nick said. 'I have to tell you about this. I ran into some people in Deathworld. They knew a couple of the people who committed suicide. But they think something's going on, something odd . . .'

He went on to lay out everything Khasm and Spile had told him, especially the part about drugs being involved. Then he summed up what he'd found when he searched the message database. Nothing much, but it might make it clear to Charlie why he was feeling a little weird about what was going on.

Finally he trailed off, not knowing what else to add. 'Just comm me at home, if you can,' Nick said. 'Not too late. Dad's been working weird hours the past week or so. The studio had to send him to California for something; don't ask me why he couldn't just go there virtually.' He tried to think if there was something else he should mention. He had the feeling that he'd forgotten something. 'OK? Comm me. And listen . . . be careful.'

Nick paused. 'Finished,' he said.

'Thank you, Nick,' Charlie's system said. 'I will pass this on to Charlie as soon as he checks in.'

'You have any idea where he is?'

'Not at the moment. I'm sorry.'

Nick nodded. 'Thanks.'

He wandered back up the steps again, not without pausing to look back at those images of kids his age, or a little older or a little younger. Wondering, he turned and headed back to his own workspace, trying to figure out what to do next.

★ ★ ★

In the VAB, dusk was drawing in, and the big sodium lights hanging from the cross-gantries in the ceiling were turned on, flooding the concrete with a harsh, bright glare. 'OK,' Mark said to Charlie, coming across the floor to him. 'Here you are.'

He held up what he carried, white and shimmering in that fierce light. Charlie looked at it in bemusement. 'It's a jacket,' he said.

Mark rolled his eyes. ' "It's a jacket," he says. Do you know how much *programming* there is in this thing? This is not just any jacket!'

'OK,' Charlie said, 'it's a *magic* jacket. Do I have to wear a bow-tie with it? And does the tie have to be magic, too?'

'I swear,' Mark muttered, 'once we both get somewhere physical at the same time, I'm going to whack you a good one with something that can't just be deleted. Here, put it on.'

He helped Charlie into the jacket, a rather formal-looking one of the kind a gentleman might wear to dinner. To Charlie, it felt completely normal. 'Nice material,' he said, patting it down.

Mark stood back from him. 'It should be,' he said, rather sourly, 'considering what it would cost you per hour if someone, I should use the word loosely, "professional," had built this for you.'

'I feel like a waiter,' Charlie said. 'Probably I look like one, too. So where's the switch?'

Mark sat on the Rolls and shook his head. ' "Switch"?' he said. '*Please!* And if you look like anything, you look like a doctor. And you'll probably make a great one someday, as long as you don't try understanding anything more complicated than a stethoscope, OK? Look, there *aren't* any switches. You just wear it into Deathworld. You wear it out again. Make sure you *don't* take it off – not only because you won't be able to record anything you're perceiving, but because it's set up to work only when it's in circuit with your own virtual account and your own implant. I haven't been able to implement a whole lot of failsafes, partly because I still don't completely understand how to subvert all their systems. But there's a real good chance that if the jacket comes out of circuit with you, with your implant I mean, every alarm in that place will go off. This would be a *bad* thing, because immediately afterwards, every security op associated with Joey Bane Enterprises, not to mention every lawyer they've got, thousands of them probably, will be chasing you down the labyrinthine ways. You're getting all this?'

'Uh, yes,' Charlie said. He was also enjoying it. It was always fun to get Mark annoyed about something. 'Had a bad time getting the details worked out?' he asked.

Mark glowered at him. 'I spent the better part of five hours analyzing Deathworld's security systems,' he said.

'Oh, well, five *hours*,' Charlie said.

'And if you think I enjoyed it, you're—'

Charlie started laughing. He couldn't help it. 'Of *course* you enjoyed it!' he said. 'You're a pirate at heart, Gridley. That's why it drives you nuts to be your father's son.' He laughed some more, unable to stop.

Mark gave him a crooked smile. 'Yeah, yeah, Mr Psychoanalyst,' he said. 'Well, you can't help it, I guess, it's your mom's side of the family. Look, never mind that. Just don't let this thing off your back, OK? You can wear a "seeming" over it – in fact, probably it'd be smart if you did.'

'OK,' Charlie said.

'I had to do some jury-rigging,' Mark said. 'The security systems in Deathworld are really complex. To keep the flow of information moving out of there and into your space, I had to do spectrum-fission on it, scatter it up and down several different kinds of in-Net communication, then reweave it to "singleband" throughput on the outside.'

'I hope that wasn't meant to make some kind of sense to me,' Charlie said, checking the jacket to see if it had an inside pocket. It did.

'That's data storage, in there,' Mark said. 'Meanwhile, just think of the outbound signal as white light broken down to a spectrum, then "welded" back to white again,' Mark said. 'The important thing is, it worked when I tested it.' He raised his eyebrows. 'Though the first couple of test cycles were interesting. What matters is that what you see and hear will go back to your site and store themselves there. One thing: when you're done with the jacket, don't leave it in your workspace. Leave it in mine.'

'Oh? How come?'

Mark gave him another of those endearing it's-like-this,-stupid expressions. 'If something goes wrong,' he said, 'or on the other hand, if something goes *right*, and in the unlikely event that someone gets cranky afterwards about what's been done, you want the Deathworld people to take *you* to court for theft of intellectual property and copyright violations, thus ruining your not-even-started-yet brilliant medical career for ever after? Or do you want them to come after *me* for it, and let me take the heat as the Brilliant But Slightly Unstable Genius Son of the Director of Net Force?

Phrased that way, the answer more or less made itself obvious. 'Uh,' Charlie said.

'Exactly, "uh",' said Mark. 'So I've left my space open for you, day and night. As soon as you're done with a run, leave the jacket here. Over the desk. When you've done that and left, the logs at my end will wipe, leaving no "electron trail" to your workspace. That much I managed with no trouble. But the rest of it remains technically a little fragile, so as I said, don't lose the jacket and *don't* take it off.'

'Right.'

'As for the rest of it,' Mark said, 'and our discussions about what you think's going to start to happen later, I've "tripwired" the outside of your own workspace. I think I can safely say that no one will be able to detect that tripwiring. The minute someone tries to hack into any of your accounts – either yours or your folks' – alarms will go off here in my space. My system will start a traceback on whoever's trying to get at your files. When that happens, your own space will alert you, if you're in Deathworld, through the links I've built into the jacket. For times when you're not virtual, you'll want to install some other alert method, to your home comms or whatever. I've left the "hot ends" of the alert routines visible for you, in your space. Hook them up whatever way you like, then camouflage them. After that, we'll have the information we need to send Net Force after whoever it is. And then you and I will be covered with glory.'

Mark grinned. 'Assuming,' he added, 'that *they* don't pitch eight kinds of fit when they find out what we're doing.' He made a pointing-upward gesture that indicated the entire adult world in general, but specifically his father, and his mother, and Charlie's mom and dad, and James Winters. 'Because you haven't told them . . .'

Charlie made an unhappy face. 'How did you know?'

'The same way I know that I haven't exactly told my dad about what we're up to,' Mark said. '*You* know you're being careful, *I* know you're being careful. But they don't understand, do they?'

'I'm not sure they would,' Charlie said, 'no.' The thought of what his father's face would look like if he told him what he was planning to do, had been haunting him the last day or so. *And as for Mom* . . . But haunting him more assiduously were the faces of Renee, and Malcolm, and Jeannine, and the rest of them. No one else was in the position to find out as much about what had happened to them as Charlie was. And more to the point, time was running out. There was only so much of the month left, at which time Charlie believed that the person who he was sure had been stalking the 'suicides,' and was somehow complicit in their deaths, might well go dormant again. A year would go by during which media and police attention to the suicides would wane, and then, there would be more of them.

No more, he had thought last night, as he'd been going over his plans, and had started putting them into operation while scanning through some of the bleak-sounding messages left in the Deathworld 'bulletin-board' system. *No more deaths.* The image of the dim hallway, the peeling paint, a huddled form lying across the room from him, intruded itself again. *No more.*

'Hey,' Mark said.

Charlie looked up.

Mark leaned back a little, let out a breath, looked the jacket up and down one more time. 'Not that it's not a good idea. But are you absolutely sure you want to go through with this?'

Charlie walked around slowly and waved his arms around a little in the jacket, getting the feel of it. There was a faint fizzing sensation associated with it, something like the sensation that came with a mouthful of soft drink before you swallowed it. 'Yeah,' he said. 'It's partly that I know I can pull this off, solve this problem, without having to run to "the grownups" for help. But there's also the time problem. If I waited to do this the way my folks, or Winters, would rather have me do them, it could get to be too late.' He shook his head. 'So

I don't see that I have a choice. There are things more important than just "being careful".'

'Yeah.' Mark let out a long breath.

Charlie sighed as he came back and leaned against the Rolls. 'Besides, for Winters at least, I'm going to need more solid evidence than I've currently got. What I'm sitting on right now won't stand up.'

'Well,' Mark said, 'you'll have some solid stuff pretty soon, if you're right.' He leaned back on the Rolls's hood. 'But if you insist that it's not going to be enough just to have proof that someone tried to hack into your workspace . . .'

'It's going to have to go a little further than that,' Charlie said. *Meaning that I am going to have to stake myself out as bait, not just virtually . . . but physically.* The prospect still made him nervous enough, though, that he was unwilling to say it out loud, even to Mark.

'I could see where it might,' Mark said. 'But the implementation's gonna be tricky. How's your research been coming?'

'Oh, fine,' Charlie said. 'There's tons of stuff available on the subject on the Net.' He smiled but the expression was grim. Suicide, even in these affluent times, was not something that was showing any tendency to go away. 'I get depressed sometimes just reading it.'

'That might be a good thing, under the circumstances. If one of the people you're interested in finding actually comes across you, you'll look more like you're really likely to do something about it.'

'Don't even joke about it.' Charlie had spent the last couple of evenings, when he wasn't busy with other things, studying the symptoms of impending suicide as carefully as if he was about to have a test on them . . . which, in a way, he was. If there was anything he knew about himself at the moment, it was that he wasn't in the slightest bit suicidal, but the descriptions of the feelings of those who were filled Charlie with pity. And the idea of such people being ruthlessly taken advantage of by someone with another agenda besides pity, a deadly one, left him furious.

Mark's expression was somber. 'I wasn't joking . . . not really. But look, the minute you decide it's enough, that you have the data you need . . .'

'I'll call.'

'Call a minute early,' Mark said, 'just to be safe. I won't be far from my workspace anytime I'm not in school.'

Charlie got up, dusted the jacket down again. 'Cut it out!' Mark said. 'It's not like it can get dirty, or wrinkled.'

'One less thing to worry about,' Charlie sighed. He looked up at the faraway ceiling of the VAB. A couple of buzzards peered down at him from the tops of their metal cliffs. 'You get it to rain again?'

Mark shook his head. 'You can't hurry nature,' he said, with a wry look. 'Besides, I'm still analyzing the phenomenon. There are some weird things about the humidity that have to be resolved. When are you going to go in and try that out?'

'Tonight,' Charlie said. 'My folks are going out. I won't be disturbed. And then again early in the morning, and late tomorrow night again, and early the morning after that.' He slid down off the hood of the Rolls. 'Until we get a result.'

'Assuming you do,' Mark said. 'Well, just be careful. I'll be keeping an eye on the jacket's link to my space tonight, and whenever I'm in from now on. Yell if you need anything.'

'Believe me, I will.' Charlie headed toward the door back into his workspace. 'I'll call you as soon as I go in, so you can check the link. Let me know if you find out you're going to be elsewhere, though.'

'No chance of that tonight,' said Mark, 'or in the next few days. At least not till I can get this thing's armor to stop going away without warning.' He tapped the Skoda's hood. It lifted itself smoothly up. A moment later Mark was half under it, nothing showing but his neodenimed legs. Charlie took in this view, smiled slightly, and headed back to his space.

No one looked twice at the lone kid, small, kind of young looking, dressed in worn slicktites and a floppy striped 'sagdown' shirt several years out of style, as he wandered around in the ash and darkness of the Eighth Circle. Banies came in all ages and sizes, and could look any way they pleased if they felt like going to the trouble of adopting a seeming, or could show themselves 'as they were' – though if this was how this kid really looked, there were doubtless those who would have found him a little strange. His sense of style needed work, and the weary look on his face alone was enough to suggest that he probably was as depressing as a Joey Bane lyric himself.

He had been here for a while now, looking around him like someone feeling slightly lost. Anyone interested enough to notice would have seen that he tended to avoid the other Banies in the area, by and large, though he spoke politely enough to them when they approached him. Almost always, after a little while, they went off and left him where he was, and he found himself alone again.

And soon enough – though perhaps not soon enough for him – someone noticed.

The boy was kicking through the ash of the outer reaches with his back to Mount Glede, while in the area through which he walked, nothing could be heard but one song, over and over again, repeating at his request to the environment: the final chorus from the Seattle concert version of 'Cut The Strings,' with the six-minute instrument destruction sequence ending in the demolition of the venerable old King Dome, scheduled to be blown up anyway that year after the Quake of '22. For about the fifteenth time in a two-hour period, that vast crash and shriek of destruction filled the air. The images accompanying it were being suppressed however, and only darkness surrounded the boy who was listening, standing there, staring at the ash around his feet, like a dark statue.

When the girl approached him, seemingly melting out of the storm of black ash that was falling at the moment, the look he gave her was less than interested.

'Hi,' she said.

'Hi,' the boy said, looking her over dully. Long dark coat, short purple skirt, black vee-neck top, purple hair, pale skin. She was taller than he was, maybe a year older, and she looked faintly annoyed. 'What?' he said then, for she was staring at him.

'Are you lost?' she said.

'No.' He turned away.

'Well, you *look* lost,' she said after a moment. 'In fact, I don't think I've seen anyone more lost-looking than you in the last couple months.'

'That's nice,' he said, glowering. 'I don't recall asking you for your opinion.'

He walked away from her, then stopped suddenly, staring down at the crevasse which had just opened up at his feet.

'There's a lot of that going around,' the girl said, sounding slightly amused. 'Get very far on your own?'

'Not really,' they boy muttered. 'This place is an exercise in frustration.'

'Life stinks,' she said.

'Tell me something I don't know.'

181

'That you're not going to get very close to the Keep without a guide,' she said. 'Even the walkthroughs mention that. Unless you've got one of the newer ones.'

He backed away from the crevasse, angling a little away from the girl. 'Maybe I don't want a guide,' he said.

'Maybe you should have brought a chair,' she said, 'because you're gonna be stuck here a good long while without someone to go "pathfinder" for you.'

He started away from her, and almost as if the environment had heard her, another crevasse came tearing along the ground and passed right in front of him. There it stopped, while black ash snowed down from the edges of it into the fiery depths, glittering in the hot light.

He stared down into the crevasse and his shoulders slumped. 'It's never gonna stop doing that, is it?' he said.

'Nope,' she said. 'But some of us get the hang of anticipating it.'

She tilted her head a little to one side, watching him. After a moment he turned, slow and reluctant. 'All right,' he said. 'What would you suggest?'

'Telling me your name, for one thing,' she said.

'Ch— Manta,' he said.

'Manta. I'm Shade,' she said. 'You're pretty new around here, huh?'

'Yeah. Well, no. I've been here a while, but I don't know the place real well as yet . . .' He breathed out then, turning again to look past the crevasses, across the dark plain toward Mount Glede. 'I don't know if I'm going to,' he said.

'You got problems?' Shade said, sitting down beside him.

'Huh?' Manta said, looking shocked. 'Oh, no . . . everything's fine.'

'I'm not so sure,' Shade said. 'You look sad.'

'How can I look sad?' Manta said. 'See, I'm smiling.' He produced a smile that even in the darkness was not terribly convincing.

Shade laughed softly. It managed, somehow, to be a sorrowful laugh. 'Yeah,' she said, 'I see that. I know that smile. I've worn it, sometimes.'

'Have you been here a long time?'

'A couple of years,' said Shade, 'in and out. I know the place pretty well.'

'What're you doing here, then?' Manta said, studying the ground. 'If you've been here that long, you should have solved the place by now.'

'Oh, there's more to Deathworld than just solving it,' said Shade, pulling her feet up under her to sit crosslegged. 'It's about people as much as anything else.'

'Seeing them get punished,' Manta said, bitterly, 'yeah. That's worth something.'

'It'd be pretty dull around here without the Damned,' said Shade, glancing around her as a few of them ran by a few hundred meters away, pursued by demons. A couple of the Damned pitched straight down into a crevasse that opened before them, and the demons stood on the air above them and peered down, watching them fall. 'Sounds like you're enjoying it, though.'

'Like to see it really happening,' said Manta softly.

'How much more real does it have to get?' said Shade. She gave him a thoughtful look. 'Or is there somebody you'd particularly like to see it happening to?' Her voice was almost playful.

'Wouldn't be much point in that,' Manta said. 'It wouldn't make any difference.' He shuffled his feet in the ash. 'Nothing will, really.'

He turned. 'Look, forget it. I gotta go.'

'Manta, wait,' Shade said, walking around in front of

183

him. 'Look, you can't just turn away from people when they're trying to help you.'

'Watch me,' Manta said, his voice bitter. 'I'm not worth helping. Let me alone for long enough and it won't be an issue.'

Shade gave him a look. 'You know,' she said, 'if you weren't such a Banie, you'd be a waste of time. Look, how'd you ever get down this far with an attitude like that?'

'When you hear it from all the people around you all the time,' Manta said, 'you learn to get things done anyway. But I'm tired of it now.' He turned and looked at Mount Glede again. 'I just want to do this one thing – and then it's going to be all over with. I'm going to cut the strings . . .'

Shade looked at him in silence for a moment. 'That's not something to joke about,' she said.

'You think I'm joking, too, huh?' Manta said, giving her a cold look. 'Get your laughing done now, then. A week or so and you won't have another chance to do it while I'm around.'

The look Shade gave him was odd. 'Manta,' she said, 'you wouldn't really—'

'I see what happened to the earlier ones,' Manta said, sitting down on a rock and looking at Mount Glede. 'Whatever else their families thought, down here they have some honor, anyway. They're the Angels of the Pit. Maybe people down here are a little crazy, but at least someone notices whether they're here or not. Not like others—' He broke off.

'You don't have a lot of friends, do you . . .' Shade said.

'I don't have *any* friends,' Manta said. 'And I don't want any. They just pretend to care about what's happening to you, then they dump you when they realize what you're really like. I don't need any more of that—' He choked off, as if holding back tears.

'It's not like that,' Shade said. 'We're Banies. We have to look after each, because no one else will. I want you to meet someone I know . . . he's felt the same way you have.'

'If you think you're going to talk me out of how I feel,' Manta said, 'you're wasting your time.'

Shade glowered at him. 'It's my time. I can waste it if I like. Right now, though, I want you to give me a virtmail address for you, so we can meet down here again, and you can talk to my friend Kalki. He's a Banie, too. In fact, he's a more serious Banie than almost anyone else you're likely to run into down here. He's got the biggest "lift" collection I've ever seen. Thing is, he was about ready to cut the strings, once, too. But it's a mistake to do that while there's still music in them, Manta. He was there. He knows. You need to talk to him.'

Manta studied the ash falling around them, and into the nearest crevasse. After several long moments, he said, 'I don't see why not. It's not going to make any difference.' He raised his head and gave Shade a long, cool look. 'If I do decide to cut the strings, there's nothing you can do to stop me. You or anyone else.'

'Of course not,' Shade said. 'But you have to be sure, first . . . otherwise Joey wouldn't like it.'

'Like he'd care.'

'You'd be surprised,' Shade said. 'Manta, give yourself a break.'

'Nobody else has,' he said. But he watched her as he said it.

Shade shook her head, and held out her hand. 'I'm not everybody else,' she said. 'Let me have an address for you, and later on, in a day or two maybe, you can talk to Kalki.'

Manta looked at her doubtfully. But at last he held

out his hand to her, and there was a little white envelope in it, the icon for a virtmail address. Shade reached out and took it from him, tucking it away in one of the pockets of her coat.

'Meantime,' she said, 'let's see if we can't at least get you in the front door of the Keep. Come on!' Shade looked right and left. 'It's narrower over there,' she said. She held out a hand.

Manta hesitated . . . then took it. Together they made their way down along the length of the crevasse, stepped across it, and vanished into the darkness.

Some hours later, just after six the next morning, Charlie blinked his implant off and got up, stiffly, to walk around the den. His muscles ached more than usual, and once more he resolved to have a look at the implant chair's muscle management routines. They weren't as effective as usual. *Or I'm spending a lot more time in "the great never-never" than usual.*

Probably the latter. Charlie stretched, then wandered downstairs to the kitchen. He glanced around and saw nothing of his mother's on the table. She was already on her way to work, possibly having another in-service today and so having to do her change-of-shift report with the night nurses on her floor earlier than usual. Charlie sighed and rooted around in the fridge for the milk, poured himself a glass and downed it. Then he poured another and glugged that straight down, too.

His father came in and headed for the coffee pot. 'Morning,' Charlie said as he went by.

'Thank you for not saying "good",' his father muttered. He was already in his whites. He got busy pouring himself a cup of coffee the size of a small birdbath in a big brown cup Charlie's mother had brought back from a nursing conference in Germany.

'Early seminar this morning?' Charlie said.

'Yup. Backbones again,' said his father, and slurped the coffee. 'Ow, hot!' he took the milk carton that Charlie handed him and poured milk into his coffee until it turned a very unassertive shade of beige. 'Better. It's just today and tomorrow, anyway, then life goes more or less back to normal.' His father sighed. 'Though I wish the school wouldn't run all these fellowship-program events at the same time that the accreditation team comes through.'

'Maybe they do it on purpose. To show how a good teaching hospital runs under pressure.'

His father looked at him with resignation over the cup. 'That thought's crossed my mind. Nasty idea. In any case, there's nothing I can do about it. Meanwhile, *you* were up late again. I passed you when I came in. Third night in a row now.'

'I'm doing research for a project,' Charlie said. *Let him think it's for school.*

'What on?'

'Suicide.'

His father sighed. 'Still thinking about those kids, huh? Your mother mentioned. Sad situation.'

'Yeah,' Charlie said. 'It's pretty depressing.'

His father chugged the much-milked coffee straight down. 'Tell me about it. Well, ask your mom if you need any more help. I've gotta get out of here.' He rinsed out the coffee cup, upended it by the sink, and headed for the door, pausing only to hug Charlie in passing. 'I feel guilty,' he said. 'The absentee parent.'

'It's not a problem, Dad.'

'I want a rematch on that chess game. You promised me best two out of three.'

'You tell me when,' Charlie said. 'Gonna stomp you.'

'Don't be so sure. See you later.'

The front door shut. Charlie stood looking out into the back garden where the first rays of sun were beginning to fall. *I have been spending too much time "down there,"* he thought. *Good old normal sunlight is beginning to look strange.*

But it was in a good cause, and Charlie thought he was beginning to make some headway. *Shade . . .* There was definitely something odd about her, a sense of her watching him closely for some reaction. *Just hope the one I've found is the right one . . .*

He slowly made his way upstairs with one more glass of milk. The information which Nick had given him was turning out to be very useful, both the "walkthrough" and the other info, the stuff about the kids he'd run into, Khasm and Spile. The rumor, confirmed to the two most recent suicides' parents, that drugs had been involved – and the information that this news was possibly being suppressed – all fit in very neatly with Charlie's suspicions. Especially the idea that they weren't genuinely suicidal. *Someone met them, probably in Deathworld, managed to get close enough to them, physically, to get sco-bro into them – then set up their suicides . . .*

Now all Charlie needed was to recreate the initial part of the setup, without becoming a statistic himself.

To this end, the walkthrough which Nick had given him had been extremely comprehensive, not as error-ridden as Nick had feared, and Nick himself had also appended some material to it as notes which Charlie had found very useful. He sat down on the sofa across from the implant chair in the den, finished his glass of milk, and thought about his next moves, the ones he would begin tonight after school. Charlie had been able to get down to Eight in fairly short order. *I wonder if the system notices things like that,* Charlie thought. But then lots of people must tell their friends how to get through it quickly, how to meet them places. *It probably all averages out in the end.*

Either way, I have to follow up this contact with Shade,

*and keep looking to see whatever else turns up. No way I'm
going to sit around and let this happen to someone else. It's
still May . . .*

Charlie sighed, put the milk glass aside, and sat down
in the implant chair. He still had about half an hour
before he had to leave for school, and this was the best
time to catch people. He closed his eyes, triggered his
implant on again, and glanced around the lowest level
of his workspace, where the 3D and 4D images still
stood. 'Workspace management,' he said.

'Here, Charlie.'

'Is Nick Melchior available?'

'Checking that for you now. This time does not
match his usual online times for the past two weeks.
Not available.'

'OK, what about Mark?'

'Mark's workspace is available as usual, and he is in
residence.'

'Good.' Charlie went over to the usual access door,
opened it. The VAB's lights were on. It was early
enough at the Cape that not much light was getting in.
Charlie wandered across the floor, where he could see
the Rolls-Skoda, its hood still up, and a pair of legs still
visible.

'That thing giving you trouble?'

'Please,' said Mark, sounding tired. 'If you see the man
who invented technology, send him up. I have something
for him.' He stood up from under the hood and made an
eloquent fist. 'I just can't get this thing's armor to stay
solid when it should.' He sighed, straightened up.
'There's always the possibility that I've found a bug in the
programming language itself, but I really don't want to
believe that. It would be big trouble.'

The desk wasn't too far away, and Charlie saw the
Magic Jacket lying over it as he had left it much earlier.
'Is it OK?' he said.

'It was fine,' Mark said. 'I "looked" in on you five or six times, just to check on it. No problems.' He looked at Charlie with a rather challenging expression. 'Except with you. You didn't seem terribly comfortable down there.'

'I hate it, the whole fake-seeming business,' Charlie said. 'Skulking and acting. I don't like not being me. Being me is hard enough, without having to fake being someone else as well.' He let out a long breath. 'But I guess this is in a good cause.'

'You better believe it is,' Mark said, 'because you've had a trip.'

Charlie swallowed. 'What? *Already?* When?'

'Yesterday. Yesterday afternoon, actually. Someone unauthorized was trying to get into your space. I tried to get hold of you, but you were offline.'

'Whew,' Charlie said. 'I wasn't expecting anything that fast.' He thought for a moment. 'Mark, that means that whoever tripped the "wire" has definitely been reading the message boards in Deathworld. I didn't actually talk to anybody until this morning, real early, before school.'

'How many people have you talked to?'

'Uh, six or seven. A couple have seemed interested in me but I'm not entirely sure yet that it's more than casual. I should get a better idea later.'

'OK. Well, you're recording everything . . .'

'I never take off the magic jacket – no matter how much it itches.'

'It doesn't itch!'

'It *does*. It fizzes. I feel like I'm wearing a can of soda.'

'Must be feedback through the implant,' Mark said, thoughtful.

'Can't you do something about it?'

'Not while you're wearing it,' Mark said. 'Let me play with it today if I have some time. I'll leave it in your space when I'm done with it.'

'Yeah, fine. But, Mark, *who tripped the wire?*'

'I don't know.'

'You don't *know?* I thought you put a trace on the tripwire routine!'

'I did,' Mark said, sounding extremely annoyed now, 'but unfortunately, your pigeon was using an anonymizer to conceal the server of origin. They're perfectly legal. I thought the routine I had running would beat it, but this "anonner" is a new one, just opened up. Among the identification routines it's been built to defeat is the one I was using. Dammit.'

'But can't you use something, you know, from Net Force?'

Mark's voice got, if possible, even more annoyed. 'The "industrial strength" identification routines at Net Force are locked down tight, Charlie. To get permission to use the "Drano" utilities, you have to have a court order and ID as a senior Net Force supervisor. Which I am not – yet. And I can't exactly ask any of them, either. So I'm winging it, using routines that have a lot less oomph. If I want to upgrade one of those to industrial strength I'm going to have to do that myself. In fact that's what I'll have to do after school today. Check out this new anonymizer, find out which protocols it's using, figure out how to defeat them. Probably take me a day or so. You better sit the next couple dances out until I can sensitize the "tripwire" to backtrack the next hit correctly.'

Charlie was fuming. 'You don't know anything about where the "trip" came from?'

'Not a thing,' Mark said, sounding just as annoyed. 'Could have been next door to you or in Ulan Bator.'

Charlie sighed. 'OK,' he said. 'Let me know when you get the new routine up again.'

'I will. But look, Charlie, just give it all a rest for the

moment. A day or so won't make any difference.'

'Yeah . . .' Charlie headed out of the VAB and back to his own space, beginning now to be actively nervous. *A day or so.* But no matter what Mark said, Charlie couldn't get rid of the idea that it *could* matter. *It most definitely could.*

Chapter Eight

Nick looked for Charlie at school that day but missed him at lunch again. He wasn't able to track him down between classes either. He had things on his mind, and he really wanted to talk to Charlie about them.

His last-period class had been canceled, so Nick stopped by the wing of the school where he knew Charlie sometimes had a late upper-level biology class. But it had been relocated or rescheduled. The room was locked and empty. Nick let out an exasperated breath and started to walk home.

His path took him by the NetAccess center as usual. Nick paused by the door and took out the last commcard he had left, the one he had fished out of his bottom drawer in his bedroom several days earlier, having forgotten that it was there in the first place.

He looked at the card and sighed. He was woefully short of cash. There wouldn't be any more allowance money until Friday, and today was only Tuesday. Yet at the same time he wanted to give Charlie the opportunity to walk through Deathworld with a friend at his side, not only for enjoyment, but now, after his conversation with Khasm and Spile, for security as well.

And there were other matters on his mind. A random thought, something about the various lifts he had brought back from Deathworld with him, had been obsessing Nick for the past couple of days. The Eighth Circle was proving difficult to crack – *and it's gonna be impossible, without some more money to spend some more time there,* Nick thought. He was noticing that the hints and whispers he had been expecting from 'plants' in the Circle had been very few. He had been wandering around in those stony tunnels and up and down the Escheresque stairways for days now and had come up against – he smiled wryly at the expression – a stone wall.

Yet there had been more lifts available than usual, so many that his pocket lift carrier couldn't handle them all anymore, and Nick had to load them in and out of the storage area in his public server. Most of them were different versions of songs Nick already had lifts of. Only a collector, an aficionado, or a raving completist would feel the need to have them all. Nick certainly fitted into the last category, at least, and it was while he was listening to some of the 'alternate' versions in bed a few nights ago that he had noticed some of the lifts were alternates in other ways as well. They had lyrics that other versions of the songs didn't have—

He shook his head and went into the access center. 'Hey, Nick,' the guy behind the front counter said. 'Early today.'

'Yeah, well, you might not see me for a few days,' Nick said. 'Running out of green . . .' He slapped the commcard up onto the reader plate.

'You're OK,' said Dilish, the guy behind the counter. 'Got a couple of hours left on that one.'

'That much? Super! My usual one open?'

'No, there's someone in there, take Eight. I'll reroute your server info over there.'

Nick went back to the booth and closed himself in, locking the sliding door and sitting down in the implant chair. A moment later he was standing in the usual white space. He reached into his pocket, coming up with the key that 'remembered' his location from the last visit.

'Deathworld access,' Nick said. The door in the air opened, a black rectangle in all that whiteness, and the copyright notice began rolling by. *Is it an illusion,* he wondered, *or does that thing actually get longer every time?* Finally it vanished, and Nick went through into the dimness of the Dark Artificer's Keep, entering into the dark stone corridor where he had been standing when he last exited.

Nick needed somewhere with a little more room for what he had in mind, so he backtracked through the tunnels to where they widened out into a round cavern, something like fifty meters across, that Eighth-Circle Banies referred to as the Bubble. Only a few people were there at the moment, passing across the empty stone space on their way to somewhere else. When they were gone, Nick said, 'Sound management system . . .'

'Ready.'

'Access lift library.'

'Got it.'

'Play "Strings5".'

Music and image faded in, and suddenly Joey Bane was there some meters away, alone and spotlighted in the darkness, sitting on the four-legged bar stool he used for these performances – one of many. (It, like every other inanimate object onstage but Camiun, always wound up getting broken at the end of 'Cut The Strings'.) It was last summer's concert in Los Angeles, at the Hollywood Bowl, and Joey was sweating. Even the Bowl's slightly cooler position in the mountains was no defense against the heatwave the LA basin had been suffering that week. Joey was looking out at the crowd with half a smile, letting them settle, and finally he touched Camiun's strings and sang:

'I ran into Astraea with her veil on,
sneaking out the party's back door:
I stopped her right there and I got her
    a chair,
asking what she was leaving for:
"The party's just getting started, my lady;
what's the rush to leave us today?"
And the goddess she looked at me and
    she said,
"There's nowhere left for me to stay . . . " '

Quietly the rest of the band came in, in that deceptively soft and easygoing introduction, as the Goddess of Virtue explains that the day she's feared has come, the day when the human race is at last entirely wicked, when she must finally hide her face and leave the world to its fate forever, and Joey responded to the news:

'. . . Nothing left to live for, nothing left
    to give for,
nothing left to care about:
Nothing left to cherish, all hopes left
    to perish,
Nowhere to go but out!
No one left to bring to, no pure heart to
    sing to,
What's the point of hanging on?
When the reason in the rhyme's all
    been eaten by crime,
when the last joy's finally gone?'

And then the great chorus of rage and desperation, crashing down in chord after chord as Camiun and Joey Bane together, full-throated, shouted down the blasting band behind them:

'Then cut the strings—
let's be done with it—
If the last night's here,
then let's be one with it—
If the songs all die, if the music's all gone,
If the night's come crashing on the last
    free dawn,
what possible point is there in carrying on?
Cut – the – strings!'

Nick stood listening for enjoyment's sake but his mind
was on the lyrics, especially the very first verse, which
he was now sure was not the usual one. Joey would
sometimes play with the middle verses, inserting
something cruelly topical that suited the venue or the
world situation of the day, but Nick had never heard
him vary the first verse. Now he glanced over his
shoulder for a second, thinking of the 'front hall'
upstairs, before you ever got into the Maze, ever came
close to the tunnels or the Stairways to Nowhere.
Now Nick started to wonder about a faint noise that
he'd heard from behind one of those doors that led off
the front hall.

The sound of the audience's upscaling howl of
excitement brought Nick around again. Bane had stood
up at the first chorus – no one could sing that sitting
down, not and do it justice – but now, two choruses
further along, he turned around, and as always,
Camiun was gone. None of the concert virteos, no
matter how you studied them, ever shed much light on
how that happened. Maybe it was an illusionists' brand
of magic, maybe it was something more obscure. But
speculation always got lost in the wake of what always
happened next, which was Joey Bane snatching yet
another of Wil Kersten's unfortunate guitars out of his
hands and smashing it to smithereens on the floor, or

on some other piece of equipment that happened to be at hand. Off he went on his expected rampage, the crowd screaming noisy approval in the background, and the concert dissolved in a shriek of tortured amplification equipment and other shattered impedimenta.

Nick let it play itself out, and when the clip finally faded into darkness, he stood there a moment later in the Bubble, with the torches flickering around him from their iron grips in the wall, and considered what to do next.

Upstairs. I want to check that door. I don't want to stay too long. I gotta save a little time on this commcard for later in the week.

But first let's see if I can find Charlie!

Charlie made his way home to find the house empty again. His mom wasn't back from the hospital yet. Waiting for him in his workspace, bobbing gently up and down in the air, was the virtmail message he'd been hoping for. He made his way down the stairs of the lecture hall to it, and looked at the little glowing sphere's exterior shell to see if it was 'canned' or 'live'. Some mails, when touched, would link live to the person who had sent them if he or she was available online.

No use taking chances, Charlie thought, even though he couldn't see anything to suggest a live linkage. 'Workspace management,' he said.

'Here, Charlie.'

'Implement stealth routine one.'

The interior of the Royal Society's lecture room went away, to be replaced by a white plain with blue 'sky,' a mimicry of a public-access space. Charlie looked at his hands and arms and saw that his workspace had settled a copy of his 'Manta' seeming about him. He could see it, thinly, over his skin, transparent.

Satisfied, he reached out and touched the mail. A moment later, Shade was standing in front of him, surrounded by a little halo of darkness. The message had been sent from somewhere in Deathworld.

'Manta,' she said, 'I got in touch with Kalki. He'll be in the World tonight around ten eastern. He really wants to see you and talk to you. Let me know if you can make it.'

The image paused, waiting for Charlie to activate the reply function. For a moment he stood there looking at her earnest face, and chewed his lip.

Mark did say to give it a rest for a day or two.

Yet at the same time the thought kept coming up in the back of his head: *It's May. Early in May* . . . And every day lost meant the chance that someone else might die. *If one of these people are involved with the "suicides," and I lose the chance to get close to them while Mark's playing with his programming* . . .

Still. He was pretty definite.

Charlie sighed. 'Start reply.'

'Ready.'

'Shade, thanks, but listen, I—' He stopped himself in the middle of saying 'I can't make it.' *Do you dare* not *take the chance?* The risk was just too great. In his mind's eye Charlie could just see the blurred look on some innocent kid's face as the drug took them, left them defenseless. 'I might be a little late,' he said, 'but I'll be there. Thanks for letting me know. End.'

The workspace collapsed the message down into a smaller sphere. 'Ready to send?' it said.

'Send.'

It vanished. Charlie looked at the empty air where it had been. Then, 'Restore normal environment,' he said.

The lecture hall came back. Charlie glanced around it, and at the six sets of images which had been restored to their original locations, then headed off for Mark's workspace to collect the Magic Jacket.

Some hours later he was standing by the front doors of the Dark Artificer's Keep, waiting. There was a fairly steady stream of Banies coming in and going out. Demons stood by the doors on either side, at attention, looking like doormen at some expensive apartment building. 'Manta' stood there off to one side in his floppy shirt and old worn black slicktites, twitching slightly, looking nervously around him. None of the Banies paid him the slightest attention.

'Waiting long?'

He didn't have to fake being startled. 'Manta' turned hurriedly and saw a tall shape looming over him, somewhat indistinct in the darkness. 'You Manta?' he said.

'Uh, yeah. I don't—'

'I'm Kalki,' the guy said. 'Come on. Who can see anything here? Let's get a little closer to the doors.' He took Manta's shoulder in a friendly way and guided him over that way.

'Manta' shivered a little. Allowing people he didn't know well to touch him had always come hard to him. It was something left over from his distant childhood he didn't readily discuss. As they got closer to the doors and the light of the great chandelier spilling out of them, he got a better sense of what Kalki looked like. He was slender, about eighteen, and not wearing a seeming – or at least not an unusual one. He wore street clothes, just neos, a slipshirt, and a 'bomber' jacket. His face was unusually handsome, with high cheekbones and eyes that dropped down at the corners a little, a look that would have been humorous if it wasn't so sad. *A seeming after all?* Manta thought. *Or am I just unusually paranoid?*

'Shade couldn't make it,' Kalki said. 'Some family thing came up, she said. She told me about you . . .'

'Not too much, I hope,' Manta said.

Kalki looked at him thoughtfully. 'Come on,' he said, 'we can go in here and talk.'

They went in through the Front Hall and Manta looked up at the great black and gray chandelier, casting its cold light. 'It gives me the creeps,' he said softly.

Kalki chuckled. 'You want creepy, you should try Nine,' he said. 'That'll raise the hair on your head, all right.'

'You've been down to Nine?'

They headed off to the side of the huge space, where there were some benches faired into the stone of the massive walls. 'I've been through the gates,' Kalki said, sounding bored. 'It looked so much like the beginning of Eight to me, that I decided not to bother. They've gone to so much trouble, hiding the lifts down there, I wonder whether they're worth it. After all, the stuff I've found on Eight so far hasn't been so great. Sometimes I think it's just a ploy by the Management to get everyone real excited about substandard stuff.'

'The more I see of down here,' Manta muttered, 'the less excited I am about it.'

'Yeah?' They sat down on one of the carved benches, watching people come and go through the great doors. 'Shade told me,' Kalki said, 'that you were pretty sad about things. I see she wasn't exaggerating.'

'Yeah.' Manta looked out into the darkness, and then after a moment said, 'She said you'd felt this way . . .'

Kalki nodded. 'A little while ago now,' he said. 'It can be pretty tough when you're right down in the middle of it.'

'I left some messages in the "board" area,' Manta said softly. 'Just to try to get someone to talk to me. No one answered.'

'Hey,' Kalki said, 'life *does* stink, doesn't it? The

trouble is that people bring the outside reality in here with them. Here, you can change things. But out there, no one does anything about the nature of reality, the way people interact with each other. Or don't. No one listens to anything Joey's saying. And why should they? To do that, they'd have to admit the world stinks, in the first place.'

'I don't have any trouble admitting that,' Manta said. 'It's been a waste of my time since I first started noticing things. Now . . .' He shook his head. 'It's like every breath hurts. I'm tired of breathing.'

Kalki let out a long breath. 'You have folks?' he said.

This was the painful part, the lying. 'My mom,' he said. 'But she's a druggie. The guy she's seeing . . .' He shook his head. 'We don't see eye to eye. And they're a long-term thing. I'm gonna be "phased out." I can see it coming. She's gonna farm me out to some cousin of hers.' Manta bowed his head, unable, unwilling to look up to see how Kalki was taking this.

'Sounds rough,' Kalki said. 'Look, Manta – you've got to believe it: It can get better. Without warning, sometimes.'

Manta's laugh was bitter. 'Is that the best you can come up with? That just *maybe* things might get better? The only way that's going to happen to me is if all this stops, if the hurting, and the yelling, and the pushing around, if it all just *stops*. I've had it. I don't mind being worthless, being in everybody's way, no use for anything, I can deal with that if I'm just left alone. But when they *make* you that way, and then they yell at you for it, when they take everything away from you and then scream at you for not acting normal, for letting them down—' The words choked off. 'I couldn't even give stuff away, give some of my stuff to the kids at school, the few things I had. They even yelled at me for that.' He laughed, that harsh sound again. 'It doesn't matter. Those things are safe now.'

'You gave stuff away?'

Manta was silent for a moment. 'When I realized my mom was going to send me off to Philly or wherever it is her cousin lives,' he said, 'and I wasn't going to be able to see my friends anymore . . .' He trailed off. 'I knew she was gonna just throw all my stuff away . . .'

He listened hard to Kalki's silence. His mom had been pretty clear that suicidal people sometimes gave personal possessions away to friends in anticipation of the act itself.

Kalki shifted and as Manta glanced back at him, he thought the other boy looked uncomfortable. 'Look, Manta,' Kalki said at last, 'this isn't the best place to be having this conversation. You're talking about the most real thing there is . . . your own existence. But places like this are *instead* of reality. They can be really attractive, or interesting, but they're not *real* contact, with *real* people.' He shook his head, glancing around them. 'So much of the uncertainty in the world, the pain . . . I think it comes of there not being enough genuine contact.'

He looked down at Manta. 'We should get together and have this out,' Kalki said. 'Not here. Contact between human beings shouldn't have to be mediated by electrons.' His voice was suddenly pained. 'Or snatched in the few minutes between online experiences and virtual appointments.'

'For what?' Manta said. 'This is real enough. You don't have anything to say that's going to convince me. If you did, you'd have said it already.' He got up. 'Thanks, but the talking time's over. I know what I need to do.'

He took off across the huge 'front hall.' 'Manta, wait!' Kalki yelled after him, and came after, but Manta broke

203

his connection to Deathworld and vanished into the darkness.

A moment later Charlie was standing in his workspace again, slightly out of breath, not from any exertion, but from nerves. He glanced over at the readout connected to Mark's 'tripwire' routine: glowing letters and numbers hung in the air, zeroed out, showing no attempts to access his space in any way.

OK, Charlie thought, *the trap's baited. Now let's see what happens.*

The next morning he came down from the den, yawning, feeling somehow faintly disappointed. Despite the fact that people seemed to have been reading 'Manta's' messages on the Deathworld message facility, there were no answers to any of them. And no follow-through from Shade or Kalki. *I wonder if I overreacted a little,* he thought. *Scared Kalki off?*

This time his mother was in the kitchen, pouring coffee from a freshly filled pot, and the sound of the front door shutting told him that he had just missed his father. 'You're up early,' she said, turning as Charlie yawned again.

'Yeah,' he said.

'Want some?' his mom said.

'Uh, you don't think it'll stunt my growth?'

She gave him a look. 'Nah. That's just a matter of time. I doubt much of anything could do that at this point.' From the cupboard she got down the mug with the double duck on it and the motto EIDER WAY UP, filled it and handed it to him.

'Thanks,' he said, and flopped into one of the kitchen chairs.

They both drank coffee in silence for a moment. Then, 'A lot of late nights, the last week or so,' his mom said.

'Yeah.'

'Dad says you're still researching suicide.'

Charlie nodded.

His mother looked slightly resigned. 'It has a kind of horrible fascination, I'll admit,' she said. 'Especially when life seems good, and it's difficult to understand how anyone could want to end it.'

'Yeah,' Charlie said, thinking of the six sets of images in his workspace, people he was not convinced had unanimously intended to end anything. 'What's your schedule like today?'

His mother raised her eyebrows at him, plainly noticing the change of subject but declining for the moment to comment. 'The usual day shift, barring emergencies.' She looked slightly relieved. 'Though you know how it is trying to predict those. You?'

'School as usual,' Charlie said. 'Nothing exciting.'

'Sounds wonderful,' his mom said, finishing her coffee. 'Look, Dad picked up some ribs last night, I was thinking of doing that thing with the hot sauce again for dinner.'

'Yes, please!'

She grinned at him, rinsing out the coffee cup and leaving it to drain, then picking up her work-satchel from where it sat on one of the kitchen chairs. 'OK. Dinner around six, then. See you later, sweetie.'

School went uneventfully. Charlie had left a message with Nick's mom that he wanted to get together with him for lunch, but at lunchtime Nick was nowhere to be found. *The most highly developed communications system in history,* Charlie thought ruefully as the afternoon went by, *and we're still playing Net Tag with each other. Oh, well . . . I could always drop by his place. It's not that much out of my way home.*

He finished his afternoon bio class and headed home after hanging around a little while to see if Nick surfaced. There was no sign of him, so Charlie strolled in an absentminded way through the sweet, spring afternoon, considering neurotransmitter chemistry and the prospect of his mom's hot and spicy ribs. There had been some discussion a week or so ago into exactly why the capsiacin molecule was able to fool mouth tissue into thinking it was injured, and triggering the release of endorphins. Charlie's bio teacher had suggested that there might be some fake neurotransmitter 'key' involved. *Doesn't sound genuine to me,* Charlie thought. *If it were, there would be a—*

The sound of a car slowing down close to him when all the rest of the traffic was doing forty or better made Charlie turn his head. A big car had slid up beside him, and just as his head was turning its door popped open and someone lunged out, reached out toward him—

It was only the reflexes of the nascent street kid Charlie had once been that now saved him, the thing that even these days sometimes made it hard for him to hold still and let his mom hug him. *Don't let them touch you! Touch is control—*

He twisted away and plunged off down Morrison Street, away from the car. Charlie heard the whine of the sonic going off behind him, someone actually trying to stun him into collapse – but he was just out of range and his legs were moving faster than his brain for once. They remembered fear more clearly and immediately than he did, and the intellectual constituent of the fear was still working its way down from his brain to his adrenals while Charlie was already running, running as if the Devil himself was after him, down the street, turn the corner, down the side alley that served that block of Morrison, turn another corner in the opposite direction, run, *run—*

He barely felt the concrete beneath his feet, he was running so hard, and though his body was panting with terror and exertion already, Charlie's brain was running ahead of him, planning his escape.

It's a one-way street. They can't get down here easily. And I know this area.

He ran. His lungs started burning, and he ignored them. *I thought they were in a hurry. I was right.* Too *right.* Charlie gulped for air as he ran. *If they're ready to try a snatch in broad daylight, they're really serious. Got to get online right away. Got to get help. The cops – or better still, Net Force!* For the cops didn't know him. Net Force did. He needed Mark Gridley, or James Winters, just as fast as he could get to one or the other of them.

Is it the killer himself, Charlie thought, *or an accomplice? Does it matter? They're right behind me—* He could hear an engine, getting closer. He didn't bother looking behind him. He turned immediately right and plunged across a brownstone's front yard, down the driveway beside it, heading into its paved back yard. There was a dumpster up against the brick back wall. Charlie blessed its name and that of District Recycling Company, whoever they were. He went up onto the top of it in a rush and from there jumped up to grab the top of the wall, having already seen as he was going up that there was no broken glass embedded in it. Charlie went over the wall into the yard of the brownstone on the other side, paused for just a second to take it in – dirty windows, all with security shutters or shades down, another dumpster, a couple of parked cars. *I know where I am,* he thought as he plunged out of the yard, into the brownstone's driveway and down to the wall in front of the building and the drive-way's open gate. He looked up and down the street. *I can't let them catch me out here, where they have the advantage – size, weapons, mobility. If there's going to be a chase, let it be where I have a chance. Not out here!*

He ran like a sprinter, terrified that as he got to the corner he would see that car in front of him. *Dark blue, a new Dodge sedan of some kind, one of those big ones, they*

keep changing the names, recent model, Virginia plates. But
it didn't materialize. Some kindly fate gave him the few
seconds he needed to fly in the door of the WorldGate
public Net-access place on the corner. He stood there
panting at the front desk. The guy who manned it
straightened up from taking something out of the
shelves behind the desk, looked Charlie up and down
with an expression of complete boredom, and said,
'Yeah?'

'I need a booth!' Charlie said.

The guy looked at him with a total lack of urgency.
'Cash or credit?'

Charlie fumbled in his pocket and came up with, to
his shock, not one of the family commcards, but
something he had grabbed off the hall table that
morning on his way to school, thinking that he might
as well use up a little of whatever comm time was on
it: a public-access commcard. Gulping, Charlie
slapped it down in the reading plate on the counter.
The guy behind the counter read what the plate and
the commcard had to say to one another, and pushed
Charlie's card back toward him. 'Only got fifty-five
minutes on that,' he said.

Charlie swallowed. 'Which booth?' he said.

'Six.'

He ran down the hallway between the booths, found
Six, slid the curved booth door shut behind him and
palmsealed it locked. There he stood for a moment,
breathing hard. Then he flung himself into the implant
chair which was the room's only furnishing. He leaned
back, sweating, lined his implant up with the chair's
pickup, closed his eyes—

Charlie opened them again on whiteness, and jumped
out of the chair. He was standing on an infinite white
plain with a featureless blue 'sky' above it, empty of
everything except a voice that said, 'Welcome to a

WorldGate public Net-access facility. Instructions, please?'

The terrible thing about it all was that the one place where Charlie would have felt safe and at least slightly in control, his own workspace, was the one place he couldn't now go. There was a better than even chance that it had been tampered with somehow, that his accessing it would trigger some tracing facility that would betray his presence here. And that door would only be closed for fifty-five minutes. Charlie had almost no cash on him to buy more time. After that he would have to go out the door, and if they had been able to track him down, one way or another, the people hunting him would be waiting there with some plausible story.

Then it was all too plain what would happen to him, what had happened to the others. If not today, then some other time real soon, at an unguarded moment, he would be snatched. Someone would stuff him full of scorbutal cohydrobromate, either with a FasJect or even just out of a spray can, the aerosol method. And when the drug took, in a matter of a few minutes, when he could not resist, Charlie would be spirited away into some private spot, a hotel room, say, and his 'suicide' would be set up. Possibly even with his own cooperation. In any case, he certainly wouldn't be in any condition to resist. *And even bearing in mind what Mom said, in this case, the odds are better than fifty-fifty that they* can *make you do something you wouldn't normally do. Think of what Nick said about Jeannine and Malcolm.*

Charlie swallowed. 'Workspace access,' he said. 'Address 77356936678822-847722—'

He rattled the number off as fast as he could, having to stop once or twice, because it wasn't one he normally had to remember. The whiteness around him flickered.

Charlie found himself standing in the middle of Grand

Central Terminal in New York. This was his father's desperate joke about the state of his own schedule, which he described as being like living in Grand Central, though without being able to go downstairs to the Oyster Bar whenever he liked. The Terminal's great main concourse was gloriously lit, with sun pouring down in great diagonally-striking rays from the tall windows on the Vanderbilt Avenue side. But there were no people in it. More to the point, to Charlie's despair, his father wasn't in it, either. Normally he had a big desk, made of the same creamy polished terrazzo of the floor, standing just west of the circular information kiosk with its polished brass knob-clock, but the desk was missing.

'Damn,' Charlie whispered to himself. There was no point in leaving a message, no time— 'Home system,' Charlie said, 'Workspace access, address 77356936678822-8472086633—'

Another flicker. A second later Charlie was standing in his mother's space, which for reasons she had not explained to him was currently a huge stretch of sand just east of the Pyramids. The view was spectacular, until you turned around and saw that the suburbs of Cairo were directly behind you, and in fact you were standing in someone's back yard, with a picnic table and a swing-set off to one side, and a lawn that was scrubby not for lack of water, but because some kids and an overenthusiastic dog or two had dug or worn it nearly flat. Charlie looked at the picnic table and saw a scatter of his mother's paperwork all over the top of it, stuff from the hospital, her computer pad, a bunch of flowers stuck in a crude vase that Charlie had made her from clay a long time ago. 'Mom?' he said softly.

Her simulacrum appeared immediately. 'Hi, honey,' she said, but Charlie let out a breath of pure desperation, for she was canned. 'Guess what? The best-laid plans have ganged agley after all. I'm going to be late again tonight, sorry. They needed some more warm bodies down in ER, they were short of staff. When you get home, be a sweetie and put some more white wine in the marinade for the ribs, OK? Otherwise, if you need me for something, call the hospital and have them page me, they'll—'

Damn. 'Home system,' Charlie said, racking his memory, and then shaking his head in frustration, for he couldn't remember James Winters' commcode or the code for his office. 'Emergency call. Net Force headquarters.'

Suddenly he found himself looking at a uniformed lady, a cool-looking blonde, sitting behind a desk. 'Net Force. How can I help you?'

'This is an emergency,' Charlie said. 'My name is Charlie Davis. I am a member of the Net Force Explorers. I need to talk to James Winters immediately!'

She smiled at him, an understanding expression, and Charlie was instantly angry enough to spit, for the look was that of someone humoring a child. He then instantly felt guilty for his anger, for there were thousands of Explorers scattered all over the North American continent: there was no reason for this woman to believe that he had anything important going on in his life at all. 'I'm sorry, but he's not available right now.'

'Then let me leave a message for him,' Charlie said. 'Please tell him that I have the data he asked me to correlate for him, but if I don't hear from him shortly, the body count may have increased by one. Tell him he can reach me here for the next fifty minutes.' He rattled off the address of the Net center and of the present workspace. 'Thank you! Workspace, new access address, 8846396677336—'

This number he knew well enough from having to input it about thirty times two weeks ago, when his address filing facility had developed a fault that it took him the better part of an afternoon to put right. Charlie gulped, then let out a breath of pure relief as the sunlight spilling in through the roof of the VAB appeared all around him, but grayed out, as if through a veil. 'You are entering a restricted space,' a harsh robotic voice said. 'Access is forbidden. Track and trace protocols are in operation.'

'Mark, it's me, it's Charlie!'

The grayness vanished immediately. He rushed out into the sunlight across the concrete, looked around him. The Rolls-Skoda was sitting in the middle of the floor. High above him he heard the buzzards softly squeaking and cheeping to one another as they worked the in-building updraft. '*Mark?*' he shouted, and to his embarrassment his voice broke in mid-word.

'Jeez,' Mark said, though Charlie couldn't see from where, 'what's up with you? You sound like a chicken.'

There were about ten possible answers to that. 'Mark, where are you? *I'm up the creek!*'

Mark appeared immediately in the middle of the floor, over by the Rolls. 'Sorry, I was doing some maintenance,' he said, heading over to Charlie. 'What's up?'

'I'm stuck in a public access near the Square,' Charlie said, 'and somebody just tried to grab me off the street!'

'I'll call the cops,' Mark said.

'*Don't!*'

Mark looked at him as if he was nuts. Charlie could entirely understand why. 'You do that,' Charlie said, 'the minute they turn up there, whoever tried to grab me will just play it innocent and vanish, and we'll be no better off than we have been. Either they'll come after me again later, at a better time, or else some other poor kid's gonna get grabbed instead. And probably killed! We've got to do something *now*. But we've got to keep whoever's chasing me on the hook, until the Net Force people can catch up with him, with me.'

'I'll hit the panic button,' Mark said. Immediately the whole space filled with an astounding howl of klaxons. He looked around him with intense satisfaction.

'It's not going to help,' Charlie said, 'Winters isn't available!'

'I bet my dad is, though,' said Mark. 'He'll call the cavalry.' He looked around him, then, with some concern, because nothing but the klaxon seemed to be happening. 'Or he would if he was in his office,' he muttered.

'Mark, we have to do something *now*!'

'That'll go through to his pager,' Mark said. 'No point in us sitting around waiting.'

'The guy chasing me,' Charlie said, 'it's a fair bet he'll realize what I've done. If he has any brains at all, he'll be in some other Net access place right now, trying to find out where I am online. Then he'll try to trace me. And I'm on limited time, all I had was a valuecard. I only have about forty-five minutes now before the door of my booth opens up.'

'Then we'd better get where you're expected to be,' Mark said, 'and stall.'

Charlie stared at Mark. 'You mean Deathworld?'

'Where else? How else is he going to track you if you're in a public access except by your Deathworld ID? And you've got a hot pursuit situation, haven't you? Well, you don't want to *lose* the guy, do you? You just said you didn't want him to go to ground! He will, if he loses you.' Mark looked at him, a challenging kind of look. 'You've got to keep him chasing you until the cavalry comes over the hill, Charlie!'

Charlie gulped. 'But you won't be alone,' Mark said. 'Come on, Charlie, the game's afoot. And it's *us*. But we won't be the ones who get caught. Let's go where you're expected to go when you panic.'

'My workspace.'

'From in here, not direct from your access.' Mark picked up the Magic Jacket from where it had been draped over the chair behind his 'desk,' and threw it at Charlie. 'He, she, or they won't expect that. My anti-trace protocols outside this space will at least slow them down. And then we'll get into Deathworld. But on the way, you think we might pick up someone else who knows his way around there?'

Charlie gulped, then began to see how it could go. And slowly he started to smile. It was still dangerous and he was still scared. But this was exactly what he had been working toward. And he now had someone on his side.

'Nick,' he said. 'Yeah. It's worth a try. Come on, Mark, let's go!'

Chapter Nine

Charlie came out into the ashy darkness between the Lake of Tears and the Dark Artificer's Keep and stood looking around him for a second with Mark. Here and there in the darkness beyond the Lake, the Damned ran by, pursued by the usual demons. Banies made their way toward the Keep, or into and out of it. There was no sign of any pursuit but then he wasn't sure what pursuit would necessarily look like. It could wear a seeming as easily as he could and didn't have to look like anyone he would recognize at the moment. *And is it Kalki? Or Shade? Or someone else they've sent after me?*

'One thing you've going for you,' Mark said, 'they'll be looking for one kid, not two.'

'Great. That means they'll either pass me by, or find me and also try to trace and grab whoever's with me,' Charlie said. 'Why leave witnesses?'

This thought made Mark widen his eyes briefly. Then he grinned. 'I don't think so somehow,' Mark said. 'I don't care who they are. They're not going to get into *my* workspace from my ID here. It's too well protected for that.' He looked around them, though, with some concern. 'But I don't think we should just be standing around. Where do we go?'

'For the moment,' Charlie said, 'safety in numbers.

There are more people in the Keep than there are out here. Let's get inside.'

They headed in through the front door. There were a fair number of Banies who used this spot as a gateway 'access' while working on solving the Eighth Circle, and most of them were heading past Charlie and Mark toward the entryway that led to the Stairways to Nowhere. 'We could lose ourselves pretty well in there, from the look of it,' Mark said.

' "Lose" would be the word,' Charlie said, nervous. 'I don't know my way around in there real well.'

'Doesn't matter. Whoever's chasing you,' Mark said, 'we've just got to keep them in here, and occupied, until the Net Force people can get in and identify them.'

Charlie swallowed. 'Will they be able to do that in forty minutes?'

'More like thirty-five now,' Mark said, not even having the grace to sound scared. 'They'd better.'

'But how are they going to find us?'

Mark tugged at the virtual 'fabric' of the Magic Jacket's sleeve. 'I left full details about this in the message to my dad,' he said. 'The tracking routine it uses is piping direct into his space. Anything you see or hear, he and Net Force will, too. And it's all archiving, storing virtual locations and addresses second by second. All we can do now is leave the tracking to him and his people, and get ourselves deep inside here . . . deep enough that anyone who comes after us is plainly doing it on purpose and not just as some kind of accident.'

Charlie looked around him, looked at the entry to the Stairways. 'OK,' he said. 'I guess we'd better—'

'Manta!'

Charlie jumped. But it wasn't Kalki's voice, or Shade's. *Not that* that *means anything!* He turned, half-furious, half terrified—

—to see Nick hurrying toward them through the

great doors. 'Ohmygosh,' Charlie said, grabbing Nick by the shoulders as he got close, 'I'm gonna kill you! *Do you know who I thought you were?*'

'I can imagine. But I didn't want to yell your real name in the middle of all this. Who knew what could happen? Hey, nice jacket.'

'Never mind the jacket. How did you know my handle?'

'I've been reading the message boards,' Nick said. 'I put some things together. Your message timings, for example. Look, can this wait? I got the message you left me about the people who're after you. Had to be the hero, didn't you?'

Charlie opened his mouth to make some angry retort, then stopped himself, for Nick's tone wasn't angry or mocking. It was a compliment. 'Uh—'

'Yeah. Well, there's something I've been wanting to try, and we'd better try it now, before somebody grabs us.' He looked over at Mark. 'Who's your friend?'

'Nick, this is Mark. Mark Gridley, Nick Melchior. Mark's a virtwrangler, Nick. He's figured a way to track our progress in here.' Charlie displayed the jacket. 'Look, we have given the bad guys a target but one that's too tough to actually catch. That means we've got to get in deep enough that the people looking for me won't be able to find me. Help's coming, but we've gotta stall.'

'Great. Come this way,' Nick said, heading off to their right. 'Nine be deep enough for you?'

'Nine?' Charlie swallowed. 'Nick, one of them, the one who called himself Kalki, he said he'd been *through* the gates of Nine . . .'

'He's full of it,' Nick said. '*No one* can come back after they get through the gates of Nine. There's a "limited resume" in place after that. The designers implemented it to stop all the walkthroughs from blowing the final solution of the environment.'

'When did you find that out?'

'Yesterday. From the Gate Guardian.'

'You found the way down to *Nine?*'

Nick nodded. 'But I put it off. I didn't want to go through until you were along. So now we'll give it a try.'

'You don't know if it works or not?' Mark said, sounding alarmed.

'We're gonna find out real quick,' said Nick. 'Come on!'

There were nine tall gray doors opening out of the lefthand side of the huge entry hall, genuine old-fashioned doors with lever handles, looking like something out of the seventeenth century, with fancy scrollwork carved around the gray stone doorjambs. 'Don't look like we're rushing or anything,' Nick said, 'just stroll.' Charlie found this extremely difficult to do under the circumstances, but he forced himself to slow down and keep pace with Nick.

'A lot of people look at this at one point or another,' Nick said softly, 'but usually there isn't anything here. There's a trick to it, though.'

He went to the first of the five doors and stood by it, idly, listening. Then he shook his head.

'Nothing,' Nick said, 'but this is gonna be easier with three of us. Each of you, quick, go up to a door and listen. If you hear anything, open it right away. Don't look obvious about it, though. You don't want anyone noticing if you can help it!'

Mark headed for the next door up, and Charlie took a long breath, trying to calm himself, and went to the door after that. He stood by it. And then his eyes widened. A soft rumor and murmur of voices, like a crowd . . .

He pulled the door open a crack and peered in.

The sound didn't change but Charlie looked and

saw that the dimly lit room was completely full of people, pushing, murmuring, moving together. It was in fact a vast dance floor, absolutely crammed with people in every kind of clothes, ancient and modern, and they were dancing hard to Joey Bane's music. Hanging up high from an almost invisible ceiling was, of all things, a mirrored 'disco ball.' It shot glitters and spots of light all around the room as it turned, picking out here a jeweled headdress, there a studded white Elvis jacket, over there a slowglass jumpsuit. Charlie looked back around the door, signaled unobtrusively to Nick and Mark. They came over, and as they did, Charlie slipped in through the door. They came after him and Nick shut the door behind him.

The instant he did, the sound came blasting up to full: the 'flap mix' of 'Don't Look Back,' banging away with its wild 11/4 beat. Mark looked around him with admiration at the dancers. 'They may be the Damned,' he said, 'but they've got rhythm.'

'They're not the Damned,' Nick said, grinning. 'They're us.'

Charlie looked at him, bemused. 'It's a party,' Nick said. '*The* Party. One of the environment-programmers' jokes. Everybody who ever visited Deathworld wanders in and out of here eventually. Not the real them, of course; just a recording of them, a sim . . .'

'You mean we're in here somewhere, too,' Mark said, sounding slightly amused. 'Someone might find that confusing . . .'

'Sorry,' Nick said, 'but I don't think it works that way. The one time your simulacrum can't be found here is when you're genuinely on site. So the Guardian told me. But other people might see it and not know for sure, for a while anyway, whether it was really you they were interacting with.' He grinned. 'There are probably some funny scenes, every now and then, because some people do just come here to dance.'

'Looks like a good place to get lost in, anyway,' Charlie said.

'Better than that,' said Nick. 'This is *The Party*. And since it is, there's a side door . . . and a Lady sneaking out of it. We've got to catch her. Come on.'

Nick started to push his way through the crowd. The other two followed him. It was hard going, hot and difficult. The oblivious dancers were packed incredibly tightly together and the music was jarringly loud. Even Nick looked like he was wincing a little at the volume.

Mark was close behind Charlie. 'Are you sure your dad's people are gonna get here before our time runs out?' Charlie yelled to Mark, that being the only way he could make himself heard.

Mark was beginning to look uncomfortable. 'Look,' he shouted back, 'I did the best I could. My dad gets busy, too! I told you, I sent a "most urgent" to his virtpager. He'd never ignore that unless some seriously important government thing—'

'Like happens every day!' Charlie yelled. But there was no point in fighting about it now. Charlie took another deep breath and went plowing through the crowd in Nick's wake.

It got harder as they got closer to the center of things. *There's this, anyway*, Charlie thought, *it's not gonna be easy for anyone to follow us*— For that moment he disobeyed the advice of the music, looked over his shoulder.

And saw one of those tall doors behind them open. A second later, he got a glimpse of a long black drapecoat, violet skirt, violet hair, as Shade came slipping in.

Uh oh. Fear and loathing both rose in him and Charlie struggled to deal with the reaction rationally. *It wasn't as if she was going to be able to spray him with sco-bro here and now. If she was even directly involved. Had Mark gotten any concrete evidence that she was? Had he even managed to track down exactly who had tripped the 'tripwire' around his workspace? And is Shade someone different from Kalki, or is she the same person? For I didn't see them together. Charlie gulped. No time to spend worrying about all this now. Just follow Nick and keep them in here, and pray that Net Force is on the job.*

Ahead of him, Nick was maybe two-thirds of the way through the crowd, moving faster now, as if it was beginning to thin a little in patches near the far edge of the room. He was making his way toward the far left corner. Charlie could just see that the crowd was somewhat sparser there. And also a black blot, a shape, leaning near a door, a normal human-sized door, not like the ones they had come through, a door that was just closing.

Nick came out of the crowd, with Charlie behind him, and Mark bringing up the rear. The black blot-shape, hard to see in the disco-ball dimness, was a tall, potbellied demon, presently standing in front of the newly closed door. He had stubby little black-leather wings, and he was wearing a uniform like the ones movie-theater ushers or hotel-lobby bellboys had worn a century ago, right down to a rather ridiculous-looking little pillbox hat pushed over to one side and partly resting on one of his big ears. Nick, coming up to him, paused and looked at him oddly.

'Hey,' he shouted over the music, 'you're not Melchgrind! You're Wringscalpel! I remember how you wear that hat.'

The demon with the flaming sword blinked at him. 'Nick?' it shouted back, squinting at him. 'Why, how are you, fella? You back again? I didn't think you were going to linger.'

'Change of plans,' Nick said loudly. 'This isn't *your* usual patch, either.'

'No, we have to rotate through all the "portal" jobs,' Wringscalpel said, sounding resigned. 'Sometimes whether we've been briefed on the fine detail or not. If I had a nickel for—'

'Neither of us is gonna be *worth* a plugged nickel if we don't hurry up here, Wringer! We're in big trouble at the moment. Someone's chasing us, and we really need not to get caught.'

'Now, you know I can't let you go through without passing the test.'

'There is no *time* for that!' Nick yelled. 'Wringscalpel, in Joey's own name will you let us through here before you have a bunch more fake suicides on your hands?!'

'Test?' said Mark. 'What test?'

Wringscalpel's eyes went wide. 'But I *can't*. It's not that I wouldn't do it for you, Nick, it's just that the machine's routines won't allow—'

'*What* test?' Charlie said.

'He's not going to ask you what's your favorite color, if that's what you were thinking,' Nick said. 'Hurry up and ask the damn questions, then, Wringscalpel! I'm answering for all three of us.'

'You two agree to that?' Wringscalpel said.

'Yes,' Mark said, and 'Yeah, yeah, just do it!' Charlie said, for he could see Shade getting closer to them.

'All right. You understand the rules? If you miss a question, you're all bumped back up to One.'

'Fine!'

'And they're not the same questions as yesterday, Nick, they change every hour—'

'Come *ON!*' they yelled at him in unison.

'All right,' Wringscalpel said. 'What is the purpose of life?'

'He doesn't want anything easy, does he?' Charlie moaned.

'Shaddup, Charlie. *Pain*, Wringscalpel! And learning how to deal with it.'

'What is the dawn of the soul?'

'Which version?' Nick said.

Wringscalpel looked surprised, then smiled. 'London 2024.'

'The other side, / where the shadows hide, / and the dark no longer falls: the night of pain, / when the final chord / Comes breaking through the walls!'

'Hey, you're serious about this,' Wringscalpel said. 'Are you sure I can't ask you your favorite color?'

'*No!* Get on with it!'

'What is Joey's middle name?'

'The one on his birth certificate,' Nick said, 'or the one from the press release?'

Wringscalpel grinned. 'The birth certificate.'

Nick swallowed. 'Illusion,' he said.

'There you go,' said Wringscalpel, and began to grow.

The floor of the place shook. The disco ball hanging from the ceiling of the Party Room started to tremble, and stalactites of crystal and onyx began to fall from way above it, causing screams among the partying multitudes, who scattered in every direction, but then returned to the dance floor as if driven there with whips.

Wringscalpel, though, was paying all of this no attention. His uniform was tearing and shredding away, falling to the floor, as the demon grew, lost his potbelly, gained wings that lost the toy look they had worn earlier and now looked seriously functional, gigantic pinions, that spread above him and out to either side. He cried a great cry that shook down more stalactites.

'Is he angry?' Charlie shouted at Nick over the din of the music, the screaming dancers, the crash of falling crystal.

Wringscalpel heard this, and laughed. 'Angry? You kidding?' he said. 'I get a bonus for this.' He held out his huge hands, and suddenly they were filled with a flaming sword that lit the whole place blindingly in actinic blue-white fire. 'And now I get to leave this job to somebody else, while I go up to Seven and kick some—'

'Yeah, great, later—' Nick shouted, and dodged under his arm, past him, through the suddenly open door.

Charlie and Mark followed him in a hurry. Past Wringscalpel, on the other side of the door, it was as dark as the inside of a dog, and involuntarily Charlie looked behind them, back toward the light.

'Whoever's behind us, they can't follow us in here unless they pass the test,' Nick said.

'Yeah, and what if they know the answers, too?' Mark said, looking around him in the darkness with some concern.

'There's still one thing I don't think they'll do,' said Nick. 'Come on!'

He ran into the dark. More slowly, they went after him, but their eyes were getting used to the dimness now. They were in a huge, huge cave, the size of a sports stadium, its stony ceiling lost above them.

'What are we supposed to be doing?' Mark said.

'Looking for the Lady,' said Nick.

Charlie looked at him as they ran. ' "She left the party early" . . . ' he said. 'Or something like that.'

'Something like that. We have to find her. She's the key.'

'Shouldn't be hard, there's nobody but us in . . . uh, oh.'

There were eyes in the darkness. They glowed. The predatory eyes blinked slowly, and looked thoughtfully at the three of them. 'Ignore them,' Nick said. 'Look for a single light by itself.'

It was hard. They walked on through the darkness, and it got hot and stifling, and the eyes pressed in close around them, and they could all hear breathing. Charlie shook his head at the oppressive quality of the illusion. And he stopped, then, hearing footsteps behind him.

'There,' Nick said. He pointed. One light, distant – not horizontal like the lights around them, but vertical, not green, but a pure white.

'What's the rush?' said a soft voice from behind them.

Charlie turned, and there she was, Shade, looking at him with an expression that was almost sad . . . but not quite.

I can't have more than fifteen minutes left, Charlie thought. *I've lost track. All I can do now is stall, keep her talking . . .*

'Kalki told me you ran off without a word,' she said. 'Without even looking at him! He didn't mean to frighten you, really. He was just going to give you a ride.'

And she's got to do more than just talk. 'Was he?' Charlie said. 'And what would we have done then? He and I. Or the three of us. If there really are two of you . . .'

'Why, talk,' Shade said. 'What else would happen?'

'I have two words for you,' Charlie said. 'Scorbutal cohydrobromate.'

She looked at Charlie and her eyes widened.

Not enough. 'And a white cotton sweater,' Charlie said. 'It must have been very new, one of those teased-cotton ones . . . because it shed all over Richard Delano's rug.'

The look on her face went horrified for a moment, just for a flicker. Then she got hold of herself again and smiled very slowly, a knowing smile. 'Scorbutal? Someone your age,' she said, 'shouldn't be messing around with drugs, "Manta." Your folks would be shocked to find out about it. Maybe some responsible adult should tell them what

225

she thinks you've been up to, hmm? How you tried to buy some from her?'

He went hot with fury.

'But it doesn't matter,' Shade said. Charlie stared at her, kept his mouth shut. 'There are always other people to work with, aren't there? It's not like suicide is going to go away. There are always mixed-up kids who stumble into nasty places like this.' She looked around her with scorn, at the eyes pressing in close. 'Or going to incredible trouble to work themselves deep down into them. Places full of sick images and soul-destroying music and ugly ideas. Who would be surprised when kids who spend a lot of time in a place come to grief? No one would be surprised at all.'

She looked at Nick and Mark. 'It's nice to see you've picked up a couple of friends here, finally,' Shade said. 'But there will always be people who need friends, and aren't so spiteful and suspicious. For them, I'll always be here. Until Deathworld shuts down, some day. Maybe some day very soon . . . because, if there's justice, nothing lasts forever.'

That smile again: self-satisfied, controlling. Charlie would have loved to have an excuse to punch her in the nose. But then he realized he didn't need to. He stood quite still and smiled just a little himself. He couldn't help it.

A second later he had the satisfaction, as hot as the fury had been a moment before, of seeing her eyes go wide as she stared at the man and woman who suddenly caught hold of her 'seeming' from both sides. 'Net Force,' said the woman. 'We have some questions we need to ask you, please, so if you'd come this way . . .'

There were suddenly about six other Net Force operatives there as well, all in their usual dark suits and coverslicks, and they closed in on the group. 'You kids all right?' one of them said.

In the background Shade was shouting, 'What? Who are you? This is an outrage! I want a lawyer!'

'Uh, we're fine,' Nick said, looking around at the ruckus with some surprise. He looked at Mark and Charlie. 'But how'd they get in here without answering the questions?'

'Either a search warrant,' Mark said, looking at them with relief, 'or a "back door". Does it matter?' He looked at Shade as the agents walked her away. 'Looks like it's gonna be a real interesting debrief. Here, wait a minute . . .' he said to the agent who had spoken to Charlie.

Mark reached up and helped Charlie out of the Magic Jacket.

'Thanks, Squirt,' Charlie said, as Mark handed the jacket to the operative.

'It's still live,' Mark said. 'The evidential trail is still hot, so you'll want to lock it down when you get it back into the examination space at HQ.'

'Thank you,' said the op.

'And,' said another voice out of the darkness, 'I would appreciate it if someone would give me an explanation of what's been going on here.'

Jay Gridley came striding out of the dark, a lithe, intent-looking Thai-American man in a business suit and tie. Right now, though, the intentness was mostly concentrated on his son. Mark was looking a little sheepish. 'Uh, hi, Dad,' he said, 'you see, Charlie came to me with a problem . . .'

'Excuse me,' said a quiet voice from out of the darkness behind them, 'but were you looking for me?'

They all turned. The Goddess of Virtue stood there looking at them, while lifting up a long pale veil that had covered her face and head. Astraea was astonishingly beautiful, a tall and slender woman all robed in Greek-classical white, and her expression was severe, intelligent, and a little sorrowful.

Jay Gridley smiled slightly. 'Uh, yes, ma'am. Routinely.'

'Yeah,' Nick said. 'Mostly to say, don't go . . .'

'But there is nowhere for me to stay,' she said sadly. 'My only dwelling is in the hearts of men, and all of mankind is wicked . . .'

They looked at one another. 'If you wait about two seconds,' Charlie said, 'not *all* . . . because a baby'll be born somewhere.'

She smiled at him. It was like the sun coming up.

'Thank you,' Astraea said. 'I think I'll stay.'

They were all quiet a moment. 'Which way to the Ninth Circle?' Nick said at last.

'There is none,' Astraea said. 'Or rather, this is it. This is Despair, after all. But after this . . . you go out the far side. That way.' She pointed, and suddenly there was a little light away off in the darkness, like an open door.

'Uh, thanks,' Mark said. He was a little bemused as he said it, for Astraea had draped her former veil around her neck like a scarf, and now she reached around behind her into the darkness and came out with a sword and a pair of scales.

'And now,' she said cheerfully, 'back to the day job. See you later.'

She vanished.

Mark looked up at his father. 'You know her, Dad?' he said.

'You kidding?' said Jay Gridley softly, but with some amusement, as he looked at the distant light. 'She's one of my bosses.' Then he looked down at his son, and his face acquired a severity more like that of Justice's. 'Meanwhile, you and I need to talk. Briefly, because I have to get back to work. But later on we are going to have a long discussion.'

Mark and his father vanished. Mark's expression was

mostly unrepentant, despite his father's sternness. All Charlie thought it was wise to do was nod and grin just a little. When they were gone, Charlie turned toward Nick . . .

. . . and everything dissolved in a mist of light, back to a white plain and blue sky. A great voice came from the heavens and said to Charlie, 'Thank you for using Net Access. You have come to the end of your purchased access time for this session. Please see the customer representative for more time or inquire about one of our monthly billing accounts!'

And suddenly he was sitting in the implant chair again. Behind him there was a little *cchk!* noise as the door of his suite unlocked itself and slid open.

Charlie was on his feet in about a second, and out into the hallway. There he stopped, open-mouthed with surprise.

The place was full of uniformed police. Two of them, right then, along with a dark-suited woman in plain clothes wearing the inimitable Net Force ID, were escorting out someone in handbinders. She was of medium height, dark-haired with some gray sprinkled through it, a little pudgy, maybe about forty. She was a profoundly ordinary-looking person, one he would have passed in the street a hundred times and never noticed. She looked like a housewife, like a mother. She was wearing a soft, fuzzy white short-sleeved cotton sweater.

There he lost his train of thought, for two more Net Force ops, a man and a woman, came walking down the hall toward Charlie.

'Charlie Davis?' one of them said.

'Uh, yes.'

'Your father wants to see you,' said the woman op. 'Right now.'

Ooops.

He walked outside, past the shocked-looking counter

guy, and saw his dad standing there, by a police car. His mother was just getting out of another. The street was full of people slowing down to rubberneck, or standing there watching and talking. It looked like a disaster area.

He was afraid the disaster was going to be his.

But Charlie couldn't say a word for the moment. The relief, and the fear, and a host of other emotions, had all come crashing down on him together as he walked out of that booth and saw her – the woman who was Shade, or Kalki, or both – being taken away from the next booth to the one he had been in. *The next booth!* Charlie went over to his mother and father and they closed in on him, and he grabbed them both and hugged them hard.

'We're going to talk about this later,' his father said, very low. 'A lot. But I want to hear all of your side first.'

'Thanks, Dad,' Charlie said.

'But I notice that someone else is wearing the handcuffs,' his mother said, 'so I guess we can assume that you've been doing something that's going to make us proud.'

Boy, I hope so Charlie thought, as they walked him away.

It was a long, long talk they had, and one that was going to take more than one evening to resolve. Charlie realized that when he was in bed that night, suffering from near-terminal embarrassment and upset, and at the same time, great pride . . . for word came down on the late news that evening that the cases of all the Deathworld 'suicides' were being reopened. Additionally, after a very belated session with his mother's hot and spicy ribs (most of the dressing-down he suffered had happened while they were all in the kitchen together, and she was cooking), the vidphone went off. His father went to get it, and didn't come back for something like twenty minutes.

'Who was it, honey?' Charlie's mother said.

'Jay Gridley,' said Charlie's dad. He sat down and began to toy with one last rib he hadn't touched during dinner.

Charlie didn't say anything, though he very much wanted to. Every word he had said earlier had seemed to trigger some new and interesting strain of the basic argument. 'He says,' Charlie's dad said, turning to Charlie, 'that you may have saved ten or twenty people's lives.'

Charlie swallowed.

'He also says you're to see James Winters tomorrow morning at eight,' said his dad. 'I assume that won't interfere with school?'

'Uh . . . no.'

'Good. Let us know what happens.'

'Uh, I will.'

And that had been all. Charlie had gone to bed in a very subdued mood. But he had not been able to avoid seeing the look his mother and father exchanged as he'd gone upstairs. It had been worried, frightened, relieved – but not angry.

The next morning, having left his workspace and taken his seat in Winters' office, he wondered if being spared last night had simply left him unprepared for a more thorough reaming-out today. Mark Gridley was there when Charlie got there, and he, too, was looking rather pale.

For a minute or two Winters just sat behind his desk, looking over documentation that was scrolling through the virtual window hanging nearby. Finally he shook his head and sat back, looking at the two of them.

'Well,' he said. 'It's taken me the better part of last night and this morning but I've finally finished reviewing the forensic and other information that our fast-response team went out to act on yesterday.' He sighed. 'Mark has already finished his debrief, but since he acted as "enabler" for you on this, Charlie, I thought it might be wise to have him here to sketch in any details that're necessary. Does that meet with your approval?'

'Uh, yes, sir.'

'With one note,' said Winters. 'The wild, I would say *profligate*, illegality of a lot of Mark's "enabling" needs to be stressed here. I would have thought,' he said to Mark, 'that after the last time, I wouldn't need to have this discussion with you again. But I see that no human agency can possibly predict your actions. You, I'm just going to have to refer back to your father. Again.'

Mark didn't quite squirm.

'Don't bother trying to play to the stands quite so blatantly,' Winters said. 'There is no one in the stands but me and I am not cheering.'

He looked slowly over at Charlie. 'Meanwhile,' Winters said, 'your mother is a very understanding woman.'

'She is? I mean, yes, sir, she is.'

'Because she has not herself insisted in having you committed,' Winters said, 'on finding out what you've been up to these past couple of weeks. I seem to remember you telling me that, as soon as you came across any information concrete enough to warrant action, that you would let me know.'

The silence settled down heavy. 'I didn't think it was concrete enough yet,' Charlie said, his voice sounding even smaller than he was afraid it would. 'It needed to be tested.'

'Using yourself as bait,' Winters said.

'When you're hunting polar bear,' said Charlie, 'that's the only bait that's any good.'

Winters looked at him hard for a moment. Then he

sat back, rocking a little in his chair. 'This much I'm going to give you,' he said. 'You were right about one thing. The woman you caught was definitely getting ready to do it again. Immediately. Besides the stun gun, we found a big spray can of sco-bro in the front of her car. And all the ropes and ligatures you could have desired were in the trunk, ready to use.'

Charlie shivered. 'It's still May,' he said.

'Yes,' said Winters. 'That much you're right about. But why?'

Charlie blinked. 'Why is it May?'

'I mean,' Winters said, 'why was she attacking these kids in May?'

Charlie shook his head. 'I never did figure that out,' he said.

'Because,' said Winters softly, 'that's very close to when *her* son committed suicide.'

Charlie's eyes widened. 'Richard—'

'Exactly wrong,' said Winters, annoyed. 'Don't guess, Charlie. There's been too much guessing in this, not enough precise use of data. Fatal for a doctor.'

Charlie swallowed.

'Mitch Welles,' said Winters.

'He was the first one,' Charlie said. 'April of 2023.' He shook his head.

'April,' Winters said. 'Not May. Now, Maureen Welles had . . . well, not exactly a collapse after her son died, but she wasn't well. After she recovered, she went on a campaign to prove that her son had been induced to kill himself by something that had been done to him in Deathworld. She spent all her efforts trying to get the legislation that I told you about through Congress. It didn't get her anywhere. She was sure that there was a conspiracy against her, but as I said, the only conspirator against her that anyone can identify was the Congressional calendar. And her own

233

single-mindedness.' He let out a long breath. 'Her marriage went to pieces in the middle of it all. She and her husband separated. He said, because chasing down her son's murderer had become her entire life.'

Winters went on rocking in his chair for a few moments, scowling at his desk. 'Sounds like she was obsessed,' said Mark very quietly.

'It sounds like it,' said Winters. 'Well, all her complaints and attempts to get Deathworld shut down got her nowhere, as you might imagine, since there was no evidence whatever to suggest that the environment, or Bane, were implicated in any way in her son's death.' He sighed. 'And then the second suicide happened. That's when we got involved. Once could be an accident. Twice could be a coincidence . . .'

'Three times is enemy action,' Mark said.

'Well, even proverbs can be wrong,' said Winters, lacing his fingers together. 'But this time, as it happens, it was indeed enemy action. Because Mitch Welles' mother decided that if the government and Net Force weren't going to do the responsible thing and shut Deathworld down, then she would do it herself.'

He breathed out. 'Well, that's the simple way to describe it. Your mom would know,' and Winters glanced up at Charlie, 'that the ways a human mind gets itself into such a position are usually a lot more subtle than people suspect from outside, or after the fact. After all, she had managed to convince herself, over time, that her son couldn't have killed himself, that it *had* to be murder. Well, acknowledging that he had committed suicide would mean admitting that it might possibly have been due to something *she'd* done wrong . . . so that was a realization that her mind buried as soon as it could. From that it was just a step to believing that Joey Bane was personally responsible for his death. And from there, maybe not such a long step to believing that anyone who was in Deathworld willingly was somehow complicit in her son's "murder".'

'Maybe,' Charlie whispered. 'It would explain a lot.'

Winters shook his head. 'It may be something like that which was going on in her head. The process itself is obscure and it's probably going to stay that way for a while, because she's not talking about much of anything now. But soon enough Maureen Welles got the idea that, if people had accused her son of being a suicide, then she was going to turn that back on them, get revenge on them for hurting her, for hurting him like that. They would be the suicides, not him. She started monitoring the new login information, and the message boards, as anyone could. Her purpose was to pick likely targets, to make sure that the ones she "worked with" in her Shade and Kalki personas seemed genuinely suicidal, people who "were going to do it anyway". Their deaths would make her son's look like what she was sure it was: something done to him, to them, by the environment they'd been spending time in. That this would also hurt Joey Bane must have occurred to her. She may even have had some fantasy of killing him and turning him into a "suicide" as well. More to the point, though, she was sane enough to realize that a string of suicides would affect the place adversely.'

'But it didn't,' Charlie said. 'It went wrong. In a lot of ways. No one put it together that the suicides were connected. And Deathworld got even more popular.'

Winters' look was grim. 'You're right. It backfired on her. Her methods were too subtle. Not subtle enough to completely prevent the suspicion, here and there, that these suicides weren't uncomplicated. But distributed over so much time, and such a large physical area, they didn't attract the attention she wanted. And she wasn't completely nuts, not yet. Her first murder took a lot out of her, scared her – scared her briefly sane. She kept quiet for a while. The next suicide, the one in October, was genuine, and had nothing to do with her. But come the next year, around April, her pain started to unseat her reason again. By May she was more than ready to murder someone else, as revenge against Bane – or as a kind of sacrifice to her dead son.' He frowned. 'And she did . . . then scared herself sane for a little while.'

'But she couldn't stay that way,' Charlie said. 'Probably the knowledge of what she'd been doing was starting to prey on her. And her son was still dead . . .'

'And Deathworld was still in operation,' Winters said, sounding a little sad now. 'It must have been intolerable for her. One part of her wanting to believe that her son had been exonerated, avenged, another part of her continually wanting revenge on whatever had taken him away from her.'

'And so she kept on killing,' Mark said. 'And then did it again, this month . . .'

'Twice,' Winters said, somber. 'But now she was getting into the pattern of serial killers. One murder isn't enough. The same kind of murder isn't enough. They have to get closer together, be more terrible, somehow, to provide the same level of catharsis. But they never do.'

'It's a drug,' Charlie said softly.

'Something like one,' said Winters. 'The addiction always getting worse, in her case, because the dose increases and increases and doesn't do any good. And then this last time, she was driven to commit two murders. And no sooner have they happened than Deathworld, her old enemy, suddenly is doing better than ever. It drove her to levels of rage she'd never experienced before. She decided to go straight out to try to kill again. And found you . . . using some pretty advanced "hunting" routines. She tripped the "wire" around your workspace, as you thought. Felt you out, to make sure you were suicidal enough. And then went for the kill.'

Winters' eyes were resting on Charlie in a way that made him even more uncomfortable than the man's anger had.

But there was only one answer to that look. Charlie swallowed. 'You remember *Helicobacter?*' he said.

Mark looked at Charlie as if he was from Mars. But Winters' expression shifted microscopically to something a little less uneasy than it had been.

'*Helicobacter pylorii*,' Charlie said. 'Forty years ago, everybody thought stomach ulcers were caused by stomach acid.' He had to laugh, for at this end of time it sounded silly. But back then they hadn't had any other answer that made sense. 'Then a scientist, a doctor, noticed that in all the cultures he took of his patients' stomach ulcers, they all had this one bacterium present. *Helicobacter*, they called it, because it was shaped like a little helix. He worked with that bug for something like five years, until he was convinced that it was the cause of stomach ulcers, and that it could be killed, and the ulcers wiped out, just by using the right kind of anti-biotic for long enough. He published papers, tried to convince everybody. They laughed at him. They said that the proof wasn't conclusive, that the evidence was all circumstantial. They wouldn't approve even animal testing, let alone human.' Charlie smiled a smile as grim as Winters' had been. 'So finally the guy swallowed a pure culture of *Helicobacter* and gave himself the fastest, nastiest case of bleeding ulcers anybody ever saw. Then he put himself on a course of antibiotics and cured them.'

Winters just looked at him.

'A lot of doctors have done stuff like that,' Charlie

said. 'Pasteur. Jenner. It's traditional.' He gulped, for Winters' look was not getting any friendlier. 'When you're sure you're right. But when it's a life and death thing . . . the only life you have a right to put on the line is your own.'

Winters just looked at him, like something carved from stone. 'Mark,' he said at last, 'would you excuse us?'

Mark threw Charlie one apologetic glance, then removed himself from the room with a speed that suggested he had recently had iondrivers installed.

A moment's silence ensued. 'Now what the *hell* am I supposed to do with you,' Winters said at last, 'when you play the moral card on me like that?'

Charlie thought it wisest to keep his mouth shut for the moment.

Winters sighed and leaned back in his chair again. 'Your mother and father,' he said, rubbing his face, 'are going to have my hide off my bones if I don't come down on you hard for this dumb stunt. Which it was.' Charlie looked down. 'The "morality card" aside. Morality starts at home, Charlie. You have *not* treated your folks very well. If you and the irrepressible Mr Gridley hadn't had God's own luck, not to mention a sense of timing developed well beyond what people of your tender years should have, you could very well have been "suicide" number seven. And maybe Mark and Nick for eight and nine. And regardless of the fact that the work and the evidence you left us would have made your death murder rather than suicide, and that your murderer would have been behind bars very quickly indeed, it would have shattered your parents' lives.'

Charlie sat there with the sweat bursting out all over him, because he knew it was true, and that one way or another, he was unlikely to hear the end of this for months.

The silence stretched out again for a long while.

'All right,' Winters said. 'We'll see what you work out with them. They've let me know that, after talking to Jay Gridley, they think you should be allowed to continue as a Net Force Explorer. You may have to get used to being, uh, monitored a little more closely. You threw quite a scare into them.'

Charlie swallowed. 'Yes, sir.'

'But there is this.' He gave Charlie a thoughtful look. 'If you hadn't done what you did, heaven knows who she might have killed next. How many more murders it would have taken to quieten her ghosts . . . and of course they wouldn't have stayed quiet, not for long.' He sat back, looking at his folded hands. 'Unfortunately, among the various kinds of serial killers, there are a few who "seal over" very effectively for prolonged periods between crimes. They're crazy as bedbugs but either they're not crazy enough to let their symptoms show where people can see them, or there's no one to see. Living by herself, her son dead, her husband pretty much permanently out of the picture, with no one to see how weird she got every April . . . this could have gone on for a long while. It could have caused Deathworld to be shut down, and left Bane fighting endless lawsuits that would not have been his responsibility. So an injustice has been prevented. Though frankly, from what I've seen of the place, I wonder if—'

Then Winters stopped himself. 'No,' he said, sounding annoyed. 'Injustice is injustice, dammit, and artistic opinions shouldn't enter into it. That way lies tyranny. Now would you mind explaining why you're looking at me like that?'

Charlie had begun to smile, just a little. He couldn't help it. 'I think there's more to that place than meets the eye,' he said. 'And really, Mr Winters, I think the media've overstated the case a little about Deathworld. It's not as kinky and cruel as they think. It's more a teaching exercise.'

'Oh, is it?' Winters said. 'Well.' He glanced down at his desk, reading something that had been manifesting under its surface for a while now.

He sighed. 'It was always forensics with you, wasn't it?' he said. ' "The noblest use of science," I heard one of my people call it. Well, some good has come of this aspect of your rifling of the records, anyway. There really should have been more cooperation among the various police forces handling the suicides. There are mechanisms set up for that but they don't get used enough. This outcome will enable us to put bugs under some people's rumps; have them look more closely at how to coordinate deaths that have similarities. A "smart" system can be coached by forensic people and profilers to start handling and correlating data like this . . . as long as the cops put it in. And that a kid beat them to a serial killer might just shame them into using it.' He raised his eyebrows. 'Fine. But at the end of the day, I suppose I might have known you'd do what you did, once faced with the evidence. Regardless of how earnestly you promised me you wouldn't jump the gun.'

Charlie blushed hot again. *This is all I need. A rep as an incorrigible gun-jumper. With one of the two men who'll determine whether I ever work in Net Force . . .*

'Don't mistake my intent,' said Winters. 'I don't mindlessly push the "team player" concept because some corporate-minded superior makes me do it. I do it because it is the *sine qua non* of this organization, the single thing that makes us effective. When you start working with other people in Net Force some day, assuming that you graduate medical school without incident and that you are somehow spared for that work by an overly kindly Universe which keeps you from getting your butt kidnapped or killed when you put it in harm's way – ' Charlie began wondering whether it was possible to feel as hot and embarrassed as he presently did without actually running a clinical fever – 'then you are going to have to do what you tell them you're going to do, for the simple reason that they're going to act on that information, and when they do, if you're *not* doing what you said you were going to do, you may get them killed. They will be depending on you to keep your word. If you can't, you are no good to anyone. So get the polar bears and the *Helicobacter* out of your system *now*, because there'll be no room for them later.'

Winters looked at him. 'Uh,' Charlie said, 'yes, sir.'

There was a long silence. 'Good,' Winters said. 'Then we understand one another. Insofar as anyone my age can truly understand anyone yours.' He shook his head. 'Which is little enough. Especially after I just heard you defending Deathworld to me.' He raised his eyebrows at Charlie. 'I wouldn't have thought you'd care much for the music, for one thing. I thought you were all for technotrad.'

'The context,' Charlie said, 'makes other readings possible.'

Winters gave him a cockeyed look. 'I hear the sound of someone managing information on what he considers a "need to know" basis.' He sighed. 'You should go away, now, because you're making my head hurt.' He glanced at the bird feeder stuck to his window, where a small brown bird was taking out one nut at a time and dropping them to the ground. 'Even more than *he* was,' Winters added, 'until I realized what he's doing. He's feeding two of his buddies on the ground. Possibly his kids. They're too big to tell.'

He made a shooing gesture at Charlie. Charlie got up. 'So get out of here,' he said.

In haste, Charlie got out.

★ ★ ★

School that day went by in something of a blur, mostly caused by Charlie having to refuse again and again to say anything about what had happened down at the public access place near the Square. The case was now officially *sub judice* and could not be discussed. By the end of the day he was thoroughly tired of not being able to say anything, and seriously relieved to see Nick.

'Are you OK?' Charlie said to him as they started to walk in the general direction of home.

'Uh, yeah.' Nick chuckled a little. 'I didn't realize whose son Mark was! James Winters called my dad.'

'He did? Oh, no!'

'No, it was OK,' Nick said, sounding completely unconcerned . . . but then he didn't have to answer to James Winters. 'My dad was really impressed.'

'Winters didn't . . . say anything awful, did he?'

'Not at all. He was nice, actually. From what my mom said, he made me sound like some kind of hero.' He gave Charlie an odd look. 'They're probably gonna hand you the same kind of stuff.'

'I wouldn't worry too much about that,' Charlie said. 'It hasn't been a problem so far.'

They headed for Nick's apartment, if only because Charlie wasn't willing to go straight home to his own and find some new and interesting aspect of last night's argument waiting for him. When they got there, though, Charlie wondered whether this had been wise, for Nick's mother was putting down the receiver of the vidphone with an odd look on her face.

Nick froze when he saw it. Charlie, not knowing what that kind of expression might mean on someone else's mother, didn't bother panicking. On his own, though, he would have been cautiously optimistic about what was to follow. 'Hi, Mrs Melchior . . .'

'Hi, Charlie honey, how are you?' She sounded very abstracted.

'Uh, hi, Mom,' Nick said.

'Nick,' his mother said, 'what have you been doing?'

Charlie saw the oh-no-what-now look cross his friend's face. 'We came straight from school, Mrs Melchior,' he said, hoping it wouldn't make things worse. 'Did we—'

'No, Charlie, it's all right,' said Nick's mother, looking dubious. 'I guess. Honey, that was someone from the service provider.'

Nick instantly burst out in a sweat that Charlie could see from two feet away, and indeed could practically feel. 'Mom, in three weeks I'll have enough to give them about two hundred—'

'I wouldn't worry about that,' his mother said, 'because they say that the last month's bill has been paid in full.'

Nick's eyes widened. 'Oh, no. If Dad went and—'

'Your dad didn't do anything, honey,' said Nick's mother, sitting down at the small kitchen table and looking at him oddly. 'It seems someone from Joey Bane Enterprises got hold of them and said that the company was paying your expenses for "your efforts on their behalf." Which they took to mean the last month's comm charges, with a cash reserve to cover another year's worth of use. And apparently they're reimbursing you for your public access in the last couple of weeks.'

'Oh, wow,' Nick said, looking almost weak with relief, and collapsing into the chair opposite his mom.

Charlie stood and watched all this with poorly concealed approval. 'Charlie,' said Nick's mother to him, turning on him what would have been a fairly fierce expression except for the confusion still underlying it, 'did you have something to do with this?'

'I don't think so,' Charlie said. *Not directly, anyway.*

Or at least not the way you think . . .

He was spared having to go through any longer mental reservations by Nick's mother sighing, raising her hands in the air, letting them fall again. 'Honey,' she said, 'it's very nice of them to come in and get you off the hook like this . . .'

'Mom,' said Nick, 'I'm going to keep the summer job, if it's all the same to you.'

She looked at him thoughtfully. 'That's the best thing I've heard all day,' she said, and got up, heading down the hall toward the rear of the apartment. 'Meanwhile, I suppose we'd better see about getting your server reconnected.'

Nick and Charlie looked at each other as she went down to the den. 'It's a miracle,' Nick said softly.

'Somehow I doubt it.'

'I wonder how much of . . . you know, what we did . . . is going to come out.'

'I don't think it'd be smart for us to discuss that here,' Charlie said softly. 'Not under the circumstances. You gonna be online again tonight?'

'One way or another,' Nick said. 'I meant it about the job. I noticed that when I'm out of the apartment more, the tension level around here goes down somewhat. I would have thought it'd be the other way around. Could it be that they wanted me to get out more or something? Even if it's just to use a public booth?'

Charlie shrugged. 'Who knows,' he said, 'what parents think?'

'I know what you mean.' Nick grinned a little. 'I like to think of dealing with them as practice for when we finally meet up with alien life forms.'

'You and me both, brother. Well, if you ever find out why it's working better, tell me. Meanwhile, let's do whatever needs doing here, and then get out before the situation deteriorates somehow.'

★ ★ ★

Later than evening Nick and Charlie met in Deathworld again, near the Keep of the Dark Artificer. This time there was no agenda, nothing to worry about. This time they could walk and talk and simply relax, debriefing each other. 'You know,' Nick said, once or twice catching a betraying expression on Charlie's face, 'if I didn't know better, I'd think you were beginning to like some of this music.'

'Oh, I don't know . . .' Charlie said as they went in the gates of the Keep, and the demons there snapped to attention and saluted them. 'Some of the rhythms are more interesting than I thought originally . . .' He grinned. 'But the lyrics . . .'

'Oh, give me a break. So they're depressive.'

'Morbid,' Charlie said, 'that's the word I would have used.'

They strolled through the great 'front hall,' while Charlie looked around him, apparently fascinated by the architecture. Nick raised his eyebrows, mildly exasperated. 'Just because some idiot critics call it morbo-jazz,' Nick said, 'isn't any reason to take them seriously. It's hardly even jazz. If you think about it, you'll see that the basic riff structure has been completely . . . uh . . .'

He trailed off, coming to a stop, slowly becoming aware that Charlie was staring at him. ' "Completely uh?" '

There was a dark form standing in their path, all in black leather, a shadow dressed in shadows. 'Hey, Nick,' said Joey Bane, dry-voiced and ironic. 'How goes it?'

Nick couldn't find it in his heart to say, 'Badly, as always,' for this was the man himself, no simulacrum, no clone generated by the machine. The look in his eyes was too feral, too amused, and too real, for any program to fake.

Camiun was over his shoulder, and for once its strings were still. 'I asked the system to let me know when you two gents came through next,' Joey Bane said. 'I believe your last visit was, well, to put it politely, interrupted . . .'

'Uh,' Nick said. 'Yeah. I mean, no, it—'

'Look, relax,' Bane said. 'Nobody's going to ream you out. You did me and mine a favor. I thought I'd try to return it, a little. Come on.'

He gestured them toward the back of the entry hall. They walked with him. 'Besides,' Joey said, 'I would have come to take a look at you eventually, anyway. You just hurried me a little.'

Nick goggled. On the other side of Joey, Charlie was looking at Nick and plainly trying not to burst out laughing. Nick ignored him. 'You wanted to look at *me?* Why me?'

Bane laughed. 'Because you're the one who's always subverting my staff.'

Nick blushed. 'I never—'

'You *always!* The DP people who do their dialogue are always saying, "There's this kid who talks to us all the time, and treats us like people . . ." '

'Scorchtrap!'

'And the others. Bluebelch and Wringscalpel and Twistlestomp and the others. Where do they *get* these names, anyway? Whatever, they say the Demons want you to sit in on their next collective bargaining session. As if I don't given them stock options, and as if we didn't just have a split? What do they want now? Do they think I'm made of money?' Joey gave the two of them an ironic look. 'But, kid, even the tables here say nice things about you. Somebody who's as kind to inanimate objects and support staff as you are will go far in the world.'

Nick grinned. He couldn't think of anything to say to that.

'So,' Joey said, 'make yourselves at home. No connect charges for you two anymore. Though I think we'll see more of you than of your friend here.' He nodded courteously enough to Charlie.

'I don't know,' Charlie said suddenly, acquiring a wicked look. 'I heard some material borrowed from Hovannes in that last lift Nick played for me. Maybe we have common ground after all.'

Bane grinned. 'Maybe we do. Stop in sometimes and find out. Meanwhile, what's your pleasure, gentlemen?'

'We were going to do the Ninth Circle,' Nick said, looking over toward the doors on the lefthand side.

'I wouldn't go that way.'

Nick looked at him in surprise. 'Why not?'

'There's a shortcut. Who wants to go through all that stuff again? The noise, the crowd . . .' He waved his hand, made an annoyed noise. 'Nick, why go through all that again? You did it once. Once is enough. Suffering for a purpose – ' he looked up, as it were, through the depth of Deathworld, somehow including in the glance all the screaming and horror of the upper levels, all the rage, and the acknowledgement of evil – 'that's one thing. Purification, punishment with an object, to deter or teach you never to do it again, that's one thing. But prolonging it indefinitely, punishment for its own sake, for the mere love of cruelty . . .' He shook his head. 'That's not how we do it in Des Moines. Come on.'

He led them toward the back of the entry wall. The place was empty for the moment, except for the three of them. 'One word,' said Joey. 'You got to the very threshold, last time, before you left. We have an agreement, which one of my clones would have administered to you before passing that last doorway you saw off in the distance. We do not discuss with anyone but other people who've passed Nine, what lies beyond that portal. Anyone who does and is caught at it is banned for life.' He shrugged. 'Every now and then someone breaks the promise and tells . . . but you know what? No one believes them. Suits me. And as for the rest of us, sometimes it's fun to have a secret. Sometimes it's fun to make a promise and keep it forever. Can you cope with that?'

They both nodded.

'Right,' Joey said.

He put two fingers in his mouth and whistled, piercingly.

Suddenly the air was full of music, the likes of which Nick had never heard before – Camiun singing, for once, not in its usual dark fierce minor, but in a triumphant clarion major that was most uncharacteristic. Around them, like a mist, like a dream, the darkness and the stone and the night all began to melt away. Light came pouring in, and the view across a green landscape scaled up and up through rolling hills. Further yet it went, to mountains stacked halfway up the sky, green at first, then blinding with snow, but snow that looked down on what seemed like an eternal spring.

The chords crashed around them as Nick looked at Joey Bane, the only dark thing in all that landscape, with astonishment.

'OK, so life stinks,' Joey said, '. . . but then you stop complaining, and get on with finding out how to make it work.'

Through waves of triumphant music of lute and bass and jazz sax the three of them walked uphill, into the light, toward the crowd of Banies dancing under the second sun.